IN FOR A PENNY
The ranny Series

IN FOR A PENNY

Kelsey Browning and Nancy Naigle

Crossroads Publishing House

www.CrossroadsPublishingHouse.com

In For A Penny

Copyright © 2013, Kelsey Browning and Nancy Naigle

Print ISBN: 978-0615844862

LARGE PRINT: 978-0-9911272-0-7

Cover Art Design by Michelle Preast

Digital release, November 2013
Trade Paperback release, November 2013

Crossroads Publishing House
P.O. Box 723
Emporia, VA 23847

The first of—hopefully—many Grannies books is dedicated to Kelsey's mom, who inspired the series concept and was willing to sacrifice herself and wear orange if she had to. Thankfully, it never came to that.

As soon as we figure out the postage, we'll send you a copy in heaven. Love you, Mom.

IN FOR A PENNY

Book One
The Granny Series

Kelsey Browning and Nancy Naigle

Chapter One

Her purse swinging from the crook of her arm, Lillian Summer Fairview pressed both wrinkled hands against the barred door of the downtown Atlanta pawnshop and pushed with her whole weight to get inside.

She glanced at the bright yellow measuring stick on the doorjamb. Frequenting this place on the seedy side of town for the past two years was bad enough, but according to that ruler she'd fallen below the five-foot mark somewhere along the way. She'd noticed it on her way out last time and convinced herself it was a mistake. Maybe a bad angle. She dang well knew she'd been five foot two once upon a time. Just one more jab on possibly the worst day of her life.

No. The worst day would arrive within the month.

Today, she wore her only pair of pricey low-heel pumps and stretched her spine like a ballerina, but she still didn't pass four-eleven. It was a sore spot but only one of them.

Having to visit J&R's Pawn at all was worse than eating potato chips with a paper cut.

Harlan, I may never forgive you for putting me in this position.

When the preacher who'd married Harlan and her all those years ago said "for better or worse," she'd had no idea the worse would come after the until-death-do-you-part.

"Hello, gentlemen," she called out as she made her way past a long counter of jewelry, coins and other collectibles.

A bald, heavyset man hustled to meet her halfway. "What'cha got for us this time, gorgeous?"

Lillian didn't have the heart to play Rick's games today. "I know your tricks. You're trying to soften me up so I'll let you steal my good stuff." She stabbed a finger in his direction. "Don't try that with me today. I'm in no mood for it." She'd developed a friendly relationship with these boys and they'd treated her right. So far no one back in Summer Shoals was the wiser about her predicament.

"Wouldn't dream of it." Rick leaned forward on the counter. "Let's see what you've got for me today."

Lillian leveled a stare at him, almost changing her mind, but she didn't have a choice. She slipped a cloth place mat from her bag, positioned it on the glass counter and smoothed out the wrinkles. Then she set her bag on it and pulled out the handkerchief she'd secured with a slip of ribbon left over from the holidays.

Her hands shook as she opened the linen package. No jewels graced her fingers these days.

She couldn't stop herself from glancing into the case under her bag. Her wedding ring, handed down in the Summer family every generation, still held a place beneath the glass. She swallowed back her longing and bitterness.

Rick pulled the bundle close to inspect the contents.

Lillian flinched at the sparkle in his eyes as he examined the five pocket watches. Two gold, three silver and not a speck of tarnish on any of them. Daddy's favorites.

"You going to swap these and get your wedding ring back?"

"Not today," she said, "but you can take this month's interest payment on the things from the money for the pocket watches."

He turned to check his computer. "Your ninety days is coming up in early July. After that..."

He didn't have to finish the sentence. After that date, he could be generous and give her a thirty-day grace period or he could sell her family heirlooms.

"I'll be back for them soon." The lie sat heavy on her tongue. She beat back the tears blurring her vision and got down to the business of negotiating.

After fifteen minutes, she was far from satisfied with Rick's offer, but she slipped the few bills into her purse. It wasn't even close to enough.

When she walked through the door this time, Lillian refused to look at the measuring stick because there was no way she was an inch over two feet tall.

Lillian's right hip ached from pressing the sticky gas pedal on the long drive home in Daddy's 1948 Tucker Torpedo. Taking the massive thing to Atlanta was pure hell on her bursitis, but it was her only choice after selling her own car. A pitcher of sweet tea and the shade of Summer Haven's veranda were calling her, but after her visit to the pawnshop and that other mandatory appointment in the city, Harlan Fairview deserved an earful.

And he was about to get it.

She slowed to take a right into Gabriel's Acres. At least Harlan couldn't walk away when he was six feet under.

Lillian inched up in the seat as she eased the Torpedo through the narrow cemetery entrance. Nash Talley had added fancy new gates decorated with swirly scrolls and thin bars running from top to bottom. In her mind, angels' harps were supposed to be gold, but these were silver and looked like some artist living in a New York loft had sculpted them. It was just one of the many changes Nash had made since taking over the funeral business from his daddy, Warner.

The pathways cutting through the rolling green grounds had not one pothole. Nash had seen to that too. The whole place should've looked pretty, with the precisely manicured bluegrass, polished grave markers and dots of brilliantly colored spring flowers. But somehow it came off as plastic as the calla lilies Nash tried to talk everyone into placing in the sunken urns.

That silly man spent way too much time trying to make everything exactly the same. Order was one thing, but decorating everyone's grave with the same flowers?

Phooey on that.

Her parents deserved fresh roses, phlox and baby's breath on their memorials, just like Momma used to tuck into her hair every Sunday for church. But Lillian drove right past Momma and Daddy's graves to the outside edge of the family plot. As far as she knew, no one had realized she'd planted Harlan's sorry butt just beyond the perimeter. A tiny seed of guilt still tickled her insides for doing it. Yes, tradition dictated her husband should have been laid to rest in the family plot. But even dead, Daddy would have killed Harlan for his irresponsible actions, and she'd been forced to find a way to keep the ghosts calm.

Thank goodness, Nash was willing to help with the arrangements and zip his mouth.

Truth be told, Daddy was probably up in heaven right this minute smoking cigars, drinking whiskey with Jesus and telling him about his daughter Lillian and how if she'd only listened to her father, she wouldn't be in this mess.

Sorry, Daddy. I know you never gave a plug nickel for Harlan.

If he'd lived to witness the mess Harlan had left her in, even more-honest-than-Abe-Lincoln William Summer might've forgiven the choices she'd made to survive it all.

She stopped the car in the middle of the lane. Nash got mighty agitated when he found tire tracks denting his grass. She'd learned that the hard way. Twice he'd moved her car while she sat out here confessing to Momma and Daddy.

She scooched out of the car, and her hip

cramped like a crawdad had clamped down on the muscle. Old age wasn't pretty and it wasn't for the fainthearted. Strength was her only option. She hesitated, but only for a moment, then forged ahead to where she'd buried Harlan five years ago.

When Harlan died, she'd been so mad at him she could've outstung a hornet. Regardless, his stone had all the elegance the town expected of the Summer family. No one had to know it wasn't high-quality granite, and no one had made mention it wasn't bronze like the rest of the family's. What it lacked in true quality, she'd made up for in size. That prefab crowned headstone had a finial that darn near came up to her waist. More than once she'd been tempted to stab a scratcher lottery ticket on top of that pointy thing.

But for all his faults and this helluva mess he'd landed her in, Harlan had had his good points, and deep down she still loved that old fool.

She took a tissue from her handbag and bent to wipe away a spider web stretching between the *A* in Harlan across the *Y* in Wayne to the *R* in Fairview.

Devoted husband, loyal friend, generous benefactor.

Umm-hmm...devoted. Devoted to stopping

by the Sack 'n Snack three times a week for those scratch-off lottery tickets. What had seemed like a harmless indulgence at the time had sure turned into a disaster.

"Harlan, honey, it's not that I think you were a bad man." Lillian stooped to snap off a stray blade of crabgrass. Her knees popped like that breakfast cereal her best friend, Maggie, loved so much. "You were just a weak one."

And what hurt the most was his weakness had been a sign he hadn't loved her the way she deserved to be loved. Now, everything she cared about was at risk because she'd stood by Harlan long after she figured out he didn't have the Summer family backbone.

Then again, how many people had that kind of spine?

"I'd like to say I've made my peace with all this nonsense, but it's been a terrible day. You wouldn't believe the places I went and things I did."

She sighed and pushed the hanky back into her purse.

"And really, it's unfair for me to blame you. I made those decisions after you were dead and gone, and now the piper's come around, demanding his price." She rubbed her arms, but even the early June sunshine couldn't warm the fear steeping in her bones. "And the

Summer family always pays its debts."

"Miss Lillian, good to see you."

She jerked around at the sound of her name. Nash Talley resembled a crane stretching with long awkward strides from one paver to the next, careful not to disturb the precious grass between the grave markers. The way he moved reminded her of that step-on-a-crack-break-your-mother's-back game they'd played on the sidewalk in front of the soda shop when she was a little girl.

Nash smiled that perfect over-whitened smile he was so well known for. Warner and Melba had invested time, love and money into him, and it showed. His blond hair waved away from his face and shone golden in the sunlight. Even though summer was fast approaching, he wore a meticulous gray pinstripe suit and muted purple tie. If she looked close enough, she'd no doubt see her reflection in his black shoes.

If the *Summer Shoals Dispatch* had a fashion page, Nash would come out the winner for best dressed every year. So sad that neither of his parents could see what a fine young man he'd become, what with Melba in heaven and Warner in Dogwood Ridge Assisted Living.

Nash stepped next to Lillian. "How are you this afternoon?"

"Doing just fine," she said. Daddy would have called that out as a bald-faced lie.

"I don't mean to horn in on your private time with Harlan, but I noticed you haven't freshened the flowers as often lately. Everything okay? Is there something I can do to help?"

This was what she'd come to, being on the receiving end of people's kindness. The Summer family was the foundation of this community. They *gave* help. They didn't take it.

But Nash's observation was true. After five years of fresh flowers each week, now she had to make them stretch a little longer. If things got any leaner she'd have to stoop to Nash's plastic lilies.

But what choice had Harlan left her? What choice had she left herself?

She rubbed her chest, trying to ease the tightness that had settled there. It wasn't likely to go away in the next thirty days. Or more accurately, twenty-nine and counting.

"As a matter of fact, yes. I could use your help. I'd like you to keep an eye on Momma's and Daddy's resting spots for me over the next little while."

Tiny lines formed at the corners of his eyes. "You're scaring me. Are you sick? Why don't we find a bench and sit you down?"

Heartsick was more like it. With no idea how she going to take care of everything that needed to be squared away, the seconds seemed to tick off in her head like she was standing next to the mahogany grandfather clock that lorded over Summer Haven's foyer.

Nash led her toward a wrought iron bench by the Odom family plot. He settled her on the seat but remained standing himself.

She raised her chin to look him square in the face. The sun flooding around him made him look like an angel. "About the graves, you will keep an eye on them?" She made sure to lilt her words into a question, but Lord, it almost choked her this time.

He tugged on his coat sleeve. "I'm more than happy to, but you already keep those plots spotless. Even *I* couldn't improve on the beautiful flowers and polished headstones. So do you mind me asking why?"

This was exactly the type of scrutiny she'd hoped to avoid. But people tended to want explanations. And if Nash was curious about her asking for favors, Maggie was going to be like a hound dog after a pile of chicken bones. Maggie knew her best of anyone still walking this earth. And Maggie was no dummy. She would figure things out if Lillian wasn't careful.

She pulled in a breath and tried to smile

with lips that weren't cooperating. "Nash, when you get to my age, you realize the world has a way of taking back what's been taken from it."

"Miss Lillian, you're not making sense." He reached for her elbow. "Are you sure you're feeling okay? Maybe we should take you to the clinic."

She shook off his hand. "Stop treating me like a fragile old lady. I'm just fine. Can't I plan for the future without everyone getting all worried?" Heaven help her, she had to be strong. There was no other option. "Please do me this one more favor without worrying too much about why. Can you do that?"

"Yes, ma'am."

Good boy.

But the frown marring his evenly tanned forehead said he still wasn't convinced she was right in the head. Lillian sighed but let him lead her back to the Torpedo.

"Nash, it all boils down to what you younger people call karma." She slipped behind the wheel and Nash bent to close her door. "But in my day, we always said what goes around comes around."

Chapter Two

Nash Talley abhorred grits. Didn't matter how they were dressed up—butter, brown sugar, maple syrup or most especially ketchup like his momma had always eaten. They were grainy and gloppy and downright disgusting. He hadn't taken a bite of them since he was a toddler.

So as he headed toward the Love 'Em or Leave 'Em Florist, why did his midsection feel full of cold, congealed grits?

Miss Lillian's slow Southern drawl replayed in his head. *What goes around, comes around.* Maybe those words were a sign it was time for him to make the change he'd been planning for the past few years. Or was it too soon?

Quit overthinking it. Obsessing. That was what his therapist would have called it, but then that guy had been a waste of good money.

He pulled open the flower shop's glass door, then grabbed the strand of tinkling bells to keep them quiet as he slipped inside. He didn't need anything else jangling around in his head.

But Winnie didn't need the sound to know someone was in her shop. "Nash, sugar, it's been a coon's age since you stopped by." The short, fluffy woman who'd been filling the town's flower needs since as long as he could remember tied an elaborate bow around an arrangement of tie-dyed mums and then scooted around the counter to squeeze him in a soft-armed hug. "How's Warner?"

He cringed at her touch, stiffening like a corpse inside her embrace just as he did every time she put that bear hug on him. Never slowed her down though.

Her rosewater scent wrapped around him, and Nash patted her once on the back with a flat hand. Least he could do for his late mother's best friend.

When she finally let go, he stepped back and swallowed his anxiety. That lump of grits rolled over. He strained to make his facial muscles respond in a smile. "Some good days. Some bad days. Thanks for asking."

"The most beautiful daisies just came in. I bet that would fix Warner right up."

If only a handful of posies could cure

dementia, people all over the world would be mobbing flower shops. It was hell watching his dad's body live on while his mind made only cameo appearances. And it wasn't cheap keeping him over at Dogwood Ridge.

She fussed with Nash's suit collar. "Your momma would be so proud of the fine young man you've become. And Warner would be proud of how you've handled the family business."

Thirty-five was hardly young, but probably seemed so to a woman pushing seventy. As far as making his parents proud, he doubted his dad would be thrilled with him. Nash was no longer doing the work his dad used to handle himself. Instead, he'd hired a staff and let them run the day-to-day operations.

"What can I do you for today?" When Winnie walked to the cooler, her polyester pants legs scratched together like a rap song. "Got some yellow roses, daisies in more colors than you can shake a stick at and some ugly old carnations."

He chuckled. "Miss Winnie, you're never going to sell those flowers by calling them ugly."

She lifted the reading glasses on the chain resting against her chest, gave him a knowing glance and then lowered them. "Ain't tellin' anybody anything they don't already know and can't see for their own selves."

"Then why do you keep ordering them?"

"What's a flower shop without carnations?"

True.

"Now, what're you takin' your daddy today?"

With the way Dad's health had been lately, it felt like each bouquet was just one flower closer to a funeral wreath. The thought of processing his own father for his last hurrah shook him down to his pedicured toes. Nash took a steadying breath. Handling other people's affairs was easy, but watching his dad's decline was like hurtling down a mountain with one snow ski and no poles. Terrifying. Helpless. Hopeless.

"Before we get to that, I need to know if Miss Lillian has a regular order she takes over to Gabriel's Acres."

"Used to be every week, just like clockwork. Now, she's doing every other week. Good stuff for her momma and daddy. Roses, lilies, baby's breath, orchids, whatever I've got that's extra special. Cheap mess for Harlan." She leaned closer and whispered, even though no one else was around. "You ask me, I think Harlan must've done something that stuck in her craw before he up and passed away. She knows how I feel about carnations but she makes me bulk up that arrangement with the sorriest of them."

Some secrets weren't his to tell.

Winnie shoved her hands into her apron. "I'm not complaining, mind you. I never have to hunt her down like I do some customers. Not that I'm one to gossip or anything."

"Of course not."

"Lillian finally agreed to let me deliver them without a fussy preapproval. You'd think she'd have trusted me sooner, but then she's a Summer and you know how they can be."

"But we'd never gossip about that," he said.

"Of course not. Everyone loves Lillian. Even if she likes to have her way all the time." Winnie's jealousy aside, she did have a point. Miss Lillian giving up control was out of character.

Nash pointed toward the case. "I'll take that bunch of bright red daisies with the white pom-pom mums today." Dad always seemed to respond best to bright colors.

"Nice choice." Winnie pulled out the arrangement and waddled to the counter to log the sale in her book.

As she was about to close the ledger, Nash stuck a finger inside to keep it open. "While you're in there, move Miss Lillian's orders to my account."

Winnie squinted up at him, her eyes disappearing into her fleshy cheeks. "Now, why in the world would you do that? You know how she is, pride a mile long and back as stiff as my ex-husband on those little blue pills."

A tidbit he didn't need to know. But then again, a man who ran a funeral home was privy to secrets. Sometimes too many.

"Anything wrong with a man being neighborly?" That Lillian had asked him the favor was none of her business. There was a time when he'd liked having a Summer indebted to him, and that first favor had been a doozy, but this wasn't like that at all.

Her right eyebrow shot up. "If you want to take your life into your hands, it's your own business. But that doesn't mean I won't be saying 'I told you so' quick enough."

Thank God he hadn't shed his suit coat or she'd notice the wet patches in his armpits.

Favors. He hated doing favors that messed up his orderly routines, but he didn't have much choice on this one. "I'll risk it."

"Suit yourself."

Nash paid for his father's flowers and headed up the street. Dogwood Ridge Assisted Living was across from the post office and catty-corner from the library. He crossed at the painted pedestrian walkway. Most people in Summer Shoals still jaywalked, but he loved those yellow stripes, evenly spaced and perfectly painted.

He keyed in this month's code at the front door. He'd donated the security system before he brought his dad here to live. Dad might not remember him half the time, but Nash never forgot his dad's safety and happiness. As much happiness as it was possible for him to feel.

"Hello, Mr. Talley!" The bright-faced nurse was a new addition to the staff, hired only a month ago. She wore a sleek blond ponytail, not a hair out of place, and her green eyes sparkled.

He'd been flirting with the idea of asking her out. Maybe in another place, another time. But here and now? What woman would be interested in a straitlaced funeral home director? Now, a man of independent means who collected art and sipped martinis, that might interest a woman like her. One day. He hoped it would be sooner rather than later.

"Afternoon, Tina." He took one daisy from the bunch and handed it to her.

She spun it between her fingers. "That's so sweet." She skirted the counter, and he noticed how her starched scrubs outlined her trim figure. She could've been perfect for him.

"How's my dad today?"

Tina patted his arm in that sympathetic manner that meant he wasn't going to like what she had to say. "He's been asking for your mother."

Never a good sign.

"But I was able to talk him into spending some time in the recreation room. He settled down once he had something to do with his hands."

Nash worried how his dad might function if he wasn't under the great care of Dogwood Ridge, and now Tina specifically. That might just rock Dad's already precarious mental boat. And Nash's own mood lifted each time he saw the pretty nurse. In their own way, they both needed Tina.

They walked down the echoing hall toward the rec room. The large space framed with windows on all sides should have felt cheerful, but even the sunlight streaming in couldn't overcome the scent of age and antiseptic.

Mismatched tables were scattered throughout the room, making it look chaotic and tired. At a square table in the corner, Dad sat by himself stringing brightly colored macaroni onto strands of yarn. He peered over his glasses as he stabbed the yarn through the holes one by one.

What a waste. At one time, Dad had been a compassionate funeral director, offering care and support to those dealing with the most difficult times of their lives. And oh, how he'd loved his work. When he'd begun to let little details slip through the cracks, Nash had covered for him.

The day his dad wandered away from the funeral home right smack dab in the middle of Harlan Fairview's graveside service, his dad's dream—and Nash's nightmare—of passing down the family business had become reality. Nash had believed his own dreams of running an art gallery and rubbing elbows with the rich and famous were over because good elder care—especially for dementia patients—didn't come cheap.

At that time, Talley Funeral Home was the only way Nash could pay the bills. But after five long years, the tide was finally turning Nash's way. Now it was just a matter of timing.

Tina left his side and rushed over to calm two women squabbling over the Wii.

Nash headed for the macaroni table. "How are you today?"

His dad looked up, his eyes cloudy and confused. Not a good day at all.

"I have to get this necklace finished for my wife. Our anniversary is soon and she's the best thing in my life." His hands shook as he lifted the tangled mass of pasta and string. "Would you help me? Could you please? Help me make more rubies just like these." Warner pointed an unsteady finger at a puddle of red-painted noodles.

"Absolutely." Regardless of the sweat stains, Nash shrugged out of his jacket, carefully hung it on the chair back and slipped a craft apron over his head. Then he sat across the table from his dad.

"I don't believe we've met." His dad disentangled his right hand and held it out to Nash. "I'm Warner Talley, owner and funeral director at Talley Funeral Home."

Nash played along, just as he always did, and shook. Then under the cover of the table, he wiped the red paint off his hands and onto the apron. "Very nice to meet you. I'm Nash."

"Pleased to meet you, Nash." Not one flicker of recognition crossed his dad's face. That gut-piercing pain should've dulled long ago, but it never did.

His dad peered over his bifocals. "Are you married?"

"No, sir."

"Too bad. Marriage is good. I have a wonderful wife." Warner looked around the room then back at Nash. "Do you know my wife, Melba?"

His heart clenched. "I bet she's lovely."

"She's a knockout and, while I'm confessing—" Warner motioned Nash to lean in closer, "—my girl makes the best cornbread dressing."

Dad was right about that, only Mom had been dead for a long time and they hadn't eaten cornbread dressing since.

Nash pulled a wet wipe out of his pocket and wiped the space before him. The pasta was sticky from the paint or maybe from too many flimsy fondles by old hands. He forced himself to pick through the pieces and separate them, then washed a coat of red over the macaroni and spread them out so they'd dry evenly.

"Gold ones too," Warner ordered.

Nash picked out more noodles and painted them with the glittery gold paint. He lifted one for Warner's approval.

"Perfect."

Nash kept his tone casual as he squirted some antiseptic gel onto his hands. "How do you like living here?"

Warner looked around as if he were seeing the facility for the first time. "Oh, I don't live here, but they let me come and stay. I live in Summer Shoals but my wife is away. The people here are the kindest souls." Warner pushed his glasses up on his nose. "Have you ever heard of Summer Shoals?"

Nash swallowed hard. *That's where we are right now, Dad.* "What if you had to leave here?"

"It's not good timing." Warner's brows knit

together. "I can't go today. I told you that Melba's away."

The worry etched on his father's face broke Nash's heart. He'd thought he could wait to live out his own dreams, but even Dad's good days weren't all that good anymore. Relocating Dad would probably be hard on him, but being away from Dad would kill Nash, so he wasn't left with many options. Especially if he was going to ever live the life he so desperately wanted.

"I have a son," Warner said.

Nash's heart flipped. His dad appeared to be searching for the name, and it pained Nash to sit there and not jump in and fill in the blank.

"My boy is smart. He's good-looking, hardworking and has a really big heart." Dad smiled and shook his head. "He's got this little thing about washing his hands, but it doesn't do anyone any harm. You'd like him. He's a good man."

Nash stared over his dad's shoulder so he didn't have to see the hope and pride there, because he wasn't so sure how he liked Warner Talley's son right about now.

Chapter Three

Bolt cutter in hand, Maggie Rawls stood on Summer Haven's sagging side porch and eyed the carriage house. It was a tiny space compared to the glory of Lillian's family estate. Or the grand place it used to be anyway.

Maggie took a breath of early summer air, felt its humid weight in her lungs, and strode down the garden path.

She stood in front of the old building feeling guilty as all get-out for what she was about to do. *It's for your own good, Lil.*

The heavy padlock hanging from the hasp was big enough to weigh down an elephant. Now what in heck was so precious Lil needed the likes of that honkin' thing to protect it?

Maggie hated to cut the lock. If it was one thing she knew after all those years running the hardware store with George, it was hardware and tools. Big as that thing was, it had to have cost close to a hundred dollars, but enough was enough.

At one time, this building housed horse carriages, as the bronze historical plaque near the door stated. The history of every building on this property was recorded, and Lillian loved Summer Haven like a family member.

In the scheme of things, the carriage house seemed the least significant part of the estate. Yes, it had been Harlan's man cave, but he'd been gone a good five years now. George hadn't been gone but a few months before Maggie had toted all his old stuff down to the thrift shop for someone to give his socket collection and fly fishing lures a new life.

Time to move on, Lil.

Today, Maggie was going to open that lock one way or another. If Lillian wanted her to stay here at Summer Haven, she would have to let Maggie clean out and move into the carriage house. Sure, there was plenty of room for both of them in the big house, but living there with her best friend felt a little too much like charity.

Like pity.

And after George died a year ago, Maggie had vowed never to let someone take over her life the way her husband had. George had been a good man. But he was big. Big body. Big voice. Big personality.

Which meant Maggie's only choice had been to stay small. Stay on the sidelines.

No more.

George's passing had left a big old hole in her heart. But she wouldn't fall into the same trap of wrapping her life so tightly around someone else again. She was responsible for her own happiness. She needed to stand up and take charge.

As much as she loved her best friend, if Maggie wasn't careful, Lillian's steel would set her right back into a comfortable supporting role. She couldn't let that happen.

Maggie tiptoed into the flowerbed and peeked into the carriage house window. It was either smeared with dirt inside or Lillian had covered it with some kind of tint. Trying to get a closer look, she pressed against the window trim, only to feel it give beneath her palms. One thing wood should never be was spongy. She knelt and probed it with her stubby fingernail. Wood rot. She glanced up. The gutters sagged and buckled. Any time it rained, the water was hitting the ground and splashing against the carriage house, rather than flowing away from the building.

Lord a mercy, next thing she'd find a mound of termites had taken up residence. What was Lillian thinking, to let the place go like this?

Maggie frowned at the sight of the paint flaking from the white clapboard exterior.

What in the name of Pete?

She'd already noticed several things in the main house that begged for her attention. Baseboards needing a coat of paint. A sticky bathroom door. And those were just the simple things she and Lil should be able to handle themselves. Surely, neither of them were spring chickens, but even if Lillian couldn't fix things around Summer Haven, she could hire someone to help her.

Goodness, maybe Lil's eyesight was going. Since they were living together again, it still felt like they were two besties back at William & Mary. It was a tough pill to swallow, getting older.

She pushed away from the building with a grunt. Her knee gave a creaky-pop as she stepped over the flowers and headed to the door. Maybe she needed to start downing those glucosamine drinks that TV doctor was always preaching about.

This was a new start, a new life, and darned if Maggie was going to let something like stubborn joints get in her way. Exercise, fresh air, healthy food. She'd already negotiated a deal with one of the church ladies to get a row garden tilled up in exchange for Maggie replacing the toilet the woman's husband never got around to fixing.

Lillian was meticulous about any change to Summer Haven. *Mental note: tell Lillian about the garden before Roscoe gets over here with the tractor. Hope she doesn't have a hissy fit about that.*

Maggie pulled on the leather gloves she'd tucked into her waistband next to the pouch holding her duct tape. A small shiver of anticipation ran through her. If Summer Haven needed this much work, she'd need to pull out her full-fledged tool belt and some power tools.

She carefully positioned the cutters around the shackle of the lock so as not to damage the door when she heard a shout behind her. She glanced over her shoulder to find Lillian scurrying up the path toward her.

"Just what in blue blazes do you think you're doing, Margaret Evelyn Stuart Rawls?"

Maggie froze. Darn. It was so much easier to beg forgiveness than it was to ask permission. She slowly turned to face Lillian. "I'm opening up the carriage house."

"Why in the world would you do that?"

"Because, Lil, I can't stay in the big house forever." She swung the bolt cutter down to her side.

Lillian's face seemed to sag. "Sure you can."

"I appreciate you inviting me to live here

with you, but I thought we agreed this was a chance for me to start over. God knows I loved George, but I went from my daddy's house to college straight to George's house. Women these days get to be themselves and I want that too. I don't mean alone-alone, but I need to strike out on my own and have a little space that's just mine. Please, Lil, you have to understand."

"Big as the house is, we barely see one another now."

Reaching out to grasp Lillian's hand, Maggie said, "Hon, that's not the issue. You know I love you and I want to see you every day. But I need my space, my own place. Can you understand that?"

"But this crummy old carriage house? It's too little. You'll go crazy in there."

Sure, like Lillian thought there was one crummy thing about Summer Haven. But Lil was staring at the small building like it was a skunk slinking across her back lawn with its tail pointed to the sky, which meant something was on her mind. Something she wasn't sharing.

"What's this all really about? I promise I won't throw out any of Harlan's things if you don't want me to. Maybe I could just store them in the house's attic."

"I don't give a hoot or holler what you do

with anything of Harlan's except what's inside there." Lillian's hand shook as she pointed at the door.

When had Lillian's skin become so pale and thin? God, they were getting old. Maggie wasn't ready to be old.

Maggie lifted the bolt cutters. "Look. It's pee or get off the pot time. I'm either cutting this lock and determining what needs to done or I'm moving out of Summer Haven."

"No!" Lillian's shoulders drooped. "Fine. I've got the key up at the house, but if you have to see inside, just cut the darn lock off. Let's get this over with."

Maggie edged between Lillian and the door and positioned the bolt cutters. She felt the pull in her chest muscles as she squeezed the long red handles together. The sharp blades cut through the metal like a hot scoop through butter pecan ice cream.

The lock thunked to the ground, and the sound of it felt like the starting pistol at the beginning of a race. *Out of the gate!*

By God, her body was still strong and she would have a mind and heart to match if she had anything to say about it.

Lillian elbowed around Maggie before she could reach for the knob to open the door. She leaned against the door, putting all her tiny self into it.

"What's your hurry?" The door hadn't opened but maybe a foot when Maggie heard something slowly slide across the floor inside. What in tarnation—were they dealing with a vermin infestation too?

Lillian turned sideways and shimmied through the narrow opening with ease.

Maggie tried to follow, but she had to wiggle like a trapped snake to get her generous bust and behind through the crack. Junk in the trunk, that was what the young gals down at the fitness center called it. Well, she had so much junk in her trunk that she felt like she needed to hold a garage sale. George had always claimed he liked a full-figured woman, but she was out of breath by the time she squeezed her way inside the carriage house.

And what she saw didn't help her catch it again.

Trash bags. Too darn many to count in a single glance. Heavy-duty black trash bags stacked one on top of the other, leaning against walls, crammed cheek by jowl. The carriage house wasn't all that big to begin with, but there was barely room to turn around in it now.

Maggie gasped. "Harlan was a hoarder?"

Lillian looked around. "Not exactly." She flipped the light switch on, but in the room full of black bags it didn't do much good.

A bag tumbled from its perch and caught Maggie on the shoulder. She spun around and wedged it between two of its brethren.

"Then what in the world is all this?" She waved a hand, barely missing taking down a whole wall of the bags. "It'll take us days to burn all this garbage."

Lillian sighed like a balloon losing its helium. "No, we can't burn them."

"Lillian, I understand you loved the man, but keeping his trash?" Maggie started to raise her finger and twirl it by her temple, but her arm froze halfway to her head. Oh, Lordy, what if Lillian was going a little...soft...in the head? An ache set up housekeeping in Maggie's chest.

"Probably be easier if they were filled with trash. Then at least I could smell the stink instead of imagining it." Lillian's tone was more vinegary than that dandelion wine Winnie down at the Love 'Em or Leave 'Em Florist had tried to make last week. Maggie's lip puckered just thinking about that godawful stuff.

Claustrophobia suddenly pressed in on Maggie. The carriage house was stuffy with all that plastic and no ventilation except for the front door.

"Geez, Lil, it's like these bags are

multiplying as we're standing here. Let me go get the wheelbarrow. Or you can leave and I'll take care of it for you. Honey, everyone has a bad habit. If this is the worst thing Harlan did, it's not really all that terrible."

"I'll agree to getting rid of this stuff, but not until we open every single one of these bags and search through the contents."

"Why?"

Lillian slid one of the bags closer and untwisted the tie. She stretched the mouth of the bag wide and dipped her hand inside. "Here's why." She lifted a handful of cards and held them under Maggie's nose.

"Lottery tickets? Is that what's in all these bags?" Maggie could barely form words as she slowly processed the potential volume and dollars this many bags of lottery tickets represented. "No way."

"Yes, ma'am. Every last one of them. My Harlan had a problem."

Maggie shook her head. "A Hefty problem by the looks of things."

"I didn't realize it until he was dead and gone."

"Why didn't you say anything?"

"Why would I?"

"I don't know. Because we're best friends. Because it had to have made you madder than a cat in a creek." She swept her arms up in the air. "Because you're not going to get through these by yourself. Are you sure they're all full of scratchers?"

"See for yourself." Lillian yanked another bag down and let it plop between her and Maggie. She bent and grappled with the tough plastic, her hands like claws. "Why couldn't he be satisfied with the Walmart brand bags? No, Harlan always had to have the best."

"Got that right." Maggie pulled another bag down. "These are 4 mil contractor bags."

"Don't be talking all hardware on me," Lillian said.

Maggie took hold of one side and they each pulled. One, two, three...the bag split and bits of paper exploded out like confetti from a piñata. She and Lillian stumbled apart and Maggie gawked at the lottery scratch-off tickets all around them.

Maggie picked one up. Then another. And another. "They're all already scratched. And none of these are winners. And, hon, most of these tickets are expired anyway."

"A couple of the games are still going and Harlan loved those." Lillian's mouth pulled down and she suddenly looked every one of her seventy-two years. Her gaze lit with a combination of fire and desperation. "What if he missed a winner?"

Suspicion swarmed Maggie. "There were

more bags, weren't there?"

"You'd think, five years later, that I would've had time to go through them all. At first, I tried to search a bag a day, but Summer Haven was suffering."

Maybe that was why the side veranda was sagging slightly. And the driveway was full of crabgrass.

"There must be a thousand scratcher tickets in each one of these, Lil. How many bags did Harlan leave behind?"

"I stopped counting." Lillian swept at her brow.

By Maggie's quick calculation of the number of bags flooding the 1200 square foot space of the carriage house, even at a dollar a ticket, could be more than tens of thousands of dollars. And the few Maggie had in her hand were two and three dollar games. "He had to have spent a fortune."

"He did. Trust me. He did, but he also collected all the discarded tickets. Harlan had sheets and sheets of paper with statistics on how many winners were left in each of the games. He seemed to think he had some kind of system."

"Not a good one."

Lillian shrugged. "He thought he'd write all these off when he hit the big one. What an old fool."

"Crazy is what it is, and it's time to let go, Lil."

"This isn't about Harlan."

If that was what she wanted to tell herself, fine, but Maggie knew how hard it was to lose the love of your life, no matter how many shortcomings the man had. "This is why you've given me the runaround on the carriage house, isn't it?"

Lillian nodded, but there was something hesitant about the motion. Sometimes tough love was the answer. Maggie grabbed a bag with two hands and started scooting it to the door. Her hips dislodged a stack of bags that tumbled in her way.

Lillian lurched toward her. "Stop. Where do you think you're going?"

"It's time to have a ceremonial bonfire."

Lillian grabbed Maggie by the elbow, her fingers digging into bone. "No, ma'am."

"Excuse me?"

"If you want to live in this carriage house so darn bad, then you're going to help me go through the rest of these scratch-offs."

Maggie's heart dropped to her aching knees. That was it, she was going to lose a good twenty pounds one way or another. *Weight Watchers, here I come.* "Have you lost your ever-lovin' mind? You already said it's taken you years to get this far."

"Sometimes friends do things for one another, even when they don't want to. Even when they think those things are crazy or they don't understand why they should."

"I guess you're telling me this is going to be one of those times."

Lillian nodded. The stubborn set of her lips—strangely pale and thin without her normal hot pink lipstick—said she wasn't going to give in.

Maggie let go of the bag and straightened. They weren't talking about lottery tickets anymore. "Lil, what's going on around Sum—"

"Remember that time back in college when you asked me to loan you my biology lab notes and not ask questions? Well, this is one of those go-on-faith times."

"Fine, but I am moving out of the big house as soon as we're down to ten bags."

Lillian reached out and hugged Maggie with surprising strength in her thin arms. Lordy, she'd always been built like a bird, but she was thinner than ever.

The scratcher ticket search might nip away at a few of those pesky pounds Maggie was trying to get rid of. Either that or she'd lose her marbles with the never-ending task and it would land them both in the loony bin.

On the bright side, at least she'd be a step closer to her own place.

Chapter Four

Lillian wandered through the second floor of Summer Haven, trailing her fingertips over a railing here, tracing the facets of a cut-glass doorknob there. She'd taken her home for granted. Assumed it would always welcome her with its pine floors, tall ceilings and wavy glass windows.

Ever since the day Momma had brought her into this world in the mahogany four-poster bed downstairs, Lillian never once doubted she'd live out all her days inside this house. How terribly wrong she'd been.

Since her trip to Atlanta almost two weeks ago, Lillian had barely slept. It seemed like all she'd done was wander the rooms, smoothing the coverlets on the upstairs beds and dusting furniture like she might touch a newborn. She felt the need to give the house extra care before she abandoned it. No one would ever love Summer Haven like she did. The least she could do is make it sparkle like Momma always had.

Was that a dust bunny in the far left corner? Lillian got down on all fours to peer at the space bordered by cabbage rose wallpaper and stained wooden trim.

Nothing. Not even a smattering of dust.

She crawled to the sleigh bed and crouched to look underneath even though she'd inspected it yesterday. All she saw was a gleaming expanse of the heart pine floors. Just as they should be. Once yellow in color, the patina had gradually turned them into a rich russet tone that felt warm even on a winter day.

But she wouldn't be here to enjoy them this winter. Her heart shriveled inside her rib cage.

Lillian pushed to her knees. Her knobby bones ground against the floor. She felt every one of her years today.

And aren't I just a pity party without cake and punch?

She entered the Magnolia Room, the last room on her sad little tour. It overlooked the grounds out back. As a little girl she'd sit in the window here and watch the horses meander the fence line. This room had always been her favorite. It's why she'd had Maggie move into it.

When Lil was gone Maggie could move into

her room downstairs, unless she'd already taken up in that godforsaken carriage house. It would save money if they closed off this part of the house.

Lillian crossed the room and closed the door with a click of finality.

Would Maggie be able to take care of Summer Haven all by herself?

Lillian rushed down to the ground floor, almost tripping over her slippers in her hurry. She would not allow herself to climb those stairs again. No more of these little pity party sessions. She needed to spend her little remaining time handling Summer Haven's growing list of maintenance needs.

That meant she had to get to trimming trees. Maybe not entirely on her own, though. She had a plan, but to carry it out she needed a ladder.

A little later, she hopped into Daddy's Tucker Torpedo and headed to Darrell Holloway's hardware store. As she entered, rather than the sweet tinkle of bells, something akin to a wounded warthog bellowed. Why the man thought that greeting was good for business, she'd never fathom.

"Hey there, Miz Lillian," Darrell called from behind the counter to her left. "What can I help you with today?"

"I need a new ladder."

"What'cha gonna do with it?" Eyes narrowed, Darrell paused, clearly waiting for an answer.

His concern for her business was like three quilts thrown on top of a feather bed smack in the middle of August—stifling, oppressive and panic-inducing. "Just some general house maintenance. Everyone needs a decent ladder tucked away in the tool shed, wouldn't you agree? I was thinking I'd buy one of those metal ones this time."

This time? She should be ashamed of herself for lying to the man. She'd never purchased a ladder in her life. Daddy had always taken care of those things and then Harlan after him. Women's lib wasn't some newfangled idea, but she'd always been satisfied to be taken care of. And now here she was scrambling.

"Well now, how tall a ladder do you need? We've got six, eight or ten foot. Or an extension ladder that goes up to twenty-eight foot."

"That's the one. I need an extension ladder. Tallest you got."

He studied her. "You sure?"

Nosy man wasn't going to let her get out of here without finding out her plans. "The yard at Summer Haven could use a little tree trimming."

"Then you don't need a ladder. You need to call Johnny Dean. He'll come out there and fix you right up. Got his own cherry-picker and everything." He reached for the phone on the counter. "Why don't I give him a holler for you?"

She forced a smile. "I'm sure Johnny does lovely work, but all I need today is a ladder. Thank you."

"All I've got is the fiberglass kind in that height. How you gonna get it home?"

Phooey. She should've brought Maggie's truck instead of Daddy's car. But then Maggie would've wanted to come too. All this sneaking around behind her back was exhausting and made Lillian's heart hurt.

But the ends were more important than the means.

"Think it'll fit in the backseat of Daddy's car?"

Darrell's craggy face split into a smile. "What were you thinking to do? Straddle it through the back windows?"

She didn't take kindly to his snarky response. "It's not that far. Wouldn't that work? I could put the top down."

"Would hate to mess up that pristine upholstery. Your daddy would haunt me for sure. Maybe we can let it hang it out of your trunk, but you'll have to go real slow." He let out a loud guffaw. "That ladder is gonna look just like a torpedo shooting out of the back of that car."

She really didn't see the humor in it.

"That should work." She'd have to chance it. If she went back to Summer Haven to pick up Maggie's truck, she might climb into her bed, pull up the covers and not come out until someone came to cart her away. "How much do I owe you?"

Darrell flipped through a catalog on the counter. "Those new fiberglass extension ladders are pretty precious. You're looking at three and a quarter."

Over three hundred dollars for a ladder. Lillian swallowed, trying to cover her shock. That kind of money for something you climbed? She'd hoped to pay cash, but that obviously wasn't going to happen. "You know, I just realized I forgot my wallet. Would you mind putting it on the Summer Haven account?" She added that to her mental list. Another thing she needed to take care of so Maggie wouldn't have to. God knew that big old house was enough of a financial burden without her compounding the problem.

"Sure thing, Miz Lillian." He jotted down the figure on a sticky note, stuck it to his register and then headed for the stockroom. "I'll just go in the back and get that for you."

Lord, if only that piece of paper would come loose and get lost somewhere.

She was just reaching for it when the warthog bellowed again.

Lillian jerked her hand back and turned to find Angelina Broussard, owner of Broussard Bed and Breakfast and the woman who headed up all the Summer Shoals holiday celebrations, entering the store.

"I saw your car parked out front. You've been hard to catch up with lately." The woman tugged an envelope from a pocket on her huge designer handbag and thrust it in Lillian's direction.

Lillian took the envelope and flipped it over. The golden seal and fancy lettering on the front were high quality. "What is this?"

A smile spread across Angelina's face. That grin was so wide and her lipstick so bright that she seemed to transform into the Joker right in front of Lillian. "Honey, I'm the president-elect of the brand new Bartell County Historical Society."

"The what?"

"Oh, yes. You haven't heard?" Angelina fluttered a hand against her chest. Lillian knew darn well that Angelina had likely gone great lengths to keep the news of that committee out of her earshot. If anyone belonged on that committee it was Lillian

Summer Fairview!

"Anyway," Angelina said. "We're doing site visits to all the historical markers in the county to ensure they are up to the standards we see fit for our reputation."

"You're mistaken, dear." Lillian folded her arms and tried to steady her voice. No way was she letting Angelina and her posse traipse around the estate. "Summer Haven is not locally registered, it's *nationally* registered."

"Yes. Exactly my point, *dear*." Angelina placed her hand on Lillian's arm. "The national registrars don't care if the place is falling apart. We're looking to raise those standards for Bartell County. We'll help you. Don't you worry."

"Summer Haven is just fine, thank you very much." Lillian lifted her chin and bit down hard to keep it from trembling.

"We'll see. It's all in the letter. Our site visit to Summer Haven is scheduled for the first week in August." That bright-lipped smile was back. "You'll want to be sure everything is shipshape or well..."

Yes, what Lillian wanted to say was better left unsaid as well.

"Oh, and by the way, while I've got you," Angelina added, "I wanted to chat about the July Fourth plans."

Lillian's heart cringed and tried to hide

somewhere behind her lungs. This woman was bound and determined to get her goat one way or the other. "So early? You're really on a roll this year."

Angelina cocked her head. "Early? It's less than a month away."

All that mattered to Lillian was that it was more than twelve days in the future.

"I know it really goes without asking, but I wanted to confirm that you'll lead the parade in your daddy's car like you always do."

Even if she were going to be around, she'd be hard-pressed to do this woman any favors after that little committee stunt. "Oh, I'm so sorry, but the Torpedo is due for some work and won't be available for the parade this year."

Angelina's jaw dropped in a most unladylike way. "You're not serious!"

Oh Lord, if she were any more serious, she'd lay right down on the floor and cry. "I'm sure you understand a car like that needs special care and attention."

"Well, of course," Angelina sputtered.

"Maybe you could ask Teague to lead the parade in his patrol car."

"Now, Teague Castro in and of himself is a draw, but a Crown Victoria sheriff's car? Even with the lights and sirens, it's not very exciting."

And now Lillian had one more thing to feel responsible for. Then an even bigger weight crashed down on her shoulders. Fourth of July was not only the biggest parade of the year, but it had completely slipped her mind that it was also Maggie's birthday. How in the world was her best friend going to forgive her for all this? If the tables were turned, Lillian wasn't sure if she could be so unselfish.

Then again, Maggie didn't have a clue about the storm coming her way.

Darrell ambled through the store with the monstrous ladder above his head. "Alrighty, Miz Lillian, here's your ladder. Since you don't have any money today, I'll put it on your account like we talked about."

A flush bloomed across Lillian's chest and raced up her throat to heat her face. "That's kind of you. Just send me the balance and I'll write a check out of the estate account." And she would, if the darn thing had any money left in it.

Darrell muscled the ladder out the front door.

Lillian turned to Angelina. "Again, I'm sorry about the parade, but I'm sure you'll find another lead car this year."

"Fine," Angelina said through tight lips, "but I'll see you in August for that inspection."

Oh, no she wouldn't. But Lillian rushed

toward the door with that threat hanging over her like a hungry black vulture. When she opened the door this time, that damned warthog fell eerily silent.

Chapter Five

Maggie sat in one of the six rocking chairs in a perfect row across Summer Haven's front porch. She was elbow-deep in her twentieth garbage bag of scratcher tickets when a tow truck pulled into the circle drive. A man, in his late thirties if she had to guess, stepped out and pulled off his baseball cap. He wore coveralls and a friendly smile as wide as the name—Christopher Cartersworth— stitched out on his shirt. "Howdy there. Is Mrs. Fairview around?"

Darn it, every time she was making progress she was interrupted. She lifted another handful of tickets from the bag and thumbed through them as she answered. "Lillian's gone to town. Can I help you with something?"

"Maybe. I'm here to pick up a trunk."

Lillian hadn't mentioned she was having something restored. Just like Lil to fix one of the family heirlooms instead of tending to maintenance first. Maggie tossed the losing and expired tickets in the pile of others and walked down to talk to the man. "Most of the bedrooms have a trunk of some type. Do you know which one?"

"Yes, ma'am. It's pre-Civil War."

"Sweetheart, just about everything around here is from that era."

"I think she said it's in the Cherokee Rose Room."

Maggie's breath caught. "There has to be some mistake." Doing any restoration on an antique like that would actually decrease its value. "Lil wouldn't have work done on that trunk."

"I'm not working on it, ma'am. I'm buying it for my wife as an anniversary present. I don't understand why my wife loves all that old shi...stuff, but she does. And I have a feeling she's gonna be *real* happy when I give her this." The smile on his face told Maggie exactly what he figured his wife would give him in return.

"I'm sorry, but you'll have to wait until Lillian gets home because this must be a big misunderstanding."

The hopeful expression on his face slid straight off his chin. "But my anniversary is today."

Her heart went out to him. It really did, but she wouldn't just hand over a piece of history out of Lil's house. Goodness knows, she would've given anything for George to have been this passionate about an anniversary gift for her. She'd always appreciated the new split-leather tool belts and wire cutters, but flowers and hand-picked furniture would've been nice now and then.

Maggie sighed. "Tell you what, we'll go upstairs and take a look at it and maybe by the time we're done she'll be home."

She hated to string the man along, but disappointing people always made her feel like she was being rubbed all over with sandpaper.

"I'd appreciate that." He situated his cap back on his head.

She led him inside. "Can I offer you a cold drink?"

"That'd be nice." He smiled, and even with the sweat and a streak of grease on his cheek, the man was attractive.

"Your wife's a lucky woman." *Did I say that aloud?* By the fact that the man's eyebrows had disappeared under the bill of his cap, the answer was yes. "I mean...I didn't mean... Oh, shoot." How was she ever going to find romance again when she acted like such a ninny around a man? And why in the world was she even thinking about romance?

"I'll be sure to tell her you said so."

Maggie poured him a big glass of sweet tea and led the way to the second floor.

Summer Haven was normally meticulous, but upstairs looked like a band of Merry Maids had waged an attack on dust and dirt. The floors shined with a recent waxing and the doorknobs had been buffed until they gleamed.

"It's this way." Maggie opened the door and found it as immaculate as the hallway. Nothing was even slightly askew on the highboy dresser.

A shiver cruised over Maggie's spine. It made her think of how she'd cleaned and arranged George's den right after he passed away. Something wasn't right at Summer Haven.

The Jenny Lind trunk sat at the end of the bed, its rich pine rubbed to a glowing patina. The four iron bands were studded by brass buttons. And the rare brass double lock still worked perfectly, with the original key tucked securely inside. Of all the treasures in the house, this was one of Lil's favorites.

"My wife will flip over this." He stared down at the trunk and lifted a shoulder. "Like I said, I don't really get all this excitement over a bunch of wood and metal, but if it makes her happy, then I'm all for it."

"Why don't I take down your phone number and I'll have Lillian call you when—"

Just then, the sound of the front door opening and closing filtered upstairs.

Good. They could clear this up now. He would go away disappointed, but at least he wouldn't have a false sense of hope.

Maggie rushed into the hallway and called down the stairs, "Lil, can you come up to the Cherokee Rose Room for a sec?"

"Maggie Rawls!" Lil's tone was as sharp as a diamond-edged saw blade. "What in Pete's sake are you doing in that room?"

Lillian's wildly swinging moods the past couple of weeks were getting on Maggie's last nerve. If she didn't know Lil had already gone through the change, she'd suspect PMS. Maggie didn't appreciate being scolded like a child, but she wasn't going to kick up a fuss in front of this nice man. "I have a gentleman up here who says he's supposed to pick up the Jenny Lind trunk. I already told him he's mistaken, but he's insistent. Can you come talk with him?"

Maggie stood there waiting for a response, but there was only silence from below.

Finally, with a weariness Maggie had never heard before, Lillian said, "It's not a mistake. Five hundred dollars and the trunk is his to take."

Maggie reeled back from the balustrade and glanced over her shoulder at the man who was already scooting the trunk away from the bed.

He gave Maggie his empty tea glass and smiled. It was an apologetic expression, but not so apologetic he was going to leave without his treasure.

"I guess you knew what you were talking about after all."

The man took a fat wad of folded cash from his pocket, peeled off five crisp one hundred dollar bills and handed them to her.

She snapped each one between her fingers as she counted them. She'd handled enough cash in the hardware store over the years to spot a fake bill with pretty good accuracy. She stepped to the window and held up each one, looking for the watermark.

"The money's good." He tipped the trunk up on its side. "If it makes you feel any better, ma'am, my wife will take real good care of this trunk. It's been on her wish list for as long as I've known her."

Maggie put the money in the back pocket of her khakis. "I can help you with that. Let me get one end," she offered.

"Oh no, ma'am. I've got it."

What—you think I'm too old to help carry something? She reluctantly stepped back and let him have at it.

He hefted the trunk and hauled it down the stairs.

It'd been quite a while since she'd seen muscles flex like that. Lord, did looking at a man young enough to be her son make her one of those...those cougars?

As he headed out the front door, Maggie stood by feeling more than a little useless and still confused. It wasn't her trunk to protect so why did Lillian selling off family heirlooms worry Maggie so much?

The front door closed behind the young husband with a finality that shot all the way to Lillian's toes. What was done, was done. That could certainly become her life motto.

At her small desk in the kitchen, Lillian scanned the list she'd hand-printed on a legal pad. Every letter of every word was perfectly formed with a Faber-Castell pencil. She lifted the top page to find those letters embossed three sheets deep. She let the pages drop, then added a few more items to the list.

Make arrangements for care of Daddy's car

Remove tree limbs over veranda

Settle up account at hardware store

There wasn't money to hire anyone to help

with that tree, and the thought of climbing that ladder she'd just bought on credit sent tendrils of exhaustion through Lillian's arms and legs. But it didn't matter how tired she was. So many things to be done. So little time.

Lillian tore the list from the pad and punched holes in the side so she could add it to the binder she'd started for Maggie.

Maggie, please forgive me for this.

The thick vinyl three-ring binder held the information to everything Lillian could think of. Legal, insurance, bank accounts, warranties and even how to get the persnickety furnace fired up the first time of the winter season.

She pulled an envelope from between two books on the desk.

Unwinding the string from the loops on the back of the five-by-seven manila envelope seemed symbolic of her life right now, hanging on by a thread. She dumped the contents and eyed the receipts. She tugged one in particular from the pile. The pawn slip from her ring. If she didn't pay the pawnshop before she went away, there'd be no getting them back.

In the top corner of the list, she wrote herself a note: *7/1 pick up b/f appt at WSPC.*

The sound of Maggie's footsteps on the stairs filtered toward Lillian, and she quickly closed the binder and tucked it back into the desk drawer, then slid the envelope of receipts back into the hiding spot.

Lillian had just hopped up from her desk when Maggie stomped into the kitchen.

"What in heaven's name was that all about?" Maggie demanded.

"He's a very nice man and his wife has been looking for a chest like that for years. They're about to have their first baby. Can you imagine all those tiny clothes she'll fold and store in there?" Lillian lifted a hand to her heart. "It's really quite romantic if you think about it."

"I'm sure it will be very sweet, but have you lost your ever-lovin' mind? Didn't you tell me once that your great-great something or other brought that chest all the way from Boston in the 1850s?"

Maggie never was an easy one to bamboozle. "Come with me," Lillian said. "I need help unloading something from the car."

"I'm certain that trunk is worth more than five hundred dollars." Maggie dug the money out of her pocket and handed it to Lillian.

Lillian stuffed it into the top of her purse and then motioned for Maggie to follow.

"You can't just change the subject and make it go away, Lil. What's going on? Please talk to me." The hurt in Maggie's voice was plain as daylight at noon.

"There's nothing to talk about. I'm not losing my mind. It's just time for that trunk to be passed on again, and Lord knows, the Summer line ends with me." The anger and guilt still felt like boiling water rolling in a teakettle after all these years. *Damned Harlan.* By the time they'd figured out her eggs were farm-fresh and his swimmers were belly-up, it was too late for babies. And this, a stately old house that took more care and feeding than Harlan ever had, was her legacy. Only now she didn't have anyone to leave it to. And really, when you got right down to it, was it a legacy or a burden?

She shook away the thought. If she lost focus and belief now, it would all be over for good. At least now she had the money to pay for the ladder. Thank goodness he'd come to get the trunk like he said he would. It was perfect timing really.

Maggie followed Lillian out to the car. "You drove like that?"

The fiberglass extension ladder poked out of the back of the car like a NASA missile ready for launch.

Lillian waved a hand. "I didn't go over twenty-five miles an hour and it's only a few blocks."

Maggie blew a breath that pouffed her bangs up. "You could have shish-ka-bobbed someone or snagged an overhead line with that thing. You should've called me to bring the truck."

"Quit your fussing. Nothing happened."

Maggie marched to the trunk of the car. Half a ball of twine zigzagged between the ladder and the metal frame of the trunk. "Don't guess it was going anywhere."

"Darrell secured it for me."

Maggie whipped a knife out of her pocket and started slapping at the string. "He should have delivered the darn thing if he wanted to be helpful." She stepped back and put her fists on her nicely rounded hips, just above her ever-present roll of silver duct tape, as the trunk flew open.

"Hope you ate your Wheaties, Lil, because this thing probably weighs fifty pounds."

"Surely not," Lillian said. "Darrell carried it on one shoulder like a sack of feed. I hope we can drag it."

"Why did you buy this thing to begin with?"

"I've got to keep things in order around here. I can't let this place fall down around my ears. And on top of everything else that snobby Angelina Broussard has conjured up some local historical society committee and wants to put her stamp of approval on Summer Haven provided it meets with their so-called standards."

"She can't do that!" Maggie's mouth tightened. "Can she?"

"I don't know. Regardless, those limbs over the veranda need to be trimmed for starters, and that woman will be here with her committee the first week of August. It doesn't give me much time."

"Don't get all in a panic. It's not even July. We've got time. Wait a minute...did you just say we're going to trim limbs?" Maggie's eyes went wide and sparkly.

"Not exactly, but it'll get done." Lillian gave her a wink even though she didn't feel all that playful today. "I've got a plan. This ladder is part of it."

Maggie shook her head. "Wish you'd discuss this stuff with me first. Some things are just not meant to be do-it-yourself jobs, as much as I hate to admit it. These fiberglass ladders don't come cheap, and you'll never use it again. I'm not sure those limbs are your biggest problem. I think I need to figure out a holistic plan for you to keep up this place."

"Well, clue me in when you do, because if this place isn't in order before Angelina prances in with her committee, no telling what will happen. She's been dying to weasel her new money in and push the Summer name out, and August is not that far away." Lillian swallowed to keep the tears from coming. If it wasn't one thing, it was another. *Maggie, I know you think I'm going crazy. You're always so capable, so sturdy. So there. So always wonderfully there.* "Have I told you lately how much you mean to me?"

Maggie's mouth dropped open wide enough to catch a swarm of flies. Her eyebrows went MIA under her dark brown curly bangs and her eyes had that popping-out-on-springs look to them.

"Where in the world did that come from?" Maggie rushed over, slapped a palm across Lillian's forehead. "Oh, hon, do you have the fever? Are you feeling okay? Maybe you should lie down."

Lillian pushed Maggie's hands away. "I'm fine. I just don't tell you often enough how much I appreciate your friendship and how happy—" relieved, "—I am you came to live at Summer Haven."

"I know you do." Maggie squeezed her hand once and marched to the car. "Come on. Let's get this puppy out of here."

They both headed for the end of the ladder, but at the end, neither of them was tall enough to reach the darned thing.

Maggie worked her way to the middle of the ladder and then pushed it up and stepped back to release its hold on the inside of the trunk. The ladder teeter-tottered hip level.

"Now, that's better, only we don't want to scratch the car."

Lillian opened the driver's door and pulled out the carpet mat. "Here. Put this under it."

"Perfect," Maggie said. Then she and Lillian walked out to the far end of the ladder, placed their hands on the top rung. "On three. One. Two. Three."

They both heaved backward and the ladder fell to the ground. Together they dragged it off to the side of the driveway.

"Help me get it over to the porch," Lillian said with a tug.

Maggie took hold of her side again and dragged it the last few feet, then slowly walked it up to lean against the veranda roof.

"Lil, you've got a little more oomph than I expected out of that teensy frame of yours."

"Together we can do just about anything, Maggie."

"I think you're right. You never cease to amaze me."

Lillian smiled at her friend. *Honey, you ain't seen nothing yet.*

Chapter Six

Bartell County Sheriff Teague Castro pulled to the side of the road in front of Summer Haven's infamous fountain. Everyone treated the colorfully tiled landmark as if it belonged to the town even though it was part of the Summer family estate. First time he'd laid eyes on it, he thought it was the tackiest thing he'd ever seen, but it had grown on him over time. Now, if it would only return the favor by granting him a wish.

Teague dug the spare change from his uniform pocket. Two nickels, three quarters, a dime and six pennies. He got out of the car and circled the fountain flipping the coins one by one into the mosaic designs decorating it.

Local lore claimed each design carried different luck. Folks said the original Mrs. Summer was a crazy old bird. She'd tiled the mosaic patterns in the fountain while her husband was away. Apparently, he'd been as angry as a bear woken too early from hibernation when he saw the psychedelic mess she called art. One of the scenes, on the back side facing Summer Haven, was so sexy that there'd been talk of having it removed. Rumor was Mrs. Summer tiled that one especially for her lover, the one she'd fancied while her husband was away on business. The whole town knew, but no one ever spoke about it above a whisper.

Teague eyed the sexy scene, lined up his coin and aimed for the center. Maybe it would bring a lover into his life.

Couldn't hurt to try.

He flipped the twelfth coin right smack dab in the middle of the image of the naked couple. Twelve coins. One wish. The thing—or rather someone—he always wished for. As much cash as he'd tossed into this thing over the past couple of years, he could have bought a damned mail-order bride or maybe two.

He climbed back into his patrol car and shot a quick glance back at the flourish of water soaring into the air.

If nothing else, he was supplementing Lillian's retirement. Yeah, like she needed his piddly change.

He might not have known the other Summer family members, but the Summer legacy was legend around these parts, and

Miss Lillian was like the queen of the town.

In the three years since he'd settled here in Summer Shoals he'd grown to respect Lillian Fairview. He loved the town her family had built and the people who made it unique. Small town, little crime and happy hour on Summer Haven's veranda were all just perks of the job.

He eased his car down the long loop of the driveway that led back to Summer Haven. When Lillian had moved her friend Maggie in with her, he'd been relieved. Those two seemed to be able to handle just about anything together, and Miss Maggie brewed up one heckuva a batch of *special* tea. It was why he usually saved this visit for the end of his shift. That stuff was more potent than some of the white lightning he'd taken in as contraband.

Just as he rounded the gazebo near the house he spotted Lillian and Maggie up on the roof.

What the hell were they up to?

The tires squealed on the vast expanse of concrete as he stomped on the brakes on what passed for one fancy driveway in comparison to the town's pitted roads.

Both women whipped around at the noise and Teague felt everything kick into slow-motion as he watched Lillian lose her footing on the shingles.

Christ Jesus.

He hauled butt out of the car toward the big old white house and made it just as Lillian tumbled ass over teacup down the side of the veranda.

She plopped into his arms with her feet sticking straight up in the air. She didn't weigh much more than his favorite shotgun.

"Oomph." That was the most unladylike thing he'd ever heard come from Lillian's mouth.

"Teague, were we expecting you?" she asked in a breathy tone.

He swallowed back the words he wanted to yell because they all consisted of four letters. "Well, seeing as I stop by once a week, I doubt it was a *complete* surprise."

"Would you mind terribly putting me down?"

He tipped her upright and eased her to her dainty feet. "You're bleeding," he said.

She limped over to one of the chairs. "Where?" She checked herself over. "Goodness. That's nothing," she said, wiping the blood from her forearm. "Barely a scratch."

Teague could already see the bluing of a big bruise coming up on her arm too. "Are you sure you didn't break anything?" As thin as she was, he'd probably cracked half a dozen of her ribs just catching her. "Maybe we should take you to the hospital and get you checked out."

She waved a hand. "Just got the breath knocked out of me."

"What do you think you—" Realization blindsided Teague like a hit-and-run driver. Oh, shit. Maggie was still on the roof. "Don't you move, Miss Lillian."

Teague ran back into the yard just in time to watch Maggie descend a ladder no woman their age—hell, no woman of any age—should be climbing. He let out a sigh of relief.

Maggie hopped off the last rung and dusted her hands across the rear of her serviceable khaki pants. "Teague, how nice to see you."

It cost him, but Teague stretched a smile across his face. He'd just thought these were sweet old ladies. Now it was clear they were menaces *disguised* as sweet old ladies. "Miss Maggie, what do y'all think you're doing up there?"

"That was some show, wasn't it?" Maggie laughed and stepped toward the porch. "I don't think I've ever seen Lillian do something quite so lacking in elegance. Did you know she was crowned Homecoming Queen at William & Mary? My, that girl had the parade wave down. Never even missed a beat when the arch of flowers we'd glued against the backdrop toppled right over beside her. Nope, she just kept smiling and waving."

It was easy to tell Lillian had been a looker and a half back in the day, but Teague wasn't about to let Maggie pull him off topic with the little trip down memory lane.

Maggie settled on the bench alongside Lillian and checked the scratch on her arm. She ripped off a piece of duct tape from the holster on her belt and slapped it over the cut. "It'll be fine."

Teague unclenched his back teeth enough to say, "Mind telling me why you ladies were on the roof in the first place?"

"Tree trimming." Lillian's smile was as cordial and smooth as if she'd been talking about a damned Christmas tree.

Teague eyed the pin oak closest to the veranda. It was a monster, probably a good century old and close to seventy feet tall.

Maggie chimed in, "Some of the branches have been rubbing the roof, and you know that's not good for the shingles."

Yeah, kind of like walking around fourteen feet off the ground wasn't good for old ladies. "What were you going to do? Shimmy to the top of it?"

"Lord no, Teague. We're not crazy."

Could have fooled him.

"We were just going to trim the ones hitting the roof," Maggie said. "We have a chain saw. We were just having a little trouble getting it started."

His insides froze at the thought of the two of them wielding a tool that size. They could cut off their fool legs.

Good thing he was finished with his official shift for the day because it appeared he'd be doing some landscaping this afternoon.

Shaking his head, he rolled back his sleeves then leveled his gaze at Maggie. "If you don't have a batch of that special tea, I suggest you get to working on it, because when I'm done with this little project I'm going to need it."

He caught a movement from the corner of his eye. Had Lillian just winked at Maggie?

Maggie rushed inside before he could figure out for sure.

Teague went to his car and popped open the trunk. It wouldn't be the first time a woman had tricked him into a few odd jobs. He stripped off his shirt, unbuckled his belt and dropped his gun, holster and the whole shebang into the trunk. He switched out his uniform hat for a ball cap then locked up the car.

He climbed the ladder to the veranda roof and took a quick walk around the area under the tree.

Damn, not only were the limbs overgrown, but a few of the shingles were loose. One job at a time. Tree trimming today. Roof repair later. He started the chainsaw with one quick tug, and swept through the wayward limbs like Edward Scissorhands.

Lillian could barely contain her smile at how easy the tree trimming had suddenly become. That task had worried her most of all the ones left.

Maggie returned with the tray of her special tea out to the front porch. She handed a glass to Lillian then set an extra glass of ice on the table for Teague.

"Cheers." Lillian held up her glass and clinked it against Maggie's.

Maggie took a sip and then tapped Lillian's arm. "Why are you grinning like a possum? That little spill you took was not part of the plan. You are okay, right?"

Lillian giggled. "I know. I didn't do it on purpose. I could have broken my neck. Thank goodness he's a good catcher. I didn't have time to tuck and roll."

"Well, I'm glad we can mark tree trimming off the chore list."

Her too. Now if she could just sell a few more pieces of furniture before her time was up, she could get her ring back and pay the hardware store for that high dollar ladder.

"You are wicked sneaky sometimes, Lil."

If you think that now, wait until you get the whole story. Lillian rocked back in her chair and gestured to the roof of the veranda. "Sounds like he's making short business out of it up there too."

A few minutes later Teague descended from the roof with the chainsaw dangling from one hand.

Maggie leaped from her chair and poured him a glass of tea. By the time he took the last step, she was at his side with it. "Here you go."

"Thanks." Teague swept the sweat from his brow and gulped half the glass down. He lifted the chainsaw. "Where do you want me to stow this?"

"Just put it in the wheelbarrow there. I'll take it back to the workshop later," Maggie said.

"I got the ones that were scraping the roof here and one that looked like it might slap against the upstairs bedroom in a good wind, but you need a professional to come out and take care of this before you end up with real damage. You girls need to promise me you won't try this kind of thing on your own again."

"Can't do that." Lillian placed her empty glass on the small wicker table. "I have a responsibility to keep this place up. I will promise to be careful though."

"Well, I'm no tree expert, but the thin bark on that pin oak has taken on some damage and I think that's going to cause some long-term trouble for you down the road."

"What kind of trouble?" she asked.

His face grew serious. "The next big storm that comes through could take it down. Could wreck the house, or even hurt someone. It's not something to ignore."

"I can't let that happen." Lillian wrung her hands. Just when she thought she was getting ahead, something else swept her off balance. A tree in the middle of the house sure as heck wouldn't pass muster with that committee review, especially with Angelina running the darn thing. That woman had been looking for a way to ruin Lillian's standing in the community for years.

"I'm sure it's hard to take care of an estate this size by yourself." He propped one foot up on the rail and guzzled his drink.

Lillian nodded. "It's always been my home. It's my duty."

Teague set his glass on the porch rail and tipped his hat back. "You know, you could probably hire a live-in handyman in exchange for room and board. I've heard of folks doing that. Doesn't cost you a dime, and this place is sure big enough that it's not like he'd be underfoot."

Maggie looked put out. "I'm quite handy, you know."

"Yes, of course," Teague agreed. "It's good you're here to help with some of it now. I was just thinking some more hands might make easier work of it and keep you off the roof."

"He doesn't know what we're capable of together, does he, Lil?"

Lillian just grinned.

"I think I'm going to have my hands full with you two girls." Teague turned to leave. "Just try to stay out of trouble, would you?"

Maggie lifted her glass. "We'll see you soon."

Chapter Seven

Wielding that chainsaw had left Teague sore. He could only imagine what Maggie and Lillian would feel like this morning if they'd used that thing to cut those branches over Summer Haven's veranda. They couldn't have thought they were going to manage that tree on their own. He had a strong feeling those two old gals had played him, but it was just as well. He really didn't mind helping. All they had to do was ask.

After a long morning sitting in court for the slew of speeding tickets the department gave out each month, he was glad to be done early for the day. Maybe he could get some fishing in.

He went back to the station and, just as he pushed his IN magnet over to the OUT slot on the board, Deputy Barnes alerted him to an emergency call from Walmart.

"There's another boondocker," Deputy

Barnes said. "Want me to handle it?"

The last time Barnes had taken one of those calls, he'd tried to arrest the boondocker for conspiracy and treason. Sometimes that guy watched too much television. "I'll take care of this one. Then I'm off for the day."

Teague was in no big hurry to run off the poor folks just doing a little Walmart to Walmart camping spree across the country. They never caused any problems, but that new manager was such a stickler for the law, and all that had done was keep Teague and his deputy busy with silly calls like this. A waste of good time and the county's money.

He stopped by his house and picked up his tackle box and fishing pole. With everything he'd need, including a six pack and wigglers in a cooler, he headed off to handle his last task of the day.

The Walmart parking lot was crowded, but even so he didn't need to go in and talk to the manager to figure out who the culprit was.

The sunshine yellow VW bus took up two spaces off to the far side of the lot. The old vehicle wasn't in the way, but next to it stood an open market umbrella with a cooler and lawn chair. A bright purple rug sprawled alongside, and a long lean blonde in a colorful skirt and skintight tank top was stretched out in a pose that, from where he sat, looked like a cross between an Egyptian hieroglyphic and a burglar on the run.

Okay, so this could be distracting.

He parked and headed over to her. She moved from pose to pose and didn't seem to notice that he was standing right in front of her.

"Excuse me, ma'am."

The woman, who he'd assumed was in her late twenties from a distance, straightened and turned to face him. He slowed for a moment. She was no kid. With the fine lines around her mouth, she had to be in her fifties or older.

Her face spread into a perfect smile. "Greetings, my friend. Isn't it a glorious day?"

Perfect for fishing. Let's make this quick. "I'm sorry but I'm going to have to ask you to pack up and move along, ma'am."

"Why?"

"There's no boondocking allowed in this parking lot."

The woman folded to the fetal position with her chin tucked tight to her knees. Her strawberry blonde hair nearly touched the ground around her.

"Ma'am? I'm talking to you."

She slowly rose with her palms together and fingers pointed to her feet. "But I've stayed in Walmarts all over this beautiful country. No one has minded before."

"I'm sorry about that. There's a nice little inn up the street."

"I've got a place to sleep." She pointed toward her van. "Right here."

"That might be the case, but you can't do it in this parking lot."

She raised her hands to the sky and inhaled. He stood there waiting and wondering what the heck she would do next. She blew out an exaggerated breath, like she was blowing away a bad smell.

He took a step back.

"Could you let me just stay a day or two?" she asked. "Please?"

"I can't."

She looked him over, starting at his Astros baseball cap, meandering down his jeans to his boots and back up. Her gaze never returned to his face, but stalled somewhere south of his waist. She waved a finger in a circular motion aimed just below and slightly left of his belt buckle. "When was the last time you got a little...you know?"

Christ Jesus, was she checking out his package? Holy hell, maybe this was what that fountain had brought him. No more quarter tossing. No matter what. "That's not relevant. What's your name?"

She tsked and shook her head. "Your

chakras are telling the story, my friend. Listen up. It's not good to stay all bottled up for too long. You've got some problems there in the sacral chakra."

"The sack what?"

"The sacral chakra. It's your reservoir of sexual energy. When that chakra is under-active, it usually shows in your face. And believe me, I could look up *poker face* in the dictionary and find a picture of you, which means yours is pent up like a dam. It should be bright orange and vibrate to the musical note D." She spun around and grabbed a guitar from just inside the van's sliding door. She placed her fingers on the frets and strummed.

"What are you doing, lady?"

"Your junk didn't vibrate, did it? See, your sac—"

"Don't be talking about my sac anything or my junk. Look, I'm here on official business."

"I'm sorry. I was just trying to help." Her bottom lip turned down and quivered.

Why did he get the feeling that quivering was an act? "It would help me if you'd find somewhere else to park."

"I don't know where else to go."

She looked like she was in good shape. What with all the maintenance Summer Haven seemed to need, maybe Lillian and

Maggie could use the extra hand for a day or two. Couldn't hurt to ask. "Tell you what. Follow me. I think I know where you might be able to park for a couple of days."

"Really?" She jumped up in the air. Bells on her right ankle jingled like one of Santa's reindeer. "I knew you would help. I felt it."

"In my sa—?" Teague cut himself off. "Yeah. No. And no more of that talk."

Teague pulled into Summer Haven's driveway with the VW van right behind him.

Surely those old gals wouldn't be doing anything crazy this time. If they could just make this happen real quick-like, then he'd still have enough daylight for a little fishing. Just introduce them and haul ass. That was all there was to it.

He put the car in park and walked back to talk to the woman before she got out and started parading around doing flips or something. If he was going to foist her off on Miss Lillian, he needed her to look normal for ten minutes. "You never told me your name."

"Serendipity Johnson."

Of course it was.

He could picture the eye-roll he'd get when he asked Miss Lillian to let *Serendipity* park on her property for a couple days. They would mix about like crude oil and ocean water.

"My friends call me Sera."

Better. Much better. "Sera it is. I need to chat with Miss Lillian for a minute. You stay there." He patted the door panel. "I'll be right back."

"All I want is a parking spot. I can sleep in my own bed." She looked up at the big house and then back at Teague. "One person lives here?"

"Two."

Serendipity shook her head. "She's a widow. I feel mourning all around. This house used to be a beauty. There's a story here." She held out her hands as if inviting something to land in her palms.

He wondered what chakra colors Serendipity was seeing around that house—if houses even had chakras.

"Sit tight," he said, then turned and headed for the door.

He knocked on the front door with two quick taps and waited. He glanced back to make sure Sera was still in her van. So far, so good, but still he was second-guessing himself. Why had he thought it would be a good idea to bring his Walmart boondocker to Miss Lillian's? She was going to chew up this little flower child and spit her out without Serendipity knowing what the hell had just happened to her.

Bad, bad idea.

Before he could figure out another solution, the front door swung open. "Teague? Come to mow the yard today?" Lillian asked with a smile.

God help him. He'd never make it to the lake. "No, I have a little favor to ask."

Her smile dimmed a little. "Ask away."

Maggie poked her head around the door and then stepped next to Lillian. "What kind of favor?"

"You know, maybe this wasn't such a good idea—"

Lillian grabbed his forearm before he could turn away. "Teague Castro, stop being so namby-pamby. You came out here for a reason, so spit it out."

He hooked a thumb toward the yellow van in the driveway. "This lady needs a place to park for a couple days. That new manager at the Walmart called her in."

"Park? What do you mean *park?*" Lillian blinked with each word.

Maggie's face drew up like she'd smelled catfish bait. "You think Summer Haven is a campground?"

Okay. So it was a stupid idea. "I'll just tell her—"

"Is she young? Strong?" Lillian asked.

"Might be nice to have someone able-bodied to help around here."

Maggie stepped back and stared at Lillian the same way she'd looked at Teague. "What am I, chopped liver? Whatever I am, it's apparently not able-bodied."

Should've let Deputy Barnes take the damn call.

"Hush, Maggie," Lillian said. "You know that's not what I meant. But one woman...I mean two women...can only do so much. Wouldn't hurt to have another pair of hands."

Maggie went on tiptoes to peer over Teague's shoulder. "I'm not sure about her hands, but her feet are nimble."

Teague spun around to see Sera hitting poses that only circus performers should be able to do. *Shit. Didn't I tell you to stay in the car?*

"What in the world is she doing out there?" Maggie asked.

"I'm pretty sure that's called Downward Facing Dog—" Lillian tilted her head to the side, "—only with a leg in the air."

Maggie locked her arms over her healthy bust. "You ask me, she looks like Dog Planning to Pee."

That couldn't be easy. Teague pushed his hat up to get a better look. Almost looked like a pole dance without the pole. *Wonder if*

Jenny Cady does yoga? "Her name is Sera. She's very...nice."

"And very flexible," Maggie added.

Lillian skirted Teague and headed down the steps.

"Lil, you can't be serious," Maggie protested.

But Lillian just kept marching toward the yellow van, with Maggie and Teague on her heels.

"Hello there," Lillian said as they got closer.

Serendipity slowly returned to a standing position. "Hey! You must be the widow. I'm Serendipity."

Lillian look gobsmacked and Teague stiffened. *Please don't say anything about her chakras.* "Sera. Her friends call her Sera," he interjected.

But Serendipity didn't seem to realize she'd been rude and took Lillian's hand in both of hers.

Teague could hardly believe his eyes. As Sera held her hands, Lillian seemed to soften and a look of peace came over her.

"I'm Lillian, and this is my best friend, Maggie."

Sera finally released Lillian's hand and grasped Maggie's arms. "So nice to meet you both."

"Teague says you need a place to park,"

Lillian said.

"I'd planned to get a few odd jobs in town and visit for a short while, but I guess it just wasn't meant to be."

A tiny smile hovered around Lillian's lips. "It might work out yet. Summer Haven needs a little maintenance work. Do you have any experience?"

"I'm a quick learner and a good cook." Sera grinned. "I'm an excellent painter. I once helped a very famous artist, who shall remain nameless, with a mural that got national attention. Well, mostly I filled in the blanks and cleaned his brushes but I learned a lot. I'm very handy. Count me in."

Maggie had disappeared around to the back of the van. She returned looking skeptical. "Lil, before we strike a bargain here, we should ask a few questions."

Lillian was already beaming at Sera. "Like what?"

"You've come quite a long ways," Maggie said to Sera. "California?"

"Yes. I've been mapping my way state-to-state across the country doing some...soul-searching. I don't stay in any one place too long."

Maggie gestured to the back of the van. "Quite a bumper sticker collection you have there. Not only are we staunch Republicans, something you might want to know, but I saw that Legalize Marijuana sticker."

Lillian slapped a hand to her chest.

Teague felt like he'd swallowed that cup of night crawlers. Hell, he'd never get to the fishing hole at this rate.

"You don't do drugs, do you?" Maggie asked.

"Very rarely," Sera said. "I try to find natural ways to heal my body."

"What does that mean?" Maggie asked. "Yes, you do drugs or no, you don't. Which is it?"

Lillian knew that hands-on-the-hips stance of Maggie's and quickly tugged her to the side. "Maggie, let's chat for a minute."

Once they were out of earshot, Maggie jerked her arm away from Lil's hold. "What in hell's bells are you thinking? Not only does she have one of those Legalize Mary Jane stickers, there's another one that says Free Love."

"We need more help around here." *Honey, you are going to be so glad you have the extra help. Believe me.*

"So hire someone. You can't seriously be considering letting her stay."

"Well, I am."

"But...but she's a walking, talking California

cliché."

Lillian leaned around Maggie and smiled and waved. "What could it hurt to let her park here and help out for a few days?" She could almost picture the growing list of to-dos shrinking with the extra help. Her days were slipping away and there was still so much to do, especially now with that August inspection looming. Under normal circumstances, she would figure out a way around Angelina's little scheme, but she was running out of time. Turning away Sera would be like looking a gift horse in the mouth. Downright stupid. "Besides, if she were into anything illegal, Teague would've taken care of it."

"She was boondocking, wasn't she?"

"Really, Maggie? That's the best you've got?"

"Well, then, what kind of name is Serendipity? She's a dippity-do if you ask me."

Think, Lil, think. How to change Maggie's mind?

"I bet she could whip through those bags of scratchers in record time." Lillian leaned closer to Maggie, dangled the biggest worm in her almost empty tackle box. "Maybe she could even help you paint the carriage house."

"Lil? Really? You're going to let me paint the carriage house?"

"Isn't that what you wanted?"

Maggie rushed back to Sera and Teague. "Serendipity, welcome to Summer Haven!"

Chapter Eight

In one week with Sera's help, Lillian was able to mark off several more items from the to-do list. Teague's request to let Sera park here for a few days had been a heavenly gift. Plus, Maggie was so happy to be fussing around with the gosh darn carriage house, and she'd made a huge dent in those lottery ticket bags. There was actually a path through the middle of that space now. She didn't have the heart to tell Maggie it was all for nothing.

She tucked the remainder of her cash in an envelope with instructions, slipped it into the front of the notebook and put it back in the drawer. She stood and pushed the chair back under the desk, then went into the parlor to peer out the front window.

Lillian watched the children bring Summer Haven's front lawn to life. It was like this all summer, every summer. The kids chased each other around the gazebo, turning cartwheels in the grass and sprawling under the trees that had sheltered generations of Summers.

At one time, Lillian had dreamed her own children would build forts and play hide-and-seek on this land. Without her conscious thought, her hand went to her abdomen. *Silly old woman.* That place was as empty as the offering plate after it passed by Deacon Jones.

Lillian smoothed her hands down the seams of her summer-weight skirt. The peach suit had been a favorite of Momma's. Lillian had kept it all these years, and wearing it today felt both right and so terribly wrong.

She caught sight of Maggie hefting a piece of plywood painted as a backdrop for the play the local children staged in Summer Haven's gazebo every July Fourth. That woman was in hog heaven hammering together the sets and making props. At least Lillian didn't have to feel completely guilty she'd begged her to move to Summer Shoals. Maggie was happy here.

At least she would be for another five minutes before Lillian walked out there, took her aside and dumped a whole load of poop in her lap.

But Maggie was strong, hardy stock. If anyone could scoop poop and get on with things, it was her.

A flash of tanned leg streaked by with half a

dozen kids trotting along behind. That Serendipity was a piece of work. She'd certainly made herself at home after parking that eyesore of a van down the hill near the creek running across the property. Maggie had tried to talk her into sleeping in the house, but Sera had insisted she had everything she needed.

What kind of fifty-something woman dressed in cut-off shorts and ran around barefoot?

Sera wasn't the kind of companion Lillian might've chosen for Maggie, but by the way the girls wore little floral wreaths in their hair, she was obviously good with children. She was pretty good with handiwork too. What she lacked in skill she made up with enthusiasm, and Maggie seemed to enjoy showing her the ropes. At least Maggie wouldn't be rattling around on this big old estate by herself.

The grandfather clock in the foyer bonged one o'clock. Lillian couldn't put this off any longer. She double-checked her handbag. Lipstick, tissue and wintergreen mints. Those three essentials and a woman could face anything.

When she walked outside, the noise level was a lovely buzz of high-pitched squeals, parental warnings and laughter. This. This was why Summer Haven had to be tended to.

It wasn't just the Summer family's home. It was whole town's home. People treated Summer Haven's front lawn as their own and the gazebo as a sort of community center. *Daddy would love this.*

Lillian stood on the porch and soaked it all in one last time.

Maggie hustled toward the house, her hair a mess of sweaty curls and her cheeks the color of that godawful shirt appliquéd with sheep. "Have you seen that case of duct tape I bought from the hardware store?" Then her brow lowered as she took in Lillian's trim suit and heels. "Where are you going? Aren't you going to watch the kids practice the play?"

"The tape is in the bottom of the china cabinet in the parlor. I have an errand to run in the city, so I won't be able to stay for the performance today." She took a breath, tried to fill her insides with courage. "But while I've got you here, I need to talk to you about—"

"Lil, can it wait until later? I just realized we don't have a rhinoceros costume, but I can make one in a jiffy if I can find that darn tape."

"Sure. We have all the time in the world." What a whopper of a lie.

Thank goodness Maggie had already rushed into the house. Otherwise, she might've seen the tears Lillian blinked back. But now, without her good-bye explanation, the binder she'd left Maggie would be more confusing than enlightening. Lillian rushed around to the back of the house and slipped inside through the veranda door. She ducked into her bedroom, pulled out another sheet of stationery and tried to find the right words to give Maggie strength and help her understand.

By the time Lillian was finished with the note, she was running late for her appointment, which meant there was no time to stop by the pawnshop today. She'd have to figure out something between now and next week or her ring would be gone. But she just couldn't lay that at Maggie's doorstep today. Lillian pulled the pawn ticket out of her purse and tucked it back between the books on the desk. She blew out a breath, but her chest didn't lighten.

In the garage, the blue Torpedo was fueled up and ready to go. Lillian got behind the wheel and navigated the curved drive, keeping her speed to a crawl and waving at the children like the homecoming queen she'd once been. When she passed the Summer Shoals city limit sign, population 8,324, Lillian didn't allow herself even one glance back.

Chapter Nine

The first hour of the drive, Lillian's hip complained. But now, as every mile brought her closer to her final destination, her body had become one big numb lump. How would Maggie react when she found the note Lillian had left? It took a lot to get Maggie riled, but once her hackles were up, she was like a badger, not letting it go until she was good and ready.

Lillian glanced out her window. What had begun as a day of blue sky frosted with clouds was now a gray swirl. God had a way of painting the right backdrop for every occasion and today was no exception.

She exited the interstate and followed the directions she'd been given. Of course, she was required to stop before entering the parking lot. She rolled down her window and tried to smile at the young man in the booth.

"Name, ma'am?"

"Lillian Fairview Summers."

"And who are you here to visit?"

Wasn't he sweet? "I'm not visiting. I'm...checking in."

He looked up from his clipboard and studied her intently. "What is this world coming to?" He said the words under his breath, but there was nothing wrong with Lillian's hearing. Tipping his clipboard at the Torpedo, he said, "I don't think you're going to want to leave a car like that just sitting in the lot."

"Someone will pick it up later."

"Be sure to have them added to the visitor list."

Like she had any idea how to do that. But she would soon. "Absolutely."

The young man handed her a sheet of paper to place between her dash and front window, and Lillian headed into the parking lot.

The gates slid closed in her rearview mirror.

She parked and sat staring at the flat-roofed white building in front of her. It stretched the length of the lot, and although it looked freshly painted, no shrubs or flowers softened the austere façade. Maybe there was a courtyard on the other side. That would be nice.

Lillian closed her eyes. She breathed in the scent of the vanilla air freshener she'd stuck in the vent to chase off that musty smell that invaded the old car. She ran her hand across the front seat. The smoothly worn upholstery was a reminder of simpler, happier days. Days when Daddy would drive her into town for a lollipop or a soda.

She tried to relax her tense muscles. Too bad she hadn't asked Sera to teach her some easier yoga moves. Right about now, she could use some of that calm Sera was always bragging about. Well, just thinking about it wasn't going to get the job done. And procrastination was never polite. Lillian snatched up her purse and jumped out before she could change her mind and speed home to hide in Summer Haven's bomb shelter.

She pressed a kiss to the Torpedo's key, leaving a pink stain on the metal. She laid it on top of the front tire, like she'd told Maggie in her good-bye note.

With a tug on her suit jacket, she lifted her chin and marched toward the building where she would receive her just rewards.

Last night, Maggie had been so darn exhausted after wrangling the kids and their parents that she'd dragged her rear-end straight to bed without eating supper or saying boo to Lillian.

As she wandered into the kitchen for her morning bowl of rice cereal, it occurred to her that she'd never even noticed when Lil returned from Atlanta. But her bedroom door had been closed yesterday evening, and now, after nine o'clock, it was still closed. Strange since Lil was normally up with the birds.

Something had been weighing on her friend's mind, probably the last of those scratcher tickets. The bags were finally starting to dwindle. Five more and Maggie could start work on the carriage house. Just the thought made her insides dance.

Unfortunately, all those bags had yielded less than a hundred bucks since three of the winning tickets were for games that had already ended.

The money wasn't much, but those winning tickets paid for the paint needed for the play backdrops, which the Summer family sponsored every year. Maggie knew that Lillian had hoped for a windfall from those tickets, and even eighty dollars had been enough to keep them from abandoning the possibility of finding more hidden cash among the losers. She prayed like heck they'd get lucky soon.

Then again, maybe just being done with it was luck enough.

Maggie was proud of the contribution she'd

made to the play. Creating the backdrops had given her a chance to use her tools and get creative too. Maybe next year, she'd talk her daughter, Pam, into letting little Clint and Chloe come to Summer Haven for a couple of weeks before July Fourth so they could participate in all the festivities. God knew, little Miss Chloe would eat up the stage like a spoonful of honey. And the thought of having her grandkids around here put a big smile on Maggie's face. Without the responsibility of the hardware store, grandma time would be even more fun.

She rose from the table and washed out her bowl. She had a little time this morning to work on those trash bags of lottery tickets, but if she had help it would go even faster.

Time to give Sera another project.

Sure, Sera'd entertained the children during play practice, but Maggie still wasn't sold on Lil's decision to let her stay at Summer Haven. And rather than setting up camp close to the house, Sera had insisted on parking her van down by the creek at the back of the property. Who voluntarily went without indoor plumbing?

Woman was a lug nut shy of a hubcap.

Regardless, the more she helped with the scratch-offs, the closer Maggie came to moving into the carriage house. Reason enough to be friendly.

Rooting around in the pantry, she pulled out a box of bran cereal with raisins and tucked it under her arm. Then she poured milk in a plastic container. No telling if Sera had anything fresh in her camper. By the time she made it across the back lawn, up a little rise and down the hill that tumbled into the creek, she was puffing like the little engine that couldn't. She tried to moderate her breathing, but her chest was still rising and falling too rapidly by the time she made it to the front of Sera's VW.

"Sera," she called. "I brought you a little breakfast."

There was no answer, so Maggie poked her head around the camper. Sera had the van door pulled back and a cute little camp set up under a tarp. Maggie couldn't help but reach out and shake the nearest pole. Surprisingly sturdy.

Okay, maybe she isn't as dippy as I thought.

A splash came from the direction of the creek. Maggie turned to see Sera wade out of the water, naked as the day her momma'd given her breath.

Lord, Jesus! Something hot and tight lodged in Maggie's chest.

Surprise? Embarrassment? No, that was

pure-D jealousy.

The woman's skin was the same lovely golden color all over. Her long wet hair streamed over her shoulders.

Lordy goodness, was that a belly button ring? Tattoos, a belly ring and naked as a jaybird. Why couldn't Maggie have aged that well? Sera's hips were a little wider than they'd looked in those stretchy pants yesterday, and if Maggie squinted hard enough, she was pretty sure she spotted a patch of cellulite right there on Sera's thigh. But a woman Sera's age with breasts that perky? God just wasn't fair.

Then again, if Maggie looked like that, she might just go skinny-dipping, or for that matter, parade through Walmart without a stitch on.

"Hey there, Maggie." Completely unselfconscious, Sera smiled and pulled a towel from her clothesline. Rather than wrapping it around her body, she dried her face and twisted it turban-style around her head.

Maggie tried not to gawk, she really did, but not only did Sera have that cute little swirly tattoo around her ankle, she also had an intricately inked angel on her right shoulder blade. "That's so pretty."

Sera glanced over her shoulder, but her

sunny expression dimmed a little. "Different times."

Finally, she stepped into some flowing pants and a tank top. No bra. Okay, Maggie might as well suck that one up because it didn't matter how much weight she lost, she was never going to be able to walk around without strapping those puppies up as tight as she could. "I brought you breakfast."

"How nice." Then Sera saw what was in Maggie's hand. "Oh, I'm sorry, but I don't eat processed foods."

"But it's bran cereal." Didn't Sera know a peace offering—or a bribe—when she saw one?

"Have you really looked at those raisins? They're coated with sugar."

No, she hadn't because she wasn't much of a fruit eater. "Suit yourself."

"I have a nice quinoa I put in the cold box last night. I glaze it with a little local honey and some flaxseed. Would you like some?"

Here it was, her chance to turn over a new leaf. Maybe this would be the path to her own remodel, and Lord, if she could look good enough to go skinny-dipping in the creek, it would be worth it. "Sure."

Sera served up two bamboo bowls of a lump of brownish grain with a stingy amount of honey and sprinkled on top what looked like fleas.

Maggie took a cautious bite. Not horrible. Not an ice cream sundae, but she could swallow it.

"I have a favor to ask," Maggie said between bites. "Think you'd be up to helping me sort through a few bags of scratch-off lottery tickets?"

"Like grocery bags?"

"Think a little bigger." A *lot* bigger.

"No problem."

When they headed up toward the house fifteen minutes later, Lil was still nowhere to be found. Maggie's chest tightened and her breath shallowed as she rushed to the detached garage and threw open the side door. The Torpedo was gone. Oh, Lord have mercy, what if Lil hadn't come home at all yesterday?

Maggie patted the pockets of her carpenter pants looking for that fancy little phone her son had bought her for Mother's Day. Heck if she knew how to use half the functions. The thing could probably build a house by itself if she just knew which buttons to use. She punched the one programmed to call Lil's phone, held it to her ear and weaved through the house. She knocked on Lil's bedroom door, but didn't wait for an answer when she heard "Für Elise" playing from the other side.

Lil's bed was made, the corners precise and the pillows fluffed. Maggie's insides contracted even more. Something had happened to her in the city. That was the only explanation. And Lillian couldn't even call for help because her cell phone was sitting on her nightstand.

As Maggie reached for the other phone to call the sheriff, she noticed a piece of Lil's monogrammed stationary propped directly in the center of a pillow.

Dearest Margaret,

Lil's use of my given name is never good news.

> *First, I want to tell you how sorry I am. I wanted to tell you. I tried, but then time got away from me. Now it's your birthday. Happy Birthday, my dearest friend.*

She's dying. Lil has cancer and has checked herself into hospice care. Maggie held her hand to her heart and drew in a breath.

> *I've done something I simply can't undo and you're*

the only person in this world I trust to keep my secret and take care of my home. If I were a stronger woman, I would have told you weeks ago.

I left you a binder in my desk drawer, along with a few hundred dollars. I know it's not enough to maintain Summer Haven fully, but only take care of what absolutely cannot be avoided. The taxes are paid up, and so is the insurance, and I've left enough money in the estate account to cover the bare essentials, but whatever you do, you are not to use any of your own money to maintain the estate. In its current condition, Summer Haven should pass Angelina's *trumped-up inspection.*

Maggie wasn't as confident of Summer Haven's condition as Lillian. She'd seen the water damage and structural concerns that maybe the average onlooker wouldn't notice. Hopefully, Angelina and her posse wouldn't be well-versed enough to notice either. She scanned the note again.

Where in the world is Lil's money? The Summer family came from money so old, rumor was Abraham had opened the family's first checking account. Had Harlan squandered all the Summer family money?

I know you'll be busy with the July Fourth celebration for the next few days, but afterward I would like to ask you one more favor. Please pick up Daddy's Torpedo. I've left the key on top of the front tire. It's in the parking lot at 5400 Ellington Boulevard, Salisbury, Georgia, as soon as you get a chance and then store it in the garage.

Maggie, I know right now you're confused. You may even find yourself hurt and angry eventually, but please know I did what I thought was best for everyone involved. There's no one in the world I trust more than you.

Thank you for being my best friend for all these years.

Love always,

Lil

An unnatural weight pressed against Maggie's bladder, and she trotted into the downstairs powder room and plopped on the toilet. What was Lil thinking, leaving her that letter, a piece of paper that no more explained what Lil was about than a man on the moon?

If you think I'm going to wait until after the Fourth to get to the bottom of this, the brain in that skinny little head of yours is going mushy.

Maggie flushed, washed her hands and face and stormed outside to find her *new* best friend, Sera.

Chapter Ten

She marched to the gazebo where Sera sat cross-legged in the grass, humming a tune while she painted fine detail on Yankee Doodle Dandy's top hat.

"Sera, I know I'm asking favors right and left today—" Maggie tried to catch her breath, "—but I need you to go somewhere with me."

"But what about the scratch-off tickets? I was going to work on those as soon as I got done with this costume."

"This is even more important." Shoot. Maggie remembered her truck had under a quarter tank of gas. "And I need you to drive."

Some of her desperation must've shown in her face because Sera popped to her feet and tossed her paintbrush into a can of water. "It'll take me ten minutes to break camp."

"I'm really sorry about this, but—"

Sera held up a hand. "You should stop apologizing. It decreases your psychic stamina, opens your brain and body to toxic chemicals."

Okay.

Sera hotfooted it around the house and across the meadow. By the time Maggie caught up with her, the tarp was down and folded and Sera was stowing the last of her few belongings in the van. "Where are we going?"

"I don't know."

Now, Sera stared at Maggie like she was a pancake shy of a short stack. And oh, didn't maple syrup sound delicious about now? Maggie shook her head. "I mean, I have an address. Do you have a GPS?"

Sera waved a hand toward the east. "I go where I'm moved to go."

"Then stop by the house and I'll grab mine."

A few minutes later, they were putt-putting out of Summer Haven's driveway and headed northwest.

An hour and a half and three pit-stops for Maggie to pee later, Sera pulled up to a gatehouse flanked by tightly woven chain link fence. Maggie leaned toward the driver's side window and said, "Hi, we're here to pick up Lillian Summer's car, but I'm not sure we're in the right place."

"Do you know when she arrived?"

"Yesterday."

He flipped through his papers. "I see it

here. It should be in slot number 56. I'll need your names and IDs before I can let you into the lot."

They passed him their driver's licenses and he jotted down something on his clipboard and passed them back. He had a patch on his shirt sleeve, but the embroidery was too tiny for Maggie to make out the words. It was obvious this was some kind of official facility though.

She said, "Forgive me—" She glanced at Sera to see if she'd caught Maggie apologizing again. *Busted.* "I mean, could you tell me what this place is? Our friend left us a note to pick up her car, but no other information."

The young man's face scrunched with what looked like pity and he pointed to the sign to the right of the gate. If it had been a snake, it would've bitten her.

The letters on the metal sign were raised and slightly faded. Strung together, they spelled *Walter Stiles Federal Prison Camp.*

Snake? That sign was nothing less than a fork-tongued copperhead.

Maggie and Sera exchanged a look but neither said a word. Sera slowly pulled into the parking lot and parked in the spot next to the Torpedo.

"Did you bring the keys?" Sera asked.

"Lillian left them on the front left tire."

"In California, you couldn't do that. Someone would boost it for sure."

Maggie stared at her. "If you haven't noticed, we're inside a federal prison facility."

Sera lifted a shoulder. "More criminals here than anywhere else. Right?"

"Good point." *Criminals.* Could that word possibly apply to Lillian? Maggie was sure as shooting going to find out.

Her every muscle shot, Maggie rolled bonelessly out the van door and plodded over to Lillian's car. The doors were locked. She felt around on the front tire for Lil's keys and pocketed them.

Sera hung out the driver's side window. "What now?"

"I'm going inside," Maggie said, then turned and headed for the door in the center of the plain white building. *You can't just dump and run on me like this, Lil. I'm going to get to the bottom of this. Today.*

Gravel skittered behind her, causing Maggie to spin around.

Sera smiled a sheepish smile. "I don't want to sit out here alone. This is a freaky place."

Maggie glanced down at Sera's bare feet. Was that even permissible in prison? Guess they were about to find out.

They hiked across the lot to the front door. The door was locked but a buzzer hung on the wall next to it.

Maggie punched the button.

After a moment, she pressed it again.

Finally, someone answered. The scratchy voice was like the worst drive-thru restaurant. *You want fries with that?* "Walter Stiles Federal Prison Camp. Please state your business."

"We're here to see Lillian Fairview." Please let that tinny voice tell her there had been some mistake. That she'd never heard the name.

"I'm sorry, but visiting hours are over for the day. You can come Monday for special holiday hours between 10 a.m. and 2 p.m."

Maggie's stomach cramped. Not only hadn't the person on the other end denied that Lillian was there, but visiting hours were smack dab in the middle of the parade and play. "So...so are you telling me that she's in there somewhere?"

The silence stretched out. "You are here to visit an inmate, correct?"

"I don't know. You tell me." That last word definitely came out of Maggie's mouth a shriek.

Sera grabbed her hand and squeezed.

"Lillian Summer Fairview voluntarily surrendered yesterday. You may visit her the day after tomorrow during the hours stated.

Otherwise, the next visiting hours are on Friday from 1 p.m. to 4 p.m."

The intercom clicked off and Maggie's knees melted to the consistency of carpenter's putty. She'd either have to miss the Fourth of July parade or wait until Friday to see Lillian.

Lil, it's going to kill me to wait, but I know that's what you would want.

Sera wrapped her arm around Maggie. "Come on. Nothing we can do here today." They walked back to the parking lot. "Are you sure you're okay to drive? Why don't you let me take you home? We can pick up the car when we come back to visit Lillian."

Maggie lifted her chin. "No. I'll do exactly as she asked. I don't know what the heck is going on, but I'll have to find a way to help her."

"You jump behind the wheel then. I'll follow you. If you feel shaky at any time, you just pull over."

"I'll be fine." Maggie pulled the keys from her pocket and unlocked the car. She looked at the flowery woman-child next to her. "Thank you for being such a dear. I appreciate it." Maggie slid behind the wheel of Lil's daddy's precious car and closed the door.

Sera ran over to the van and fired it up.

Maggie cranked the Torpedo. *Lil, I never thought I'd be driving your daddy's car. What have you done?*

On her way out of the lot, she glanced once more at the prison camp sign. *They said she's really here. That she surrendered.*

Lillian. Her Lil. A jailbird.

After the orientation session, Lillian's head was reeling with all the dos and don'ts of federal prison life. She stepped out of the changing area wearing her prison-issued khaki shirt, khaki pants and a pair of steel-toe shoes.

She looked down at herself and wiggled her toes. Too bad they didn't issue a handbag to match this fashion *faux pas*. She'd need extra makeup if she was stuck wearing this. Khaki just wasn't her color.

She pushed her lips together hoping to pinken them up, then carried the paper sack with the rest of her assigned wardrobe out into the hall as she'd been instructed. The stiff cotton scratched at her thin skin and she'd had to turn the bottom of the pants under so they didn't drag on the floor.

The line of women who'd gone through orientation with her stood single file like a row of naked paper dolls waiting for some colorful clothes. Some of them looked so young. Too young to be locked up like this. Yes, this was a minimum security facility with supposedly the best amenities a lawbreaker could expect, but it was prison just the same. Most of these folks probably weren't dangerous criminals, but were here on white-collar crime and drug charges. Still, it was such a shame.

As they marched through the front building to their assigned dormitory, she noticed many of the young girls' pant hems dragging across the cloudy-looking floor. If only she had a thread and needle she could fix this problem in a quick hurry. She hadn't run the Summer Shoals Quilting Bee in her home every summer for more years than she cared to count without becoming quite adept with a needle and thread.

Lillian studied her surroundings. The whole place looked as if it could use a fresh coat of paint, and some color would be nice. Flowers maybe? *Don't be setting up housekeeping. I won't be here that long. If I keep my head down, hands busy and mouth shut, I'll be back home at Summer Haven before I know it.*

The group was led into a huge room holding at least a hundred metal bunk beds. Each was partially surrounded by a chin-high cinderblock wall painted with a number. Those thin mattresses certainly didn't look as comfy as her pillow-top at home. Nary a throw pillow in the place either.

Lillian put her limited wardrobe away and then turned to see a red-headed woman standing behind her. Well, at least the bottom half of her hair was red. Her roots were about six inches of dark brown with wiry grays springing out in three directions.

"Heard I was getting a new bunkmate," the woman said.

With her best Summer Shoals meet 'n' greet grin, Lillian extended her hand. "I'm Lillian Summer Fairview. So nice to meet you."

The woman raised a brow and stepped back instead of toward her. "That's a lot of big names for a woman little as you. What the heck did you do to end up here?"

Her tongue went numb. Oh, Lord. She should've considered this question would come up right out of the chute. She dang sure wasn't going to roll back to Harlan squandering all her money on lottery tickets every time someone asked what she'd done. If she had to guess, there were nearly a thousand inmates. She'd probably still be telling the story when she walked away at the end of her sentence.

"Fine, so you don't want to share. I'm Dixie. How long you in for?"

Hmm...what about not wanting to share hadn't she understood? But still Lillian said, "Not as long as they said, I hope."

"Don't we all?"

Lillian dug a long sleeve T-shirt out of her bag and pulled it over top of her shirt.

"You have to wear that under your other shirt," Dixie said. "It's the rule."

"Certainly you're kidding."

Dixie shook her head. "Seriously. The shirt with your name identification and bar code has to be worn on the outside of whatever else you're wearing. All the time."

Lillian frowned. She wasn't particularly interested in undressing down to her bra in front of this stranger, but she was cold and the bathroom was a trek from here. Probably wasn't the last humiliating thing she'd be subjected to in this place.

Unbuttoning the camp shirt was difficult with her aching fingers but she managed to get them undone. She slipped it off and put on the long sleeve T-shirt and then pulled the camp shirt back on and tucked it into her pants. She tugged the waist of her shirt out and pouffed it a little to make it look a little nicer. The shades of khaki didn't even match. Yellow-tones and blue-tones together. Might as well have been plaid and stripes.

Once Lillian was re-dressed, Dixie said, "You gonna tell me what you done?"

Lillian folded her arms across her chest. "I spent some money that wasn't mine to spend."

"Embezzlement, huh? Usually it's the other way around. Old ladies being embezzled. Not old ladies doing the embezzling. Good scheme. I like it."

"I'm not proud of it."

"Hey, whatever floats your boat. I'm in no position to judge you."

"What brought you into this unfortunate circumstance?"

Dixie laughed. "Unfortunate? Honey, after the amount of bad checks I wrote, there's not a darn thing unfortunate about landing in Walter Stiles Federal Prison Camp. Compared to real prison, it's like living in luxury. I couldn't ask for more."

Only Lillian knew better. She'd had more. She knew what more felt like, and this was not luxury.

"They give you a work assignment yet?"

"Cleaning the bathrooms."

Dixie wrinkled her nose. "Yeah, lots of the newbies catch that one."

"I've taken care of a four-bathroom home for many years."

"Betcha there ain't five-hundred women traipsing in and outta your shitters every day though."

Lillian closed her eyes. Just the very idea of cleaning up after all those people exhausted her, especially after everything she'd done trying to get Summer Haven ready for her absence. "Surely they can't make us work all the time."

"Nah, lots of other stuff going on around here after work hours. Kickball in the rec area, bingo, aerobics, church and stuff."

"What about personal hygiene?"

"I'm sure they already told you that you can buy stuff in the commissary."

"Yes, but—"

Dixie cocked her head. "Sweetheart, if you think we got a mani-pedi chair around here or one of those salons, then you're SOL."

"SOL?"

"Shit outta luck."

Lord, yes, I am so SOL.

"What are you doing here?" Dixie was staring over Lil's shoulder.

Lil turned to find a woman—probably in her forties with black hair, acne scars and big, rough hands—standing hipshot in the so-called doorway.

The woman pointed at Lillian. "You need to come with me."

"Janisse, leave her alone," Dixie said.

"Who're you to tell me what to do, Dixieland?"

"One of these days, girl—" Dixie, her chest puffed out, crowded the other woman, "—you are going to be so sorry you ever spoke to me that way."

Oh, no. These two women were obviously not friends. It wouldn't do to be caught between them.

"By that day, I'll be long gone." Janisse motioned at Lillian. "C'mon with you then."

Lillian took a step forward. "Where are we going?"

"Big Martha wants to chat with you. Now."

Like the Welcome Wagon? How nice. "Excellent." Lillian tucked her hair behind her ear and plastered her smile back on her face. "Shall we?"

With her mouth open and eyebrows raised, Janisse stared at Lillian and finally said, "Well, let's go then."

Janisse strode out of the dormitory and through the courtyard. Lillian tried to take in the small patches of grass and anemic flowers, but Janisse's stride was so long, Lillian had to darn near jog.

"Excuse me," Lillian called out. "Can you slow down?"

"Can't you speed up?"

"Are we in a hurry?" Lillian asked. "Because I'm quite sure I'm not going anywhere for fourteen months, or less if I get lucky."

Janisse spun around, loomed over Lillian. She raised her hand and Lillian swallowed, but didn't flinch.

Never let them see you sweat.

Janisse grabbed Lillian's wrist and lifted her hand, then smacked it in a high five. "Put it there, sister. Love your spunk."

Lillian relaxed. Well, fine then. She could do this.

They entered a cottage and Janisse stopped at door 7C, grabbed the knob and pushed open the door but didn't enter. "Go on in."

Wasn't that sweet? Lillian stepped through the door. But when the door slammed behind her, she jumped two feet in the air.

"Welcome to Walter Stiles Federal Prison Camp."

"Thank you." Lillian scanned the room to find a woman sitting on the left-hand bed with her back propped against the wall. Her uniform was nicely pressed, her hair needed a trim but was recently washed, and her nails looked freshly painted. Maybe the federal prison system should do a little roommate Match.com to pick bunkmates in these places because this woman looked more Lillian's style. Maybe she'd suggest it when she met the warden.

"Have a seat."

The command in her voice shot through Lillian and made her knees shake. "Who did you say you were?"

"Martha. They call me Big Martha around

here mostly."

"Well, Martha, as much as I appreciate your hospitality, I really can't stay. Count is in less than fifteen minutes and it took me ten to walk here from my dormitory." Which meant she had a five minute cushion, if that.

"Sit. Down."

"If you insist." Lillian's knees gave out and she plunked down on the other bed. "But only for a minute."

"I heard Dixieland is your bunkie."

Lillian just nodded.

"That girl is no good. You hang with her, she'll get you into trouble."

"Hang with her?" Dixie had certainly seemed nice enough.

"Do you understand what I'm saying?"

"Not entirely."

"I'm saying, Miss High and Mighty, there are a couple things you need to know. One, you need to mind your own damn business. Two, if you throw your loyalty to Dixie, then you've declared yourself my enemy."

Prison politics already? And just when she'd sworn she was going to keep her head down and mouth closed. Worked so well for all of an hour. Sure hadn't seen this coming.

Lillian buried her hands in her lap to hide the nerves making her fingers twitch. "I take it the two of you have differing interests."

Big Martha's laugh wasn't pleasant. "I figured you for a smart one."

"Well, thank you for your concern, but I'm not interested in pledging loyalty to anyone. I plan to do my work, do my time and that's it." Lillian slid off the bed and stood to leave.

"No, Miss H&M, that's not it. You can't make up your own set of rules around here. You play by what we've already set. Understand?"

Lillian lifted her chin but refused to respond.

"Tell you what, I'll be generous, give you a little time to think about which decision is in your best interest. Understand?"

Oh, she understood all right. Understood that she'd already landed in a big ole heap of horse dung. Lillian nodded and shot out the door. Janisse was standing guard and Lillian lifted her hand in a little wave. Then she took off as quickly as she could toward the dormitory, every running hop-step ramming her toes against the steel plate in her shoes.

As she hustled through the courtyard minding her own business, a big busty woman hip-checked her, causing her to stumble. She didn't even give the woman a second glance, just kept rushing back to her cube.

By the time she made it back, she had less than a minute to spare before count and she was pretty sure she'd lost a toenail.

Chapter Eleven

On the Fourth, Maggie woke up to a sunny day but in a dark and cloudy mood. She'd slept in Lil's bed, needing to feel close to her. First she'd lost George, and now she might well have lost Lillian.

Lillian, how could you leave me in this position? This isn't the kind of seventy-second birthday present I expected.

Caring for this big ole place and figuring out what the heck she was supposed to do to help her best friend was way more than she'd ever bargained for when she moved to Summer Shoals.

Dear God, was this happening because she'd been so whiny about having personal freedom and space? She'd just wanted to use the carriage house. She hadn't meant to get it like this.

She rolled out of bed and shoved her feet into her slippers. "Careful what ya wish for, I guess."

When Angelina Broussard had seen the Torpedo parked in front of Summer Haven yesterday, she'd been so excited that Maggie hadn't even realized what she was agreeing to until the woman was walking away. Lillian must have told Angelina the car was going to be in the shop to cover her absence. That also meant Lillian had known she wouldn't be around for the parade when she spoke to Angelina weeks ago.

Would have been really swell if you'd have shared that little tidbit with me, Lil.

That was what she got for neglecting to park the Torpedo back in the garage. Now she had to come up with a plan to cover her mistake. How was she supposed to pull off Lillian leading the parade with no Lillian?

She sure couldn't tell anyone Lillian Summer Fairview was in prison.

Prison. And prison sure wasn't a place for a William & Mary girl.

If people found out Lil was up the river, it would be the biggest scandal to ever hit Summer Shoals. And if Lil thought Harlan's scratcher tickets were worth keeping hidden, then Maggie sure knew to zip her lips about Lil's little *vacation.*

Maggie jumped to her feet. *Lil's parade outfit, that's the key!*

She ran across the room, threw open the double doors to Lillian's closet and shuffled through the clothes. Although she'd never personally come down for the Fourth of July parade, Lillian had sent her enough pictures over the years for her to know that Lillian wore the same red, white and blue outfit every year. It had to be in here somewhere.

She pushed past a dry cleaner bag of clothes, then paused. "There you are." She peeled away the thin plastic and admired the red-and-white striped jacket with silver stars embroidered on the epaulets.

Off went her nightshirt and she tried to pull the jacket over her bulky shoulders. "Oh, yeah. That's not going to happen."

She tossed the jacket on Lil's four-poster bed and plopped down beside it.

Suddenly, her brain conjured up the image of Sera coming out of the creek looking as fit and perfect as Bo Derek in that movie where she wore those cornrow braids. "Sera, you're doing Lil a favor this time."

Maggie shimmied into a red shirt decked out with appliquéd flags and rhinestone stars. She tucked it into a pair of khakis, then hurried to get to Sera. They had not a minute to lose.

She started to head for the back door, but caught the shadow of movement out the windows flanking the front door.

Oh, no. People were here for the parade already!

Hoping to head them off, Maggie hotfooted outside. But the crowd gathered on the Summer Haven lawn was worse—much worse—than early birds for the parade.

There in the middle of the yard, Sera was leading a group through yoga poses. No less than ten men were out there in blue jeans and T-shirts sweating like pigs and looking anything but elegant or relaxed. She could barely see Sera on the other side of them.

"Lord, please let Sera be fully dressed," Maggie whispered.

She hustled toward the contorted bodies, and relief streamed through her like a tall glass of her special tea. The tight little shorts and skimpy tank top Sera wore weren't much, but they covered her essentials even if that diamond belly-button ring was peeking out with every move.

Maggie skidded to a stop next to a trio of women.

"Look like a bunch of jackasses, don't they?" one woman said.

"I heard she's from Cal-ee-forn-i-a," another added. "And you know what they say about those women."

Wait a minute. Maggie might still be trying

to make up her mind about Sera, but these women had no cause to be talking behind her back. "No, what do they say?"

"They'll steal your menfolk in a New York minute."

Maggie pointed to the group, where half the men, chests heaving, had collapsed to the grass. "You think she wants to steal the likes of that?"

The woman frowned and nudged her friend. "She's got a point."

Maggie marched across the lawn. "Sera," she called. "Can I talk with you for a minute?"

"Friends, please move into triangle pose and I'll be back."

Maggie drew her out of folks' earshot. "I need your help."

"Of course, anything," Sera said.

"You have to pretend to be Lillian and ride in the Torpedo during the parade."

"But that's dishonest. Why can't you just explain that Lillian is in jail and can't be here?"

"That's not the way things work in a town like Summer Shoals." Steam gathered in Maggie's head and trickled out her ears. There was no time for debate. "Look here, Lillian brought you into the bosom of her home during your time of need and one good turn deserves another."

"But—"

"But nothing. Lillian has a reputation to uphold. If you want to stay at Summer Haven, you have to be loyal to her."

"Fine, but I'm not wearing shoes."

"Deal." Maggie's knees went loosey-goosey. *We can do this. Everything will be A-okay.*

While the entire town milled around Summer Haven waiting for the parade to start, Teague stood by the fountain, but he kept his hands—and his loose change—in his pockets this time.

He eyed the whole damn fountain with suspicion. His last wish had apparently conjured up Serendipity, and he could do without any more mention of his sac chakra.

The water spewed high into the air, rode the breeze and sprinkled down on the kids nearby. They squealed and ran away, but came right back.

Nash Talley was around the other side tossing in pennies one after the other. Teague meandered over, but Talley had his eyes closed, apparently concentrating on all those wishes.

"What'cha wishing for?" Teague asked.

Talley's eyelids popped open. "I can't tell you."

"Why? You got illegal wishes?"

Talley swallowed. Why did skinny men have such big Adam's apples? "No...no, of course not."

Teague slapped him on the back. "Just messing with you." He nodded at the shiny coins filling Talley's hand. "Looks like you've got a few more to go."

The guy nodded, but his eyes darted as if Teague had shined his flashlight into them. "Look, the parade's starting."

The kids and adults alike lined up along the side of the driveway.

Teague stepped closer. As she had every year since he'd moved to Summer Shoals, Miss Lillian rode on the back of her daddy's convertible. But this time, she shaded herself with a giant red and white golf umbrella. She turned his way to wave at the crowd. If he hadn't known who she was, he wouldn't have recognized her in those huge movie-star sunglasses and with her hair covered with some kind of wild-patterned scarf that clashed with her patriotic jacket.

The children shouted and begged for the candy Lillian always tossed from the car. As she smiled and flung a handful, her jacket hiked up and something at her midsection winked in the sunlight.

Teague said to Talley, "Did you see that?"

"See what?"

"Nothing. Never mind." Like he was going to tell the guy he thought Miss Lillian was wearing a belly button ring. Reelection wouldn't be so easy if folks thought he was losing his mind.

"Aww," whined a nearby child. "What's this? Where's the suckers and chocolate?"

All the kids who'd hit the ground to scrounge for candy wore puckered lips and scrunched-up eyes. And every last one of them was holding a handful of unshelled peanuts and dirty raisins.

What the hell was Miss Lillian thinking?

Chapter Twelve

With the Fourth of July behind them, and no one the wiser that Lillian had missed the parade, Maggie only wished for one thing. To know what the heck was going on with Lillian. Her emotions were still reeling over Lil's betrayal, so she asked Sera to drive on the ninety-minute trip to the prison camp again this morning. Finally, today she'd get answers.

Maggie barely paid attention while Sera chatted with the guard. The parking lot at Walter Stiles Prison Camp was near empty because visiting hours didn't start until 1:00 p.m. and it was only 11:30 a.m.

What in the world was she going to do with herself until then? Maybe it was long enough that she could decide if she was more angry than hurt about this whole situation before she saw Lil.

"Maybe we should've stopped for lunch," Maggie said. Then again, she'd felt guilty about every bite she'd put in her mouth since she found out Lil was in prison. Whatever they served in there, it couldn't hold a candle to Maggie's biscuits and white sausage gravy.

"We could find someplace to eat. I'm sure that nice man at the gate would help us," Sera said.

"Forget it," Maggie said. "I can't eat anyway."

"If you change your mind, I have some snacks. Waiting here is fine by me. I need to stretch after the drive." Sera hunched at the shoulders and duck-walked from the driver's seat to the back of the bus.

She stretched out in the middle of the floor and pointed her toes. The heavy breaths she was sucking in and blowing out sounded a little like someone on life support.

Maggie cranked down the window to get some fresh air and propped her elbow on the door. The heat and the funky smell permeating Sera's van were making her nauseous. That scent had to be the marijuana. Medicinal or otherwise, it wasn't pleasant.

Was it possible to get a contact high from residue left in the carpeted ceiling?

After doing a whole routine of VW van-modified yoga and a meditation session, Sera finally crawled back into the driver's seat and handed Maggie a little baggy of what looked like bark.

"What's this?"

"Anise and pumpkin seed granola. Go on. Try it. It's good for you."

Good for you was the kiss of death to a snack as far as Maggie was concerned. But she glanced over at Sera, in her flowing skirt and body-hugging top. *If there's a hope or prayer of me ever having a body half that amazing, it won't kill me to try it.*

Maggie poured some into her palm, then tossed it back like a shot of Gentleman Jack. "Blerg!" Half of it came spewing back out just as fast as it had gone in.

"What?" Sera leaned back trying to escape the sputtering spray of seeds.

Maggie grabbed her water bottle and guzzled to clear the nasty licorice residue from her throat and tongue. She popped open the glove box in a frantic search for relief. All she found was a small piece of cardboard. She tore it in half and scraped it down her tongue.

"What are you doing?"

"Clllng my thung."

"Quit being so dramatic. It's no worse than that marshmallow-filled cereal you have hidden in the back of the pantry."

Maggie rinsed out her mouth again, opened the door and spat. "Way, way worse." She capped the water bottle. "If that was all I had to snack on, I'd never snack again."

"It might be an acquired taste."

"No, Sera. Scotch is an acquired taste. That is like eating gardening supplies. No, thank you." Maggie looked toward the building, then grabbed her purse. "People are already lining up to get in. I'll be back in a bit."

"Can't I come with you?"

"Umm...if you want." Let the prison people be the ones to tell Sera that Lil hadn't put her on the visitor's list.

Once in line, it took them a good fifteen minutes to make it to the staff member checking IDs.

Maggie handed over her driver's license. "Margaret Rawls here to see Lillian Summer Fairview."

"You're on the list. Do you have anything on your person that would threaten the security of this institution?"

Not unless they counted heartburn from bad granola a security threat. "No, ma'am."

"You're clear."

"We're together." Maggie nodded toward Sera.

"Lillian Fairview doesn't have anyone else on her visitor list."

Even though she expected this, Maggie's heart squeezed. *Poor Sera.*

Sera's back went stiff. "I'm Mrs. Fairview's Minister of Record."

Maggie practically got whiplash as she spun around and gawked at Sera. *Her what?*

The guard checked another list and looked Sera up and down. "You're Reverend Marcus? If so I need your ID—"

Sera quickly laid a palm on the guard's shoulder. "Lamb of God, how long has it been since you prayed? I feel the sin invading your body. Your every thought. Let us pray together." She jerked her head toward Maggie.

Maggie lowered hers along with the guard, but watched Sera from the corner of her eye.

Sera's voice was smooth and comforting. "Father, we ask you this day for wisdom and the courage to do what's right." She scooted around the check-in table. "Let this woman no longer walk in sin, but rise up into the sunshine of compassion and love. Amen."

"Amen," Maggie murmured and tailgated Sera into the visiting room. They sat at a small round table and Maggie leaned toward Sera. "What was all that?"

"I used to really be into one of those crime shows. Guess it paid off."

This Serendipity Johnson was smarter than she looked.

"Nice furniture," Sera commented. "Sure is decked out for jail. Who needs a television that big? It's one of those hi-def jobs too. I'm not even sure it would fit in the back of my van."

Maggie hadn't even noticed. All she was able to absorb was that she was sitting in a federal prison waiting for her best friend. In all her years, it was the last place she'd ever expected to be.

A tiny colorless woman walked through the doorway, smiled at Maggie and waved her fingers in her direction. Maggie glanced behind her, looking for the woman's visitors, but no one was there. She turned back and gasped. *Lillian?*

In khaki from head to toe, Lillian could've disappeared like a soldier wearing camo in the desert. Not a flattering look. Lord, if this was what she looked like in just a week, what would happen to her if she had to stay here for long?

Lillian sat down at the table next to Maggie and across from Sera. "How've y'all been?"

"That's where you're going to start?" She hadn't meant to snap at her right off the bat, but really? *How've we been?* "Lillian, what in the world is going on? What have you gotten yourself into? What have you gotten *me* into?"

"Now, calm down."

"We're best friends." Maggie felt her lips tremble. "I want to know what happened."

"I'm so sorry. I wanted to tell you. I tried to tell you that last day, but you were so busy and—"

"Don't you dare lay this at my feet. I was busy that day, but you had every opportunity in the world before that. How long have you known?"

"A while. A long while, but the final date was just set last month." Lillian leaned over and laid her hand on Maggie's shoulder. The guard gave her the evil eye, and she dropped it again. "I really didn't mean to hurt you. I'm sorry I left you with such a mess, but I just need you to look out for Summer Haven while I'm here. I don't expect—no, I don't want—you to waste hours every weekend coming here to visit me. Please spend that time taking care of my home."

"I'm supposed to just babysit Summer Haven and yet you haven't even explained how you landed here, the worst place I could ever imagine."

"Might not be as bad as being checked into Dogwood Ridge Assisted Living. That tired old place doesn't have near the amenities. Nash Talley had a fundraiser in the Summer House gazebo to raise money for a gigantic television and a piano for the community room when he put his daddy in there. Trust me, neither of those are as high quality as the ones here at Walter Stiles Prison Camp."

"Lillian, you're worrying me. If you're trying

to convince yourself this isn't so bad, you just back up the bus. And before you do that, I want to know how the heck you landed in this godforsaken place."

"It all started so innocently. When Harlan died and I realized he'd squandered nearly every last cent we had, I had to do something. I needed to bury him the way folks would expect, so we held off just a little while on the paperwork to get a few extra Social Security checks—"

"*We?*" Maggie asked. "We who?"

Sera elbowed Maggie, bowed her head and said, "And the good Lord sayeth, be careful. The man is listening." Then she flashed her eyes wide and acted out the charades versions of the-walls-have-ears and zip-your-lip-and-throw-away-the-key.

Maggie inhaled. "Oh, she could be right."

Lillian glanced at another table where a forty-something woman was holding court with a couple of men.

"Nash—" Lillian paused, "—ville helped me."

Maggie's mouth opened, closed and finally formed words. "Nash-ville. That place that's to *die* for?"

"Right. That one."

"Lord love a duck, Lil." She'd pulled an innocent man into her scheme. "What were you thinking?"

"I never meant to do anything that would hurt anyone. I just wanted to bury my husband."

"Should have put him in one of those heavy-duty contractor bags," Maggie muttered under her breath.

"Don't think I didn't consider it," Lil said. "But I wanted to keep up appearances. I was so embarrassed. And hurt. And broke."

"And so you went to Nash-ville to bury him?"

"That was the only place I could think of."

"But those Nash-ville funerals are pretty cheap. You know with the pine boxes and all. I wouldn't think your Uncle Sa—" Sera cleared her throat and Maggie said, "—Sal would care much one way or another where Harlan was buried."

"Apparently, there were some extra expenses I didn't anticipate."

"Just how expensive was this funeral?"

"Somewhere in the $12,000 range."

"That's not so bad," Maggie said.

"Well, I'm not exactly sure how that twelve thousand turned into nearly eight times that in just five years, but that's what the government says I owe them once I get out of here."

Maggie sputtered and coughed. "Nash-ville

took you for a ride, Lil."

"What do you mean?"

"She means," Sera said, "something is rotten in the state of Nash-ville."

"Oh, please. Nash-ville is a lovely young...place. Stop trying to pretend I'm not guilty. I did break the law. Summers always pay their debts. You know what they say...you do the crime, you do the time."

Lillian sat next to Dixie in the dining facility with her head down and her focus on her plate of what the dining staff called chicken-fried steak.

Maybe, just maybe, Big Martha had forgotten about little ole Lillian Fairview. After all, she hadn't summoned Lil back to her cottage, nor had she demanded a show of prison fealty.

Lillian picked at the green peas on her tray. They were so mushy, the only way they were fresh was fresh from the can.

"Shit," Dixie hissed from beside her.

Lord, this girl needed a language makeover. "Dixie, if you don't stop talking that way, you'll never—" Lillian glanced up to see Big Martha striding toward their table. "Shit."

"I shoulda known better than to poke at Janisse the other day," Dixie said. "Big Martha don't like anyone who threatens her authority. You even look like you're gonna be more popular and powerful than her? Wham! There you go."

And by the way Big Martha was bearing down on them, it was obvious she expected Lillian's vote in the Most Likely to Succeed in Prison Camp race. Her uniform—as always—was neat and pressed, but her face was just as starched. "Well, Miss High and Mighty, it sure looks like you've made your choice."

Lillian's back went rigid at the sneering tone. "Martha, I'm simply enjoying lunch." She gestured to the bench across from her. "Feel free to join us."

Dixie shot her an *are-you-outta-your-gourd* look.

"I don't dine with losers," Martha said.

Lillian poked at her food again. If this was dining, she'd hate to see plain old eating. "Suit yourself."

"So this is it? I sure thought you were smarter than that." She turned to Dixie. "You don't want to make her my enemy, you hear me?"

Dixie flicked a hand toward Lil. "For Jesus sake, Big Martha. Lil is a hundred years old if she's a day."

Okay, now Lillian's spine was a flagpole.

"Why you want to go hating on a woman

who's old enough to be your grammy?"

"Wait a minute—" Lil started.

"You may be too stupid to recognize breeding, Dixieland. But women like Grammy Lil here? They can snatch away everything you got just like that." Big Martha snapped her fingers in front of Dixie's face. "You mark my words. Both of you."

The tight feeling in Lil's chest eased marginally as Big Martha strode away. She turned to Dixie. "What did you say that woman is in for?"

"I heard she was some kinda procurement specialist. This time she's up for some computer hacking scheme, I think."

"Procurement specialist. What does that mean exactly?"

"It means, one way or another—" Dixie stabbed at her peas, "—that whatever Big Martha wants, she gets."

Chapter Thirteen

Maggie pulled her hair back into a ponytail and plopped down on the floor in front of the old porcelain farm sink.

Since Lillian wasn't around to sidetrack her, Maggie had been able to check a few tasks off that long list of things that needed attention around Summer Haven. Of course, her prioritization of that list and Lillian's were not a match, and she'd already added as many new things as she'd marked off it. She could only venture to guess what would be most important to Angelina Broussard's so-called committee, but she could only worry about one thing at a time.

At least this one wouldn't cost much.

She made quick work of fixing the leaky faucet. It must have been dripping for a good long while. The tall stockpot was over half-full of skanky water. With a final twist of her wrench, she tightened the coupling and then slid the pot out from under the sink. As the stagnant water sloshed, a horrid smell filled her nose, almost making her gag.

Maggie clambered to her feet and flipped the faucet knobs. With the water flowing full blast, she pulled a penlight from her tool bag and looked for more leaks.

"Good as new." She wiped down her tools and placed them back in her handy tool tote. *A place for everything and everything in its place.*

Sera was still upstairs getting her shower. That girl took way too long in the shower. If she had any idea just how many gallons of water and kilowatts of power she was using, that yoga-drunk eco-lovin' weed of a woman would probably fall out. Maggie was tempted to install one of those shower timers that cut the water off after eight minutes.

She crossed to Lil's desk in the kitchen. The binder Lil had left her had so much stuff in it that she hadn't gotten past the list of to-dos yet. She checked off the line item REPAIR LEAKING KITCHEN SINK with a feeling of satisfaction. Much better than when she'd scratched through PAY OFF SUMMER HAVEN'S ACCOUNT AT HARDWARE STORE. That had taken most of the money Lil got for the Jenny Lind chest.

One more down.

She flipped the binder closed and stood it up to slide it between a set of bookends on the edge of the desk. As she wiggled the binder between the dictionary and Lillian's precious autographed copy of *Gone With The Wind,* something crinkled against the binder. Maggie reached for the slip of paper.

The yellow customer copy of the receipt was similar to the carbonless forms she and George had used in the hardware store. The familiar texture of that paper made her miss him a little. As she reached to tuck the receipt in the drawer, her eyes caught the merchant name J&R'S PAWNSHOP.

Now, why in the world would Lil have a pawn receipt?

She pulled her glasses from the top of her head and leaned back to get a better look.

Her hand went to her chest. "No."

The ticket detailed the item pawned: One 1.6 ct emerald-cut diamond w/ 4 1/3 ct baguettes, platinum setting.

"Lil, your wedding ring?" Maggie sat there staring at that slip of paper. She knew what that ring meant to Lillian. She must have been desperate to hock it for a measly three thousand dollars, because it was worth about ten times that amount.

Then she spotted the pawn date. April 10. Weren't pawned items usually sold after about ninety days? If that were the case—her heart squeezed—she'd come across this ticket four days too late.

Maggie snatched up the phone and dialed the pawnshop.

"J&R's Pawn. This is Rick."

"Rick, thank goodness. This is Maggie. Margaret Rawls."

"Do I know you?"

"No, but you know Lillian Fairview, don't you?"

He was quiet for several seconds. "I don't discuss my clients' business with other folks."

"Listen up, Rick. If you've sold Lillian's wedding ring, I'm going to drive directly to Atlanta, wrap my hands around your neck and wring it."

"Ma'am, there's no need for that kind of violent talk."

"Because you've already sold them?"

"No, because I gave Lillian an extra thirty-day grace period. I know how much that ring means to her, and it's not my intention for her to lose them. That being said..."

"You need the loan repaid."

"There's no help for it. I need the money no later than August tenth."

"I swear on my husband's grave that you'll have it." Maggie hung up and tears filled her eyes.

How can I handle all this? I can't. I just can't. She swept at the tears and sniffled as she smoothed the receipt and put it in the front of the binder, then added one more thing to the list.

Get Lil's ring back.

The fancy envelope from Angelina Broussard sat on the desk's corner. Maggie pulled out the letter and read it...twice. The committee consisted of Angelina, Nash Talley and Darrell Holloway. That was it. Three people were going to decide if Summer Haven was worthy of its historic designation, and one of them was the hardware store owner. Talk about a conflict of interest. Maggie didn't even bother putting the letter back in the envelope. Feeling the pressure from all sides, she chucked it in the center drawer.

Now, just how the heck she'd ever keep things afloat while Lil was gone was a whole other issue, but if she stopped to think about that right now she might just start crying and never stop. Her only idea for raising enough money to repay that loan was those doggone trash bags.

Alright, Harlan. You screwed up in a big way. Help me make some of it right, buddy.

While Sera was in the shower, Maggie trudged to the carriage house and grabbed another bag of lottery tickets. She schlepped the bag across the yard toward the porch, wishing she could bring herself to just burn the whole blessed pile of bags and be done with it. But now that she understood just how desperate for money they were, she couldn't chance giving away a windfall.

Maggie heaved the bag up the last step and grunted in relief. Those little lottery tickets added up to a lot of pounds when you had a giant bag of them. Too bad she couldn't get big dollars for recycling them.

She settled into a rocking chair, but rather than riffling through the bag, she sat there in a stupor. Not sure whether to laugh, cry, or scream like a stark raving lunatic, she did something she hadn't been doing enough lately. Pray.

Dear Lord, help me find the strength to take care of Summer Haven for Lil. Not only that, but if you'd toss a few bucks down from heaven, I promise to do my best with them. I've got willing hands and a willing heart.

Wait a second. Where there's a will, there's a way.

Summer Haven was the key to its own upkeep. If everyone in Summer Shoals loved the estate, maybe other folks—cash or credit card-carrying folks—might love it too. Might shell out a few dollars to look around the place. Heck, just a peek at the fountain was worth a fiver.

That thought brought Maggie to her feet and she danced a little jig right there on the porch. No sooner than she'd executed a technically perfect shuffle-ball-change, a crash came from inside the house, followed by a screeching holler.

"Sera?" Maggie raced inside, leaving a flurry of scratchers behind her. "Sera? Are you okay?"

"Help me! Call 9-1-1!"

Maggie lunged for the phone on the desk and dialed.

"Your emergency?"

"We've had an accident out here at Summer Haven. Quick! Send help." She dropped the phone and ran up the stairs. Gasping like a fish out of water, she pounded on the bathroom door.

"Open up, Sera!"

"I can't."

Maggie twisted the door handle and raced inside the bathroom. Then froze. Where the toilet used to sit—right there to the left of the sink—there was nothing but a giant hole. Open copper pipes protruded from the wall, spilling water onto the tile and through the subfloor.

After hunkering down to crank the stubborn turn-off valve, Maggie knee-walked through the spreading puddle, braced herself on all fours and looked down. Sera sat in a crumpled heap with her skirt all hiked up around her middle-parts and her leg splayed in opposite directions.

Maggie stuck her head in the hole for a better look. "Oh, Lord, are you hurt?"

"Bit my tongue on the landing and my tailbone is still in shock, but other than that I'm in one piece."

"What happened?"

"Nothing. I was just sitting there doing my business and saying a little mantra, and next thing I knew it was like I was on the water flume."

A wild—and completely inappropriate— laugh bubbled up in Maggie's chest. "What the heck have you been eating?"

"Quit that. You know it wasn't that. Come help me."

Maggie inspected the area where the floor had given way. Years of water damage had taken its toll.

One more thing to add to the list. She got to her feet, grabbed a towel and ran downstairs to help Sera.

Maggie whipped around the thick wooden box newel at the bottom of the staircase, almost losing her footing in the toilet water stream her wet clothes were creating. "Sera?

Where are you?"

"Here! I sure as hell haven't gone anywhere."

Maggie followed the frantic call to the parlor. That laughter in her chest broke free at the sight of Sera.

"Are you laughing at me? Don't you laugh at me." Sera tugged on her skirt, her feet flipping in the air with each word.

"I always thought having another toilet down here off the parlor would be convenient, but that was the fastest demolition I've ever witnessed."

Sera reached a hand toward Maggie. "This isn't funny."

No, it wasn't. Heart sinking in her chest, Maggie grasped Sera by the wrist and tugged her to her feet. There was no way they could charge people to see inside a house with a toilet smack dab in the middle of the parlor, yet she needed money to fix the bathroom. Not only had her repair list become longer and more urgent, but her last hope of moving into the carriage house had just been flushed as surely as if she'd pulled the toilet handle herself.

"This is going to leave a bruise," Sera said.

"I'm sure it will, but if that's all you get out of that wild ride, it's a blessing."

A clatter of stomping feet raced through the

open front door.

Maggie whipped around to see two EMTs running toward them.

Sera wiggled her panties up. "I'm sticking to bathing and doing my business in the creek from now on."

A siren wailed outside.

Maggie wished now that she'd checked out the situation before calling 9-1-1.

"I'm fine." Sera swatted the EMT away from her as she carefully stepped between the wood, plaster and broken porcelain.

Then, a familiar voice boomed behind them. "What the...?"

Sera and Maggie spun around.

Teague pulled off his mirrored sunglasses and assessed the damage. "Now, that's going to cost a pretty penny to fix."

Pennies, pretty or otherwise, were the one thing she didn't have plenty of.

Sitting outside the warden's office brought back childhood memories of waiting on the wooden bench outside the principal's office back in Summer Shoals Elementary School the time Lillian had been caught selling lipstick to the girls in the lunch room. Only this time she wasn't sure what she'd done wrong. Unless Martha was making good on that promise to cause her trouble.

Her insides spun. What if they wouldn't let Maggie visit her anymore? She looked down at her feet. Her toes still throbbed every time they so much as grazed the ends of her shoes. She was forced to hobble around, and her skin had taken on the consistency of alligator hide. Beautiful on a handbag, not so lovely on her legs. She balled her hands into fists, trying to ease the ache caused by all that toilet scrubbing. Some decent shampoo and body lotion would be wonderful about now, but she hadn't had the heart to ask Maggie to deposit money into her commissary account. Summer Haven needed every measly dollar Lillian had left behind.

The warden's assistant poked her head into the locked waiting area. "The warden will see you now."

"Thank you, dear." Lillian pushed herself up from the chair and walked into the warden's office.

Nell Proctor was a handsome woman, with square shoulders and a wide face. Although she was seated, it was easy to see she was tall.

Warden Proctor's face softened when she looked up and saw Lillian walk in. "How are things going for you here?"

Lillian took a seat in the straight back chair across from the warden. "I'm fine, thank you."

The office was in sharp contrast to the rest of the facility. In here the windows were softened with flowered valances and framed artwork. Even the ink pen in the warden's hand was snazzy.

The warden leaned forward. "I really want your feedback. Positive or negative."

Relief streamed through Lillian. She wasn't in trouble. *Just smile and be polite. Follow the rules and get out of here. That's the plan.* "I haven't been here that long. I'm still getting settled in, but I'm quite sure everything is as it should be."

"I should have guessed a woman like you wouldn't complain."

"A woman like me?" The words tumbled out before Lillian could stop them.

"Well-bred, refined, rich."

Not rich anymore.

"I've got a special assignment for you."

Assignment? She sure hoped it wasn't worse than cleaning the bathrooms.

"No doubt you've already noticed we have several personal development programs available here at WSPC."

"Yes. I've heard."

"Etiquette training has been added to our list of offerings for our guests."

Guests. Did this lady think she was a cruise director?

Sometimes this whole prison stay felt like a dream, but then her crappy outfit snapped her back to reality. On her worst day she wouldn't wear these clothes on purpose.

"Here's the suggested outline." Warden Proctor shuffled papers on her desk and held out a sheet to Lillian. "I'd like to present you as the teacher for this curriculum."

"Teacher? I don't know anything about prison etiquette. Surely someone else who has tenure here could help with this."

"Oh no, not prison etiquette. I mean *proper* etiquette. Lots of these girls come from harsh environments. Manners that are second nature to someone like you are completely foreign to them. What fork to use at a nice meal, proper greetings, the dos and don'ts of a good conversation."

Lillian glanced through the curriculum. The list was a no-brainer. "Nothing on here I wouldn't expect from a school child."

"Exactly my point. But you and I both know these skills will help once these women reenter the outside world. Not only in social situations but in job interviews."

Lillian ran her finger down the page. Tempting, so tempting. But her little run-in with Big Martha had already taught her it was best to just stay quiet and lay low.

Warden Proctor must have sensed her

hesitation because she started talking in a quick clip. "If this goes well, we have the chance to pull in some contemplative programs, too, like meditation or yoga. I think we can soften the hard edges on some of these women."

Lillian didn't know if there was an emery board tough enough to wear down the chips on the shoulders of the inmates she'd met. But Momma had always said that everyone had grace inside them, they just needed to know when and where to pull it out and use it.

"What happens if I don't do a good job?" Lillian's thoughts raced back to the warning from Big Martha about minding her own business.

"I wouldn't ask if I didn't know you'd be perfect for this assignment." The warden patted her desk like it was a done deal. "And this happens to be one of the highest-paying jobs in the prison. With what you owe, I thought that might make it even more appealing."

Well, that did change things.

It might mean she could possibly have a little for her commissary account too. Her heart beat a little faster at the thought.

But she'd already heard inmates didn't get the coveted jobs this quickly. Maybe this assignment was in addition to bathroom duty.

"But I'll still have my day job, right?"

The warden laughed. "Oh, heavens no. Why would you think that?"

Because scrubbing toilets would keep her safe from the likes of Big Martha.

"Honey, with as many women as we have here, you'll be teaching at least one class a day," the warden added. "And it could also mean we might get some days shaved off of that sentence."

Now, Lillian's heart was pounding. After all, it wasn't like she was taking someone else's job or an inmate had to take part in the class. So Big Martha would have no reason to get her panties in a twist.

It might even mean Lillian could develop a small group of trusted friends here.

She looked up and leveled a stare at the warden. "I'd be happy to help." Her momma hadn't raised no fool. If she could repay her debt and get out early...that was a win-win if she'd ever heard one.

"Perfect, because I want to announce it while everyone is in the dining hall. That's just about now. Come."

The warden led Lillian out of the office. When they entered the dining hall from the restricted entrance at the rear, the lunch chatter muted immediately. The smell of tomato sauce and garlic permeated the air.

The line for food snaked around the wall and outside the room. Sometimes it took an hour to get through that line and find a seat because the dining hall couldn't accommodate all the inmates at once.

Lillian felt all eyes turn toward her and, if they could have killed, she'd have been dead a hundred times over. No one looked impressed that she was standing there next to the warden. In fact, it was quite the contrary.

One of the guards flipped the lights on and off, and everyone who wasn't already staring stopped in their tracks.

"Good afternoon, everyone," the warden said.

The last of the whispered conversations drifted quiet, and a niggle of worry vibrated in Lil's stomach. No spaghetti for her today.

"I have some exciting news. Inmate Fairview has graciously agreed to teach a new class here at Walter Stiles."

"How to be a snob?" someone called from the back.

Warden Proctor went on her toes to look over the crowd, but apparently couldn't identify the guilty party. "No more of that. We're fortunate to have someone who's well-versed in this new curriculum."

Lillian swallowed to cover her nerves.

"This week, Inmate Fairview will begin

teaching a daily etiquette class."

Grumbling rose from the tables.

"And in case you're wondering, this course is required for every inmate at Walter Stiles. You'll attend once a week, minimum."

What? That lump in Lillian's stomach hardened and sank.

But when she met Big Martha's malicious stare across the room, that lump jolted up Lil's throat and she had to slap her hand across her mouth to keep from vomiting right there on the floor.

Chapter Fourteen

Maggie sat on the front porch in a rocker, sipping a glass of her *special* tea to calm her nerves after the big toilet ruckus. So what if it was nine in the morning? Just when she thought she might have a hope of buying back Lil's ring, everything else was falling apart around her. If she didn't get hopping on that bathroom and launch those tours, she'd watch her best friend lose her home and she'd be out on her fanny too.

She eyed Sera's VW van. She could never live like that. A camper shell on the back of her pickup truck just wasn't going to cut it for this old gal, not even if she were as fit as Sera. And seeing as starving wasn't her idea of a good diet choice, she wasn't going to look like Sera anytime soon.

Oh, Lil. How the heck do you think I can keep all this afloat until you get home?

That was the question she hadn't nailed

Lillian down on, just how long she would she be gone. And the discrepancy between what Lillian said she *leveraged* in Social Security checks after Harlan's earthly departure and what she was incarcerated for bugged Maggie.

Why hadn't Lillian kicked and screamed over that? She must have had one of those bargain billboard lawyers. Probably too doggone prideful to use the family attorney.

After all those years keeping the hardware store's finances, Maggie knew her double-entry bookkeeping. And this just didn't balance.

The tea eased the stress that was making her whole body ache. Lil had said that Nash Talley helped her. Maggie stopped midrock. Now that she thought about it, he'd also been listed as a committee member on Angelina's letter. That man was popping up in every situation where Lil was coming out on the losing end. Lil might not be ready to admit that straitlaced pretty boy had helped himself a little, too, but Maggie couldn't get it out of her head.

She lifted the sweating tea glass to her lips and gulped.

"I think it's time Nash Talley filled in the blanks," she said, sounding a little like Dirty Harry and liking the way that felt. She left the glass sitting on the porch rail, grabbed her keys from the hook just inside the door and headed for her truck.

The funeral home was locked up tight, and there was no sign of Nash at Gabriel's Acres either. No one could hide in a town the size of Summer Shoals. She'd stumble across him one way or another.

But Maggie wasn't going to run around town like a chicken with her head chopped off either. She'd watched enough episodes of *Castle* to know a body needed to be discreet about this kind of thing. Ask some seemingly innocent question so the person of interest didn't get spooked and bolt.

It would look a lot less obvious if she had a wingman, so Maggie swung by Summer Haven to pick up Sera.

Maggie turned in the driveway and spotted Sera picking dandelions in the side lawn. Sera lifted a fluffy-headed stem to her mouth and blew. Tiny seeds whisked into the air all around Sera and Maggie winced.

Lillian would've had a cow if she'd seen that. But Maggie closed her eyes and made her own wish on the dandelion, just in case, because she could use all the luck she could borrow right about now.

"Sera, I need you to come with me."

Sera dropped the stem and ran across the lawn. She moved like a teenager, and Maggie yearned to be that free. Sera climbed into the truck without hesitation. "Where are we going?"

"To the Atlanta Highway Diner. And I can promise you right now you're not going to much like what they have on the lunch menu. Just keep your mouth shut about all that, okay? We're on a fact-finding mission, not a health food quest."

"I'll try, but good healthy eating is everyone's business."

"Not around here. You just tolerate it, okay?"

"I can do that."

"Good girl."

Maggie zipped down the road and parallel-parked in front of the diner at just a few minutes after eleven.

Nearly every table and chair in the diner was filled and the gossip was throbbing loud. A smile pulled at the corners of Maggie's mouth. This was the perfect place to get some answers.

She craned her neck, hoping she'd spot Nash Talley among the diners. No such luck.

The last table open was right in the center of the restaurant. Normally, that wouldn't do for her at all, but today it was the perfect spot.

Dottie, a striking ash-blonde waitress, rushed over to greet them. "Maggie, honey, we've missed you and Lillian the past few weeks. I've got some of those cheese grits you like so much in the back. How 'bout I spoon you up a bowl?" Dottie leaned over the counter and whispered, "I made 'em with half and half just the way you like."

Maggie winced. If she didn't watch out, Sera was going to know exactly why she was packing those extra thirty pounds.

"How about two specials?" She decided the surprise of whatever today's special was would be a better gamble than a lecture from Sera on what she'd selected.

Sera took the seat across from her.

A few minutes later, Dottie delivered two heaping plates of ketchup-smothered meatloaf, garlic mashed potatoes swimming in butter, and a fluffy cloverleaf roll.

"Where are the vegetables?" Sera asked, panic in her eyes.

Dottie plunked down a bowl of crispy fried okra beside each plate.

Maggie kept an ear cocked for the conversations in the booths and tables around her. This was definitely the over-sixty crowd. The ones who had nothing better to do with their time than to watch what their neighbors were doing.

To her left, two sisters were talking about their niece's upcoming nuptials and how she'd chosen orange for her wedding color since it was in October.

The name Nash Talley came from somewhere behind Maggie and her ears pricked. Sera was saying something but Maggie just let her ramble as she leaned back in her chair and strained to get a better listen.

"The flowers were set up all haphazard and the whole service ran late. This would never have happened when Warner Talley was running things."

"I thought Nash was making good changes over there. He's spruced up the place with those new chapel pews and aisle runners. This is the first complaint I've heard. That guy's so anal about things I can't believe he'd let the flowers be all cattywhompus."

A man at the next table threw in his two cents. "Anal, hell. That boy is downright OCD. Has to have everything in its place or he dang near gets a rash over worrying about it. His little problem is way more than just that hand washing Warner used to talk about."

The young woman at the counter got up and joined the man at the table. "That might be true, but Nash Talley is nowhere to be found. He's up and done one of his disappearing acts again. Not that it really matters. He practically lets the staff run that place now. Warner would have never done that. Figures Nash would fly the coop when one of my relatives died. I knew he never liked our family."

"That's not true."

"It is. I'd complain to Warner if there was any chance he could do something about it. Poor old guy is halfway to heaven already from what I hear."

"I know. I heard the same thing. Bless his heart."

Disappearing act? So this wasn't the first time Nash had been difficult to track down.

Sera hadn't touched her plate, but Maggie stabbed a piece of fried okra with her fork. Sera's face contorted as she watched the morsel get closer and closer to Maggie's lips, until Sera finally just closed her eyes. Maggie stuffed the okra in her mouth and enjoyed every chew.

At a booth catty-corner from them, one of Lillian's Bunco pals was talking about the recent pizza party she'd thrown for the Dogwood Ridge residents.

"What were you thinking, buying those old folks pizza? I bet they had the farts for a week."

"They sure seemed to enjoy it. I just thought it would be nice for them to feel like it was a good ole Saturday night. I even brought my record player so they could listen to good music. Warner Talley was doing Elvis impersonations. In fact, I'm not a hundred percent sure he doesn't think he *is* Elvis."

That's it! Warner could probably shed some light on where Nash was.

The woman was practically glowing with pride. "It was the least I could do for those poor old folks."

Dottie stopped at their table with a pot of steaming coffee. "Girl, you ain't no spring chicken either. Did I hear you right? Pizza isn't so cheap anymore. How'd you manage that?"

"It's the strangest thing." The lady pulled her freshened cup of coffee toward her. "Our government is so darn mixed up that they sent me an extra Social Security check. Well not technically me, but for Randall."

"Randall? Really?" The woman's companion drew back and cocked her head. "He's been dead and gone for a year. Now, why on Earth would they send him a check?"

"Finders keepers is what I say. Showed up right in my mailbox, just like old times. I deposited that sucker right into my account and used it for good. It felt nice to play Robin Hood for a day."

"Well, honey, as nice as that is, I'm sure it can't be legal. That's stealing. How will you pay it back when they realize their mistake and come a knocking for it?"

Robin Hood's face drained of its color.

"Excuse me, girls." Dottie turned to man hobbling in, step by painful step, on a walker. "Hollis, what are you doing here?"

"That goddamned Meals on Wheels. You can't trust nobody these days to do what they say they're gonna do. It ain't like I can just run right out to McDonald's and pick myself up a Big Mac." Hollis paused next to Maggie. "Hello, beautiful."

"Hi, there. Doesn't Nash Talley drive the Meals on Wheels truck?" Maggie asked.

Hollis thumped the walker against the floor. "We ain't seen him for nigh on two Wednesdays now. I'd resorted to eating Cheez-Its and nuts the kids gave me at Christmas, but now all that's gone."

Maggie's trouble-o-meter was just a clanging. "Has anyone seen Nash?"

Murmurs rippled through the diner, and the final consensus was no one had set eyes on him.

A blue-haired woman in a bright red shirt spoke above the crowd. "Maybe he's done up and died and he's just festering away in his house. Anyone checked on him? Maybe we should call the sheriff."

"Nash is only thirty-five. I don't think he's in danger of a random heart attack," said one of the other diners.

Sera leaned toward Maggie. "Nothing random about a heart attack after eating a few of these lunch specials."

"Shsh." Maggie gave her a warning look.

"Well, you never know about people," said a man at the counter.

Maggie didn't think Nash was dead, but had another bad feeling tugging at her gut.

Lil, I know you want me to keep your deal with Nash quiet to save face, but there's something rotten going on in Summer Shoals. I don't think you're the only person Nash pulled the wool over. Mr. Nice Guy has something else up his sleeve and it's probably a devil tattoo.

Maggie leaned across the table and whispered to Sera, "What if Nash helped himself to more than just a few of Harlan's Social Security checks?"

Sera bit her lower lip. "What do you mean?"

Just then, Teague walked in the door and Maggie waved him over.

"Teague, we've got a problem," Maggie said. "A big one."

Chapter Fifteen

Teague paused next to Maggie and Sera's table. Was it too much for a guy to pick up a to-go box and eat with his feet up at his desk? Maybe he needed to start wearing a ski mask when he wanted a break.

Nah, then someone would just call in a robbery.

It wasn't but a few years ago, when Teague worked for the Houston PD, that every day there'd been a new fire lit under his ass. Overwork and stress had defined that job. Even so, at the time he'd thought nothing could be worse than what happened his college senior year.

He'd been wrong.

Dead wrong.

Now, Summer Shoals was supposed to be his happy place after everything that had gone down. When he'd left Texas in his rearview mirror, it was for a promise of better days. His new home was still busy, but trouble was different here. Zany things like seniors slipping off rooftops and prize pigs running loose in the church. Apparently, the baptistery still smelled of slop and hog crap on a hot day.

"Teague, it's meatloaf day." Eighteen-year-old Sue Ellen, the diner's other waitress, sidled over. He sidestepped, but she gave him a big wink, then blurted loud enough for everyone to hear that she'd be happy to slide herself right between the slices of his meatloaf. *Christ Jesus.*

"I'll have mine to go." *Far, far away.*

He turned his attention to Maggie, who was strung so tight today she was practically vibrating in her chair. Just past her sat his boondocker, Serendipity. Lord help him. He nodded cordially. "Maggie. Serendipity."

"You can call me Sera. All my good friends do."

"I remember." Teague kept Maggie between Sera and him. He didn't really get the cougar vibe from her, but after all that nonsense in the Walmart parking lot, it could be a mistake to get too close. "Everything okay after the toilet incident yesterday?"

"Yes, but we've got bigger trouble than that."

He craned his neck to look over her head. "By the way, where's Lillian?"

And didn't that innocent question get Maggie's hands to fluttering around her silverware and tea glass. "She's feeling a little under the weather."

"I'm sorry to hear that. Tell her I'll stop by for a visit later today."

"Oh. Oh, no." She lowered her voice. "It's, you know, some female stuff."

How much female stuff did a seventy-year-old lady have left? That was probably more than he needed to know. "What's this about big trouble?"

Maggie glanced around the diner like she expected to find someone hiding, crouched behind the booths ready to jump out and attack. "Maybe we should talk outside."

His mom, normally a pie-baking and retirement-center-visiting sweetheart, had gotten a touch paranoid and more than a little mean when she went through the change. Could Maggie be experiencing the same thing?

Sue Ellen delivered his paper-bagged lunch and flashed him some plump cleavage and an eye-blinding purple bra. Sweet girl, but he wanted a real woman, not someone a month over jail bait. He averted his gaze, pulled out his wallet and gestured toward Maggie's empty plate and Sera's full one. "Put these ladies' lunch on my bill."

"You don't have to—" Maggie started, but

Sera covered her hand.

"Remember. Be gracious and accepting. Expect the best and the universe will deliver it." Serendipity lifted herself from her chair. "Thanks, Sheriff."

The three of them stepped outside and huddled under the awning. The July Georgia sun was such a bitch and a half, he could feel it through the thick material of his uniform shirt. "Why so secretive?"

"What if I told you that no one has seen Nash Talley in ten days." Maggie arched her brow.

"So?"

"Hollis just said he hadn't seen him for two Meals on Wheels Wednesdays," Maggie told him.

"I'll drive by his place and check on him." *But not until after lunch, dammit.*

Maggie swallowed. "I think he took—"

Teague's phone rang. "Excuse me, ladies." He angled his body slightly away to answer his phone. "Castro." When it rained, it poured. By the time he got back to his desk, everything in this bag would be stone cold.

"Teague, thank the sweet baby Jesus and all those damned wise-ass men." The whiskey-smooth voice on the other end of the line shot from his ear through every nerve ending in his body until even his toes were tingling.

He opened his mouth, but her name got stuck in his heart. He cleared his throat. "Jenny. It's been a while."

"How many times have I asked you to call me by my proper name?"

More times than he could count. But to him, she'd always be Jenny. "Jensen, to what do I owe the honor?"

"Have you talked to my mother?" Jenny pronounced the last word *mutha*. She'd damn well been up north too long. If he had anything to say about it, she'd move her heart-shaped little ass back south. But he'd given up that right over ten years ago. And she'd moved on too. Got married and had a little boy.

"Not recently, why?"

"Because she's gone crazier than a bed bug high on Pixy Stix."

Sounded about like the woman he'd always called Aunt Bibi even though they weren't technically related. "And this is surprising, why?"

"You don't understand. Since the newspaper forced her to retire, she's taken it to an entirely new level." And Abby Ruth Cady was a hot-barreled pistol under normal circumstances. "She called me yesterday from a campground in Ohio or Iowa or some flat place like that. Pretty as you please, she sold her house and took off from Texas in her dually. Bought a brand new horse trailer and is pulling it behind. Says she's gonna see every state and then maybe head to South America."

Teague didn't bother to hide his smile because Jenny sure couldn't see him. "She's a grown woman."

"You mean a child in a grown woman costume."

Suddenly, something occurred to him. "Wait a minute. Your momma doesn't have horses."

"Exactly," Jenny huffed. "Do you know what she's got in that thing?"

Shit. His gut cramped as though he'd eaten six diner lunch specials. "What?"

"Her guns."

Sometimes it sucked being right.

"She is completely out of control. And I can't break away from my job right now to track her down in whatever wheat field she's stomping around in."

"Oh, yeah?" He took a few more steps away from Maggie and Sera. "Well, I've got a whole flock of out-of-control mature ladies down here in Georgia that I'm trying to keep an eye on."

"Maybe we should ship all these crazy red-hat women to one state and throw away the key. And you know Georgia started out as a penal colony."

Just the kind of thing Jensen Elaine Cady Northcutt would know. He'd never once won a game of Trivial Pursuit against her when they were kids. But Jenny's suggestion pinballed around in his brain. Something wasn't quite right at Summer Haven, if only that the old house needed more sweat and muscle than those women could provide, no matter how many tool belts Maggie Rawls owned.

"That's actually not a bad idea. Why don't you call your mom and suggest she pay me a visit? You could tell her I've put on a big ole beer gut and can barely get my lazy ass out of my recliner."

"Have you?" And didn't those two soft-spoken words arrow right down to his sacral whatever-the-hell Sera was yapping about the other day.

"Still at fighting weight."

Jenny sighed.

Frustration with your mom or possibly regret over what could've been between you and me?

Hell, no. Jenny Cady didn't do regret.

"You know she never listens to a damn thing I say," Jenny argued. "If I push her to come down there, she'll do the exact opposite and race right up to the North Pole. But you? That woman will listen to anything that comes out of your mouth like you're spouting NFL statistics."

Jenny knew her momma, that was for sure. And he could use a pair of eyes and ears out at Summer Haven, especially after that toilet incident, and his something's-up meter was off the charts when it came to those old gals. "Tell you what, I'll see what I can do. But if I get her down here, you have to promise to come visit her before long."

She scoffed, and he knew that sound well. It wasn't that Jenny didn't love her mom, but Abby Ruth could drive a Baptist preacher to drink. "It's a deal. Call me as soon as she gets there, okay?"

"Sure thing." He'd take any excuse he could get to call the woman he'd been in love with for more than half his life.

Maggie eyed Teague's back as he talked on the phone. One minute he was smiling and the next frowning. From the sheriff's tone, it was clear the woman on the other end meant something to him. There was just something different about a man's voice when his libido and heart were going crazy.

He was a good man. He could help her sort through all this social-security-check-prison-funeral-Nash-Talley nonsense.

Sera gripped Maggie's wrist and drew her

close. "What are you thinking?"

"I'm thinking we need help."

"You're Lillian's oldest friend and yet less than two weeks after she asked you to keep things quiet, you're willing to ignore what she wanted? She told you not tell anyone about what happened."

"Teague's not just anyone," Maggie insisted.

"He's worse than anyone." Sera looked him up and down, mistrust clear in her expression. "He's the law."

"Oh, for the love of Pete. You asked him to call you Sera, like all your good friends do."

Sera shifted from foot to foot. "I don't want him to be suspicious of me."

Maggie stepped back, looked at Sera through narrowed eyes. "*Should* he be suspicious of you?"

"That's not the point here. Lillian and her trouble is the issue right now. Don't you go switching this all up on me. If we turn over the little we know to the sheriff, it's all over. He's going to tell us to go sit in those rockers on the veranda and sip tea while he chases down the truth. Or worse, what if he's in on it?"

"Sera, that's just downright ridiculous, and by the way, I make good tea."

"Is that what you really want?" Sera tapped her foot, setting those little bells she wore tinkling.

Maybe Maggie was giving Teague too much credit. Maybe she was just desperate. "But I'm afraid it's too much—trying to track down Nash and fix the bathroom."

"What's wrong with the downstairs one?"

"Nothing, but we've got a historic approval committee coming out in a few weeks. There's no way Summer Haven will pass muster the way it is now. Plus, I was hoping to offer some tours to bring in some money. It's like a catch-22. No cash to pay for the damage and yet we can't host tours with a huge hole in the ceiling."

"If there's one thing you are, Maggie Rawls, it's handy. And together, we'll patch up that bathroom." Sera's voice carried an unexpected edge. "Do you really want to stand on the sidelines while someone else takes care of all your problems?"

"No," Maggie said. "No, I absolutely do not want to stand on the sidelines. I can take care of myself. And this."

"Which is exactly why Lillian asked you to handle her affairs, not the sheriff."

Maggie swallowed back a frantic feeling. No. She was done being small, huddling in the background.

Teague finished his phone call and strode back to them. "I apologize. A fugitive we've been trying to run down for years has been spotted somewhere up north."

That girl must be really special if he was concocting a story to cover for her.

"Goodness," Maggie said. Even if that call had no more been about a fugitive than she was a *Sports Illustrated* model, those criminal type words all sounded so harsh. Not words she wanted attached to her best friend, so she couldn't tell Teague about Nash because that would lead him straight to Lillian in the big house. No. It was up to her to figure this out.

"Now, what was it y'all were going to tell me about Nash Talley?" Teague asked.

Maggie gripped the duct tape at her waist to keep from making any nervous gestures. "Some folks are a little worried about him. But I'm sure there's a perfectly good explanation for why he hasn't been around. Vacation. The flu." *Or foul play.*

Teague's eyes narrowed. "That's not what it sounded like before."

"Oh, hon, we just wanted to get you away from Sue Ellen." Maggie patted his arm and nodded toward his sack lunch. "She has her talons out for you, if you hadn't noticed, and I've heard she's not such a nice girl. Now, you better get that to-go order back to the office so you can enjoy that meatloaf while it's still hot and fresh."

"You're sure there's no problem?"

Sera nodded, and Maggie did too. "You'd be the first to know."

"I sure hope so." Teague tipped his hat back. "I'll stop in and check on him. Make sure everything is okay. I doubt you have anything to worry about though."

"We're not worried." Sera chimed in. "Everything is going great. Perfect."

"Are you going to stick around for a while?" he asked Sera.

"I haven't decided yet."

Teague's eyes narrowed, but he slipped on his sunglasses. "Let me know if I can do anything else for you ladies."

"Not a thing," Maggie said, pouring on a cheerful lilt.

He nodded once and headed toward the sheriff's office.

When Teague turned the corner, Sera squeezed Maggie in a one-armed hug. "That was close. Good girl."

Chapter Sixteen

Maggie pushed the buzzer at Dogwood Ridge Assisted Living while Sera stood next to her scanning the parking lot.

"What are you doing?" Maggie asked. "You're making us look suspicious."

"These places make me nervous."

First the jail and now the old folks' home. What normal place didn't make Sera nervous?

The lock clicked and hiccupped before the mechanism finally released.

Maggie hurried inside with Sera tailgating her. When the door latched behind them, Sera spun around and pushed on it. "They locked us in. Why would they do that? I don't like to be locked in."

Sera's pot was a little cracked, but Maggie couldn't look into the Nash Talley business all alone. "Settle down. I'm sure they do that for the residents' safety."

"It's creepy." Sera tucked in tighter to

Maggie.

"Don't be silly." Maggie looked around. Clean white linoleum floors, pale peach walls and florescent lights. A little sterile, yes. But creepy, no.

Sera pulled her sweater around her. "Gives me the heebie-jeebies. All the negative air. Don't you feel it?"

"No." *All I feel is you up in my space.* Maggie approached the main desk.

The blonde, ponytailed girl sitting behind it looked barely old enough to be out of college. "Hi, I'm Tina. How can I help y'all today? If you're here for a tour of our facility, I have to tell you we only have one vacancy."

Maggie gasped, and nothing else came out. *A tour? I'm not that doggone old. I sure as heck need no assistance to live!* Maggie was learning to do that all on her own. She grabbed the clipboard and signed in to visit Warner Talley.

Sera gave her a nudge. "Told you it sucked."

Maggie tried to smile. "We're here to visit our old friend, Warner Talley."

The young woman's eyes brightened. "I'm so glad. You know he doesn't remember much on most days, and his son is so wonderful to come and spend time with him, but he's out of town and Warner could really use a visitor. This is perfect timing. He's still in his room."

Maggie feigned disappointment. "I was so hoping to bump into Nash too. When will he be back?"

"I'm not sure. Every once in a while he has to travel, but soon, I'm sure. He never lets too much time pass between visits."

Tina cocked her head, studied her. "I don't suppose you'd know how long he'll be gone or where he is?"

Oh, no. She was suspicious. "Never mind. I'll talk with Nash when he gets back. Can we visit with Warner now?"

"I'll show you the way. Follow me."

Maggie and Sera fell in step behind the woman. Tina gave a quick double rap on the door and peeked her head in. "Mr. Talley? You decent? You have some company."

Warner Talley must have snorted out of a deep sleep because they heard that raspy snore all the way in the hall. "Yeah, yah, yah. What? Melba? Is that you?"

"It's me, Mr. Talley. Tina. You've got some beautiful ladies here to visit you today."

"I like my girls pretty. You know that's true. But there's no way they'll be prettier than you."

Tina turned to Maggie and Sera. "Were you friends with his wife, Melba, before she passed?"

Sera grabbed Tina's arm. "Oh goodness,

yes. She was the nicest woman on earth." She leaned in. "She was a lousy bridge player, but that suited me just fine. I do so love to win."

If Maggie hadn't known for a fact that neither of them knew Warner Talley or his wife, she'd have believed every word Sera said.

"He's been asking for Melba again today. He might not recognize you."

Oh, I can guarantee that man won't recognize us. "We'll try not to take it personal."

"I'll let y'all visit. Let me know if there's anything I can do."

Sera watched from the doorway until Tina turned the corner. "She's gone."

Maggie was already sitting on the love seat across from Warner's recliner. Sera rushed over, her flip-flops snapping under her feet the whole way, then plopped down alongside Maggie.

"How are you doing today, Warner?" Maggie wasn't even sure what she was going to say to the man, but hopefully he'd shed some light on where his son might be.

Warner's eyes glassed over. "Melba, honey, you've come back." He lunged toward her and took her hands into his.

"No," Maggie said, pulling away.

Sera put her hands on top of their heaping pile of fingers, holding Maggie hostage in

Warner's cold hands. "I'm sorry I kept her away so long, Warner. She was helping me this morning."

"Do I know you?" Warner looked at Sera for a long moment. "I don't think I do."

It broke Maggie's heart to see him so confused. And here she was, pretending to be his loving wife just to get information about Nash, who might be as innocent as his father. But then again, her instinct was telling her otherwise. "Warner, dear, you remember Sera. Quit teasing her. Have you seen Nash? I can't seem to get a hold of him."

"Nash? He always follows the cash."

"What?"

"Sometimes he comes, sometimes he goes," Warner crooned. "When he returns, he always shows."

"Where does he go?" Maggie asked.

"I wonder where my boy could be. I can't leave, but I can give you his key."

"Do you think he realizes he's talking in rhyme?" Sera whispered to Maggie.

She hadn't even noticed. "The key to what, Warner?"

Warner lifted himself from the chair and shuffled across the room. He returned with a single key on a paper clip and a grungy handkerchief tied corner to corner like a hobo sack. With a knobby arthritic finger, he motioned for Sera to move.

Sera darted over to his recliner, and Warner eased into the love seat next to Maggie.

Not good. Maggie made *save me* eyes at Sera, but she just mouthed, "Sorry, but he's so sweet."

"Melba, my beautiful wife, you've given me a handsome son and a wonderful life." He pressed the key into her hand, gazed into her eyes. "Dear, please take this key. Go check on Nash for me."

Darned if he wasn't rhyming like a geriatric Dr. Seuss. "I'm sure he's fine. I don't want you to worry one bit."

"He's a good boy. We're lucky, you and me." Warner reached out with shaking fingers and touched Maggie's cheek. He drew back and dropped the little handkerchief sack into her lap. "This is something special for you on our anniversary."

"Oh, Warner, I can't."

Sera cleared her throat to get Maggie's attention and nodded toward the package like a deranged woodpecker.

"I'm sorry I didn't bring you a gift." She untied the knotted ends of the hanky yellow from age and folded back the thin fabric. Her heart squeezed and she rubbed it to ease the ache. It didn't work. A single tear streamed down her cheek.

"You like it?"

"I love it, Warner." She lifted the bright red-and-gold macaroni necklace from her lap and slipped it over her head. "It's the best gift I've ever received."

He folded her in his arms and rocked her.

The dried pasta dug into her collar bone. The tiny pain was the least she deserved. Maggie patted him on the back.

"Whoops, look at the time," Sera said. "Walk me out, won't you, Melba?"

Warner drew back and his smile was so sad that Maggie hesitated. Sera yanked her off the love seat and hustled her toward the door.

"When will you be back?"

"Soon," Maggie choked out.

Sera half dragged her down the hall and out into the sunshine, leaving behind the smell of arthritis cream and lost dreams.

"We're going straight to hell for lying to that man," Maggie said.

Sera stopped in the middle of the parking lot. "Honey, you made his day."

Maggie twisted the gold sparkly macaroni necklace between her fingers. No matter what they discovered about Nash's disappearance, she'd make sure his daddy didn't suffer the consequences.

Nash stood against his balcony rail, sipping a martini—gin and vermouth only—and watching a yacht ease into the Intracoastal Waterway from the marina across the street. The view from this condo was only one of the reasons he'd bought it three years ago.

Hmm...how much would a small yacht run me? Surely my stash would cover it and then some.

But before he could consider a yacht seriously, he needed to get his daddy settled out here on the island. Tomorrow, he'd research every assisted living facility within reasonable driving distance. Although this was ahead of his original timeline, he'd felt an increasing drive to cross off this final task of his plan since running into Lillian at Gabriel's Acres a few weeks ago.

His phone sounded from where he'd left it on the glass coffee table, and his heart hitched. He'd programmed Lionel Richie's "Hello" ring tone for only one caller.

He dashed inside and scooped up his phone, gasping hello. Not manly at all. He cleared his throat and deepened his voice this time. "Hello, Nash Talley speaking."

"Nash, it's Tina."

"Tina, what a surprise." *Not.*

"I hope you aren't upset I called." She had such a sweet voice, like dark molasses. Too bad molasses was so sticky. Just so messy.

"It's just that—"

"Something's happened to Dad?" Because why else would she have called?

"No, no. Your daddy is fine," she rushed to say. "Well, not fine, but the same. Sorry to scare you like that. I shouldn't have called."

"You obviously had a reason." Maybe she missed him. He wandered back to the balcony, stopping every few steps to sweep his foot through the footprints in the plush white carpet. He pulled the sliding door closed behind him and settled into a teak lounge chair to sip his drink.

"I just wondered...if you..."

He slipped a daisy from the arrangement he'd purchased and stroked the petals as Tina's voice stroked his heart. *She loves me. She loves me...more.* "If I what?"

"If you're okay?" she blurted.

She loves me.

"Never better, why?" Nash smiled and his hopes floated up, up, up. If only Tina could see him here. In this life. If she liked boring Nash Talley, funeral guy of Summer Shoals, what would she think of him here? She couldn't be anything but impressed. He stretched out his legs and admired his leather boat shoes. Casual but pristine. He'd grown to like the no-socks look, and these Quoddy shoes had been a splurge. His white slacks were starched to a high sheen with creases so sharp, they just might slice a man's fingers.

"Well, you haven't come to the center lately and I didn't think anything of it since you travel sometimes. But then your daddy's friends came to visit him today and wondered when you'd be back in town. I realized I didn't know."

"Which friends?" He sat up straight, the air around him suddenly heavy. It wouldn't do to have folks gossiping about him. Not when he was this close to breaking away. Yes, he'd altered his original plan to spend more time here. He needed this place. Adjusting the plan had made him uneasy, and now the thought of people noticing his comings and goings made his neck itch.

"Maggie Rawls and a blonde woman. I couldn't really make out her writing. Sarah? I think Mrs. Rawls may have called her Sarah."

Those were Lillian's friends. The scene from the Fourth of July parade slowly flickered through his brain. The blue Tucker Torpedo idling down the parade route with Lillian sitting up on the back of the convertible. Lillian shading herself with an umbrella. The sheriff asking Nash if he'd seen something. Those peanuts all over the ground instead of candy.

The gin burned a hole clean through Nash's stomach.

Whoever had been riding in that car, it hadn't been Lillian Fairview.

They were hiding something out there at Summer Haven, and now they were slopping around in his business. He unbuttoned the top button of his shirt.

Did Lillian know what he'd done?

Trying to sound nonchalant, Nash lowered his voice and forced his back to relax against the chair. "How nice of them to visit Dad, especially since I'll be on this business trip for even longer than I anticipated. I hate being away from him so long. Could I ask you a favor?"

"Anything."

"Could you call me once a day? Let me know how Dad's doing and if he's had visitors?"

"At this number?"

Crap. It wouldn't do to leave this trail. "Actually, I'm getting a new phone tomorrow. Give me your cell number and I'll text you my number." He could get one of those prepaid phones. "And I don't want the calls to be long distance from the center, so why don't you call from your cell?"

"Whatever you want."

If only. "Thanks, Tina. I owe you."

"I'm happy to help." She laughed in a lighthearted way that made his own heart—even heavy with fear—do a little flip. "We need more guys like you around here."

He went back inside and fixed himself another martini—a double this time.

In a series of gulps he chugged it back, then lifted the glass. His hand shook with his need to hurl it across the room out of sheer frustration, but that would make a mess. He carefully placed the glass back on the table and walked over to the Ilya Bolotowsky painting hanging on the wall. The sharp clean lines in black, red and blues were calming.

He stared at it until the colors seemed to bleed into one another.

I can't wait any longer.

He lifted his hand to the left side of the painting and swung it out on the hidden hinge. The wall safe was well concealed right there in the middle of the room. No grooved spinning knob to collect germs, but rather a nice slick keypad.

The series of numbers sounded like the first few notes of "Row, Row, Row Your Boat." The mechanism clicked and the door opened. He hummed his favorite part, *Merrily, merrily, merrily, merrily...life is but a dream,* as he extracted the journal that held the detailed plan for his disappearance from Summer

Shoals.

Chapter Seventeen

Lillian stood in the rec room ready to present her first Walter Stiles Federal Prison Camp Etiquette 101 class. Her heart hammered as the attendees filed into the room. The only friendly face in the crowd was Dixie's. And Dixie gave a little finger wave but found a chair near the back. Unfortunately, the women settling into the front row were Lillian's worst nightmare. Big Martha and her entire posse. How in the world had they managed to be assigned the same class night? Martha had more pull around here than Lillian had even realized.

It worried the dickens out of her, but she sucked in a breath, pasted a smile on her face and handed a thick stack of papers to the woman in the first seat.

"Please take one and pass them around."

Someone in the back said, "That old woman thinks she can tell us what to do?" and it upped Lillian's blood pressure a tick.

Still, the woman snatched the handouts from Lil and passed the stack to the person sitting next to her.

"Thank you," Lillian said with all the charm and kindness of a true Southern lady.

"You're welcome."

The woman's words were a bit snarly, but regardless Lillian banged the shiny call bell the warden had provided.

Ding-ding-ding.

The room fell silent. Lillian was surprised the tiny bell had had that kind of impact on this unruly group. When the warden had given it to her, she thought the silly bell would be a waste of time.

"Point for you," Lillian said, turning her attention to the woman in the first seat in the first row.

The woman cocked her head.

Lillian paced across the front row, beginning to feel her normal sense of confidence return even though Big Martha was scowling at her. "The first lesson in etiquette. Please and thank you."

Big Martha muttered, "You've got to be kidding me with this shit."

Lillian flashed her a warning look. "Excuse me. Did you have something you'd like to share with the group?" *No sense letting her think she can run over me in here. If I shut her down from the get-go maybe that'll nip it in the bud.*

The bully glared at her.

"Apparently not." Lillian held her ground. Inside she was complete Jell-O, but she would never let it show. They'd chew her up and spit her out if she did.

"Alrighty then, the handout you've just been given includes everything you need for this week's curriculum. This may feel like a beginner's course to some of you." She looked in Big Martha's direction. If Martha felt respected, maybe she'd turn out helpful rather than a heckler. "Many of you are probably comfortable with these things, but let's work together to help each other remember those simple little gestures that help separate us from the...well, you know."

"No, I don't think I do know. Are you calling us out?" A scraggly-haired woman glanced around at the others. A few of them nodded, garnering support.

Lillian sucked in a breath. "When we're on the outside, we may have opportunity to engage in activities that require poise. That's all I'm saying."

"What makes you think poised is what we want to be?" The straggly-haired woman slumped down in her chair.

Add posture to the etiquette list.

"You think you're better than us?" another chimed in.

Lillian raised a hand in the air. "Enough. I'm surely not here to pass judgment on anyone. We're all at Walter Stiles for doing something that was not appropriate. So no one, me included, has any right to judge." Why had she thought for even a moment this might be fun?

Dixie stood and whistled at a pitch that made Lil's ears ring. "Y'all pipe down. This is a required session and Lillian didn't volunteer for this job, she was picked. She's already helped me with a few things. Let's give the old bird a listen. If you have to sit here, you may as well give it a go."

"Thank you, Dixie."

"You're welcome."

Lillian dinged the bell. "Point." She spun around to the stack of materials. "Oh goodness, I almost forgot. Every time you get a point, you get one of these commissary dollars."

"Well, why didn't you say that to begin with?" The women muttered between themselves, but only for a moment, and then suddenly almost all eyes were on Lillian.

She distributed the first two commissary dollars.

"There are up to twenty of these up for grabs in every session. So, participate and it can be quite a little boost for you." Lillian winked at Dixie, thankful for the prison jargon she'd shared with her to help her better communicate with these women.

She turned the page of her notes, then started working her way through the handout. Everyone in the room, except Martha, participated. But then with the nickname Big Martha, she had something to prove.

By the end of the session when the warden walked in, everyone was seated with a formal place setting arranged in front of her, even Big Martha, but then one of her people had set up hers. Of course, not many of the settings were right, but it was a start.

Warden Proctor, a small smile tugging at her lips, strolled by each woman.

Lillian turned her notes facedown on the table. "We're all done with this week's session."

The warden gave the ladies a nod. "You can leave."

Not a word was uttered as the women shuffled out of the room.

Lillian stacked the supplies back into the box that the warden had assigned her, then turned to leave.

"Lillian?"

She turned. "Yes, ma'am?"

"Did anyone give you any trouble today?"

Lillian only hesitated for a moment. It wouldn't earn her any points if she ratted Martha out, and who knew, next week could be a whole different game. "None at all. I think your program will be a big success."

"Thanks to you."

"It's my pleasure," Lillian said, and quite honestly, it had been by the end of the hour. As she walked out of the dining hall, she saw Big Martha's best girl hustling around the corner. She'd probably heard Lillian's whole conversation with the warden.

Lillian pushed up her sleeves. She would just have to make that work to her advantage.

Teague took a folder off the top of the stack in his inbox. He flipped it open, reviewed it, then signed off on the papers inside.

"Uh...Teague?" Deputy Barnes tapped on the open door.

He looked up from the stack of case files. "Yeah?"

The deputy cocked a thumb toward the street fronting the building. "Pretty sure you've got a visitor outside."

"I'm not expecting anyone." He stood to get a look out the window.

The deputy grinned, a broad slash from one earlobe to the other. "Said she's family."

Yeah, she was his visitor all right. "More like extended family, but I've got this, Deputy." He strolled outside as Abby Ruth Cady stepped down from a shiny white Ford dually. The truck and her trailer took up nearly six parking spaces. *Only Aunt Bibi.* In the twenty-five years he'd known this woman, she'd only become more outrageous.

"Tadpole!" She threw her arms in the air and stomped a booted foot on the ground. "Damn, you look fine."

Teague winced at the pet name he'd been saddled with after a little incident with Jenny when they were kids.

Abby Ruth strode over to hug him, ending the embrace with a big whack in the center of his back. "I swear, boy, you get better looking every year. My daughter doesn't have the smarts God gave a rock, that's for damn sure."

Not going there.

He nodded at her long-bed crew cab truck. "That's some ride."

She elbowed him. "Yeah, I figure if I was a man, people would say I was compensating for something."

Teague just shook his head. This woman lived to shock folks. Was that a shell casing around her neck? Never thought he'd see jewelry made out of .22 shells. Leave it to Aunt Bibi. That woman did love her guns. "You're looking good."

"So the men at that KOA camp told me." Abby Ruth patted her steel-gray hair, chopped short around her face. At sixty, she would still turn men's heads. Only a few inches shorter than his six-two with a long, lean build. She wore her trademark white shirt with slim jeans tucked into a pair of screaming red cowboy boots.

He looked down at her feet. "Lucchese?"

"Custom. Had 'em made by a gal up in Oklahoma."

"Nice."

"Tell you what, that drive from Ohio numbed my ass something good." She rubbed her hands over the seat of her jeans. "But you said on the phone you had a situation, so I got down here as quick as I could." The volume of her voice probably carried her words all the way back to Oklahoma.

He chose to ignore the five parking violations and took her arm to lead her inside. "Let me buy you a cup of cop coffee and tell you about it. That work?"

Her grin went wide and just a little evil. "You bet your sweet ass it will."

An hour later, he drove out to Summer Haven with Abby Ruth following. They both parked, and her rig took up a good quarter of Lillian's driveway.

Abby Ruth checked out the genteel Georgian house as they approached the front door. "Some digs."

"The Summer family practically built this town."

"Power-mongers, huh? I knew a few of those back in Houston. Oil men. Good in bed, but they always wanted to be on top."

Teague's palms twitched with the need to cover his ears. God, he loved this woman, but he needed earplugs sometimes. "Lillian is the last of her line. A real sweet and refined lady."

"A doormat."

"No, she's got spine to spare." She'd gotten his ass up on that roof well enough, hadn't she? "Problem is, Lillian's a prideful old gal and she and her friends have their hands full with this huge place. And I haven't seen Lillian in a couple of weeks. Just doesn't seem right. If you can get on the inside, it would sure help me out. You know, keep them out of trouble and keep me in the loop."

Abby Ruth stuck her nose in the air and sniffed. "Smells like a story to me."

Exactly what he'd hoped for. She could keep him informed and feel like she was still working at the same time. Forced retirement wasn't her mug of beer. Teague punched the doorbell and stood back.

Maggie opened the door while wiping her hands on a stained garage towel. "Teague, if you're stopping in for special tea, I hate to tell you, but I haven't had time to mix any up what with trying to repair the bathroom after Sera took that flume ride."

No, he'd come to plant a spy in their midst. "No, ma'am. I came to ask you another big favor."

"Abby Ruth Cady." Abby Ruth stuck out her hand.

Maggie hesitated, but finally shook. "Margaret Evelyn Stuart Rawls."

Abby Ruth slid Teague a look that said *Are you shitting me?*

"Abby Ruth's an old friend of my family's." Teague smiled in what his mom described as his old-lady-and-baby-charming smile and edged Maggie backward through the door without her realizing what he was doing. He took a step closer. "She happened to be in the area—" he coughed to cover Abby Ruth's snort behind him, "—and my place isn't big enough to host guests. I was hoping, what with all this room here at Summer Haven, you'd be willing to let her stay here during her visit."

"What about the Broussard Bed & Breakfast?"

Shit.

"I'm allergic to cats," Abby Ruth spit out, "and I heard the Broussards have one of those big coon-sized Persian cats. If I had to sleep there, I'd be one red-nosed sneezing, sniffling, weepy-eyed girl."

Maggie's eyebrows drew together. "When in the world did Angelina get a cat?"

"Here recently," Teague said.

"Well, with Lillian away, I'm not sure how she'd feel about opening her home to someone else."

"She's away? I thought she was under the weather." Teague shared a glance with Abby Ruth.

"Uh...well..." Maggie stammered.

"Can't you call her and ask?" Abby Ruth's smile was less charm and more bite.

"Oh, well...hmm..." Maggie scrubbed the towel over her knuckles. "You know, now that I think about it, we have plenty of room upstairs. In fact, you'd probably be comfortable in the Sweet Vidalia Room."

"Maggie," Teague said, relief steaming through him like a cold beer on a hot day, "I can't tell you how much you've helped me out."

Chapter Eighteen

A few days with Abby Ruth Cady underfoot was enough for Maggie to know that it wasn't going to be easy to shake her long enough to get out to visit Lillian as planned. If she and Sera tried to sneak off, that woman would be hot on their heels.

Rocking on the porch enjoying a cool breeze, Maggie uncovered another winning scratcher ticket. Fifty bucks was fifty bucks and that was good enough to call it a day even though most of the tickets in these bags would expire in a couple of weeks. She'd work extra hard tomorrow. Besides, it was Sera's night to cook and it was just about dinnertime.

Maggie trudged upstairs. She knocked on the door to the Sweet Vidalia bedroom and peeked around to find Abby Ruth shoving something between the mattress and the box spring. She let the yellow coverlet fall and plastered on a smile as fake as Hollis Dooley's teeth.

It was bad enough they'd have to delay their planned weekend visit with Lillian because Teague dropped this woman off at Summer Haven like she was a stray pup. But now it looked like Abby Ruth was harboring a secret on top of it all.

Granted, Sera had turned out to be a blessing. But those Texans, with their penchant for double names, should've dubbed this woman Trouble Maker.

Something about her sharp fox face, hip-shot stance and miss-nothing eyes made Maggie's skin tight. But as long as Abby Ruth was staying at Summer Haven, she would be hospitable. Lillian would expect nothing less. "Sera cooked supper tonight. We've been taking turns since Lillian...left on her...trip."

Abby Ruth hustled into the hallway and shut the bedroom door firmly behind her. "Good. I'm starving."

"I have to warn you, Sera's not much on meat." Maggie craned her neck to look up at the other woman. Abby Ruth had at least half a foot on her. What was it with all these darned skinny gals around here? Didn't they know a woman was supposed to get pleasantly plump as she aged?

As she followed Abby Ruth down the stairs, nothing on the woman's backside jiggled.

Nothing. *Note to self: don't let anyone walk behind me and see my jiggling parts.*

Rather than eat in the formal dining room with its flocked wallpaper and twelve-person fruitwood table, they gathered around the small farmhouse table in the kitchen.

Sera passed around a platter of cooked onions, bell peppers and—Maggie peered closer—long brown strips that looked like french fries.

"What in the name of Mary, Joseph and the three wise men is that?" Abby Ruth poked at the food with her fork.

"Tofu fajitas." Sera smiled and offered Maggie purple-tinged tortillas.

"They say Jesus forgives anything—" Abby Ruth scooped veggies into a tortilla, but passed over the tofu, "—but I'm not so sure about that."

"So, Abby Ruth..." Maggie nibbled at her fajita wrap. "Tell us a little about yourself."

"I'm on sabbatical, just traveling around the U.S."

"What fun!" Sera said. "I'm doing the same thing."

Abby Ruth grinned. "Yeah, it's getting more and more exciting by the minute."

"How do you know our Teague?" Maggie asked.

That smile dimmed a tad at the word *our*.

"His family owned a house down the street from us in Houston. He and my daughter, Jenny, grew up together." Abby Ruth made a show of taking a big bite of her food.

Hmm. History there she didn't want to share.

"So your friend Lillian's on a trip. I've traveled a bit myself. Maybe she's someplace I've visited."

I sincerely doubt it. "Oh, it's a real hush-hush retreat place on the outskirts of..." Maggie's mind darted, "...the city."

"Which city?"

"You know, she didn't even tell me." Like she was going to blab Lil's secret to some stranger. Some *skinny* stranger at that. Not happening.

"More wine?" Sera poured all around without waiting for an answer.

"The house and property are beautiful—" Abby Ruth gestured with her wineglass, "—but I noticed the whole place could use a little work."

If it got any worse, Maggie would have to take off her shoes and use her toes to plug the holes in the dam, but at least she'd laid tile in the bathroom. It would take another few days for the grout to cure and the sealer to dry. But after that, she could place the toilet and they'd be ready to roll on offering tours. "It's kind of like a child. You can't turn your back on it for a minute or you'll find it's stuck a raisin up its nose while you weren't watching."

Abby Ruth's laugh was low and surprisingly pleasant. Otherwise, she was just so *so*. So tall, so thin, so confident.

Maggie splashed more wine in her glass and drank. An hour and a half later, they were still drinking and Abby Ruth's stories were becoming more and more outrageous. But darned if they weren't funny.

"So you were telling me why Lillian doesn't just hire a bunch of folks to come in and fix this place up," Abby Ruth said. "It could really be a showplace."

"There's no money for all that." Maggie hiccupped. "Summer Haven used to be a real beauty though. When we'd come down here on summer break from college, it was like becoming a princess for two weeks."

"Teague told me the family was some big deal around here, so what happened to the money?"

"Lil's late husband blew most of it." Maggie clapped her hand over her mouth and squinted at the wine bottle before her. How many glasses had she put away? She'd lost count after three, but two empty bottles sat on the table and the third was only half full.

Abby Ruth leaned back and kicked her

boots out in front of her. "Oh, now that sounds like a story."

"It's not mine to tell." Maggie pressed her lips together.

"Well, the money problem is easy enough to solve, you know."

Maggie sat up so fast she bumped her glass with her right breast and it crashed to the table and bled red wine all over Lil's white lace tablecloth. She scrambled to pick it up and save the last few sips. "How?"

"Have you paid any attention to that thing parked out in the garage?"

"How do you know what's in the garage?" Maggie demanded.

"I took myself on a little tour while you were down for your senior citizen's nap."

"I didn't...I don't..." Darn it all. The one time she'd taken an afternoon siesta and Abby Ruth had to catch her at it. "Don't call me a senior citizen."

"What's that AARP card in your wallet say?"

"How do you know I carry—" Maggie caught Abby Ruth's sly look. "Fine, but I don't *feel* like a senior citizen. And stop trying to distract me. Are you talking about Lil's daddy's car?"

"Sugar, that's not just any car," Abby Ruth said. "That there is a Tucker 48. Only fifty-one of those suckers were ever made. And a convertible?" Abby Ruth made a sucking noise with her teeth. "There's no way that came off the line. Somebody put that together after they stopped regular production. I bet you've got at least a million bucks sitting on top of those four whitewall tires out there."

Maggie nearly shot wine out her noise. "A million?" She wiped the wine she'd just dribbled down her shirt. "You're crazy."

Abby Ruth's right eyebrow cocked in a sharp arch. "I won't deny I might be crazy, but I will tell you this right here and right now. There are three things Abby Ruth Cady never lies about. Sports, whiskey and cars."

"What about men?" Sera chimed in.

Abby Ruth raised her glass and toasted Sera. "I put them under the sports heading."

"Oh. I see," Sera said, chugging the rest of her wine.

Maggie deflated against her chair back. "Well, it doesn't matter what that car is worth. It's staying right where it is. Lil made a deathbed promise to her daddy that she wouldn't sell it." A million dollars? There was no way Lil knew that car was worth more than a few grand.

"Now *that's* crazy," Abby Ruth said. "I'm assuming her dad's gone to that great scrap yard in the sky, so I can't imagine he gives a crap anymore. And if he did, would he want their family home to just crumble and fall apart?"

"It's sad when people get old," Sera said. "Like your boyfriend, Maggie."

Abby Ruth looked interested. "Your boyfriend?"

"Shut up, Sera." Maggie didn't mean to snap, but the wine was doing a number on them all.

"He gave her a necklace. Rubies and gold." A tear slid down Sera's cheek. "It was really quite romantic."

"That's quite a boyfriend if he's giving you rubies, Maggie." Abby Ruth lifted her glass. "Way to go, girl."

Maggie looked at the ceiling. "He is not my boyfriend. The old man has lost his memories."

"And the rubies were made of macaroni," Sera admitted.

Maggie told Abby Ruth, "He's confused. He thought I was his wife and it was our anniversary. He'd made a necklace. Yes, it was made out of macaroni, but he didn't know that either."

Sera's face went stoic. "I'm sorry. You should've been there, Abby Ruth. It really was the sweetest moment. Warner Talley's heart was on fire when he laid eyes on you, Maggie."

"The old timers, that's heartbreaking. Lots of sad stuff happens when you get our age,"

Abby Ruth said, sounding gentle for the first time. "Did you know him well?"

Maggie shook her head. "No. I'd actually never met him before."

"Now wait a minute. So you just go visit people down at the old folks home just to be nice? That's kind-hearted of you."

Abby Ruth looked so impressed that Maggie wasn't about to tell her that they'd been up to no good.

"We weren't really there out of the goodness of our hearts exactly," Sera said. "We needed information about his son, Nash. Warner was so smitten with Maggie that not only did he give her the macaroni necklace but he gave us the key to Nash's house."

"Stop it, Sera," Maggie scolded. "That sounds way worse than it is."

"Oh, you two don't need to put a filter on for me," Abby Ruth said. "Trust me, I like a good time as much as the next gal."

"I don't how fun it all is," Sera said. "Some of the places we've been going are right skeevy." Her words were muted because she'd tipped her glass up to her mouth. "You wouldn't believe what all's going on."

"There's more?" Abby Ruth perked up as if she'd been drinking mineral water all night and looked back and forth between Sera and Maggie. "You two are hiding something bigger than a limited-edition car out here. What is it?"

"Lillian's in the slammer," Sera blurted out.

Maggie sucked in an audible gasp and glared at her.

Sera froze.

"The what?" Abby Ruth's eyes darted like a slot machine.

"Sera, maybe you should call it a night," Maggie said, jumping to her feet to clear the table. She turned to Abby Ruth "She's hammered, doesn't know what she's saying."

Sera rested her forehead in her palm. "Did I say that out loud?"

Sera, what are you doing? You can put on an Oscar-winning performance when it doesn't matter for a guy who can't remember his own name, but you can't keep a secret? After guilting Maggie into keeping all this from Teague, she just spilled everything to a woman they didn't know. And Maggie didn't trust the Texan further than she could throw her. Doubtful she could even pick Abby Ruth up, much less toss her.

"She said the slammer. Come on, Sera, spill it. What's really going on around here?" Abby Ruth was practically rubbing her hands together. "If Lillian were in the slammer, wouldn't Teague know? He *is* the sheriff."

"No. The real slammer. Prison of the federal

variety," Sera admitted. "You know, khakis and shower shoes prison."

"Sera!" Maggie felt the room spin. What if Teague had sent Abby Ruth to spy on them?

Okay, that was just the wine-crazies talking.

Still, Maggie asked Abby Ruth, "What did you say you did for a living?"

The woman's smile was wide and toothy. Big-bad-wolfy. "I'm an investigative journalist."

What was left of Maggie's liver after tonight's wine overdose shriveled and turned black.

We've just led a wolf right into our little flock of sheep.

Chapter Nineteen

The next morning, Maggie's head felt like someone had poked a thousand upholstery tacks into her skull while she slept. Red wine was straight from the devil. And once Sera had started spilling Lil's secrets to Abby Ruth, Maggie hadn't been able to shut her up.

She'd felt so bad she couldn't even bring herself to sleep in Lil's bed, so she'd slept upstairs. She stumbled downstairs praying the ibuprofen bottle in the cabinet by the sink was at least half full.

"Morning, glory." Abby Ruth sipped coffee from a huge mug at the kitchen table.

The woman looked like a fresh spring day, short hair perfectly tousled, crisp white shirt, jeans and boots.

"Why aren't you hungover?" Maggie's whisper felt like a shout reverberating in her head.

"Because, sugar, I can hold my liquor."

Abby Ruth pointed to the countertop. "Help yourself to the coffee."

Sure made herself at home, didn't she?

Maggie grumbled under her breath all the way to the painkillers and then the coffeepot. She poured herself a cup, inhaled and sipped. If that red wine had been brew from hell, this coffee was a special delivery from heaven. "You made this?"

Abby Ruth grinned. "Worked in a newsroom with a bunch of men. It was do or die on the stuff they made. But you better bet they poured their own damn coffee."

She bet they had. Probably brought Abby Ruth her cup on a little golden platter too.

Maggie Rawls, when did you turn into a shrew? You need to stop it right this minute.

"So," Abby Ruth said, "what's the scoop on Nash Talley's house?"

Maggie coughed, and scalding liquid raced up her nasal passages and dripped from her nose. "Excuse me?"

"Sera mentioned last night that you have a key. You must have wanted that for some reason. Do you think he's up to no good or was that a cougar move?" Abby Ruth's eyebrow shot up. "You're not leading on both daddy and son, are you? Why, you—"

"No. Lord, no. I am not leading anyone on. Either one. And that key was a mistake. I decided we shouldn't use it." Maggie eased her behind around the table to sit, sending the chair screeching across the wood floor. Her brain did a jitterbug against her skull. "That would be breaking and entering."

"It's not breaking and entering if you have a key."

"Regardless, I should talk with Lillian about this. It's her problem, after all." Lil had made it clear Summer Haven should be Maggie's focus and she'd have a conniption fit if she knew Maggie had fronted the money for the bathroom. But then again, if Nash had stolen some cash away from Harlan's Social Security above and beyond what Lillian knew about, it was high time he forked it over. Between that and tour income, Maggie could pay herself back and Lil would be none the wiser.

Maggie dropped her head into her hands and closed her eyes. Just thinking about the problems surrounding her made her head throb harder.

Abby Ruth set her coffee cup on the table and glared at her. "That's just silly. If this man duped your friend and she's taking the fall, you need to do something about it. This isn't the kind of thing you wait for permission to do. You just do it and ask for forgiveness later."

Maggie's back went as stiff and straight as

rebar. "Why are *you* so fired up about finding Nash Talley? You don't know Lillian. You don't have the whole story. *I* don't even have the whole story. For all you know, we could be lying or just plain nuts."

"True." One of Abby Ruth's shoulders lifted. "But I figure it's the most interesting thing happening in this small town."

"We're not here to be your source of entertainment. I'll talk with Lillian about all this the next time I visit. Until then, we drop it."

"Fine, you skedaddle off to ask your precious Lillian for permission, and I'll have lunch with Teague." Her words were even, but Maggie heard the threat behind them.

Who did she think she was, coming in here and sticking her nose into Lil's business, giving orders like she expected to be obeyed and issuing threats to keep Maggie in line?

Maggie tried to stare Abby Ruth down, but this woman was a master at eye contact. "You wouldn't."

"I don't really want to." Abby Ruth tipped her head back to drain her mug and then sauntered over to the sink to wash it out. "I'd rather investigate this situation. Help you get to the bottom of it."

"That's blackmail."

"In Texas, we like to call it gentle

persuasion."

"Y'all are truly a breed apart."

Abby Ruth just smiled an I've-gotcha smile.

"We'll need an alibi," Maggie said.

"Of course."

If she was going to give in, she'd do it in a take-charge way. "The Cocklebur Cloggers are coming out to practice in the gazebo later today. You could park one of the cars down the road beforehand so we'd have transportation. Then we could make an appearance and the cloggers would vouch for us if anything went downhill."

"Sounds perfect."

"Abby Ruth Cady, you may be getting your way today." Maggie tried to slap on a mean face as she stared at Abby Ruth, but she had a feeling it looked more like an expression of constipation. "I'm not about to forget that you strong-armed me into this, do you hear me?"

"Sugar, I am not hard of hearing."

The Cocklebur Cloggers were stomping and clomping and clapping in the gazebo when Maggie, Sera and Abby Ruth snuck off down the road to hop in Abby Ruth's gigantic truck. Beforehand, they'd smiled and served sugar cookies and punch to everyone and then claimed they were retiring to the house to take naps. Abby Ruth had sneered at the excuse, but Maggie told her it would keep anyone from knocking on the door asking to use the powder room.

Alibi in the can, they approached Nash's house, a modest redbrick ranch with crisp white trim. But the lawn sprouted a few taller patches. Maggie looked closer. The edging was also going scraggly, which meant no one had mowed and trimmed for at least a week.

Didn't have to be Jessica Fletcher to figure this out. He was neglecting the yard. Based on those rumors about his need for order, she'd bet that he'd never let his landscaping go wild like this. This investigation stuff wasn't so hard.

They cruised by Nash's and parked two streets over. "Remind me why we didn't bring my truck," Maggie asked. It sure would've been less conspicuous than this great white whale.

"I don't like to ride," Abby Ruth shot back.

Of course you don't.

"We should go in through the rear," Sera said.

"And remind me why we came in broad daylight?" Maggie glanced to her left and right. On the other side of the street, Mr. Dooley was shuffling along on his walker, his ancient bloodhound by his side, and Maggie ducked down in the seat. No one here really knew Sera or Abby Ruth, but she was becoming part of this community. "Tell me when he's gone."

"Dear God, get that man a Buick or at least a faster dog," Abby Ruth said.

Finally, the street was clear.

They slid from the truck and Abby Ruth led them in a kind of crouching run. By the time they made it to Nash's back yard, Maggie's breath was rasping in and out of her throat and her armpits were filled with as much water as the Atlantic.

This investigative stuff is hard as H E double L.

Maggie stood in the shade of the back porch and fanned her overheated face.

"You know yoga will help with aerobic capacity, right?" Sera whispered.

God help them all. If anyone saw her doing that peeing dog pose, they'd be struck blind. "I'll keep that in mind."

"Can we skip the fitness advice and get inside?" Abby Ruth said.

The key Warner had given Maggie slid cleanly into the lock and turned with a muted click. Her galloping heart and hitching breath smoothed a little. "We're in."

The door opened into a mudroom, if a room tiled in wall-to-wall white could be called such a thing.

Abby Ruth sucked in an audible breath. "Damn, I needed to marry a man like this."

"Probably has a maid," Sera said.

"You've got a point there."

Maggie tiptoed into the kitchen, floored in the same pristine ceramic tile. The cabinets gleamed in a high-gloss white finish and the countertops sported gray soapstone. This man needed some color in his life. "What are we looking for, exactly?" she asked.

"Pretty much anything suspicious," Abby Ruth said. Well, that certainly narrowed things down. "We should each take a room and search it. Look for scribbles on random bits of paper, open bills, dig through the trash."

"I'll check the bathrooms," Sera offered and off she went.

After the kitchen, the first room Maggie and Abby Ruth came across was the den and Abby Ruth broke off there. Maggie continued into a bedroom that had been converted to an office. The floor was done in a slate tile, and the desk and credenza were—surprise, surprise—white lacquer accented with glass and chrome.

Maggie hurried to the credenza. The first drawer held six matching bamboo trays filled with office supplies. The paper clips were all silver and there was no mingling between them and thumbtacks.

The second drawer was empty except for a super-sized lint roller. Must've had five-hundred sheets on it.

The cabinets underneath weren't much more exciting. Printer paper with perfectly aligned edges, ten extra ink cartridges and a label maker.

Maybe they were wrong. Maybe Nash was exactly what he appeared to be, a well-dressed, upstanding young businessman. Because none of this was suspicious unless his stapler and tape were involved in some conspiracy.

From down the hall, she heard Abby Ruth and Sera comparing their finds.

"What'd you get?" Abby Ruth asked.

"I don't think the guy is sexually active," Sera said. "Or if he is, he's not sexually responsible."

"And you figure this how?"

"No condoms," Sera replied. "What about you?"

"I don't have any condoms either, but this guy is a freak and a half, that's for sure. His remote controls are not only dust-free, but they're lined up perfectly. What man does that?"

"None I've ever met."

"Ain't that the truth?" Abby Ruth shot back.

"Okay, I'm heading for the master bedroom."

"I'm moving on too."

Maggie crawled under the desk and knocked her head against one side. As she rubbed at the bump already forming, a drawer slid out, pretty as you please, from the kick plate. Maggie scrambled back out and snatched up the heavy leather-bound book filling the drawer.

She flipped it open to find rows and columns outlined in red and green. Someone had written in those little boxes with a sharpened pencil.

Oh, Lord. A ledger. A ledger with lots of entries and lots of zeroes.

The air in Maggie's lungs stalled. Those zeroes meant money. Meant they were right about Nash Talley.

Maggie pushed herself to her feet and race-walked to the kitchen.

"All I know," Abby Ruth was saying, "is this guy ain't right in the head. Look what I found in his pantry." She gestured to the pile of Ivory Soap and hand sanitizer sitting shoulder high on the kitchen island.

"I've got one better." Maggie slipped the ledger onto the counter, pushing aside soap with her elbow. "I don't know what it is, but if it's kept in a secret drawer, it's probably something he doesn't want anyone else to see."

Abby Ruth hip-checked her. "Good work, sugar."

A warm glow settled in her chest. They riffled through the pages. The entry descriptions were in some kind of code, but the numbers didn't lie. These double entries balanced perfectly, and not only that, there appeared to be a repeating pattern each month.

Nash Talley had been keeping track of thousands upon thousands of dollars. Whatever he was into, it was way bigger than Lillian's desperate Social Security fraud. Anger simmered in Maggie's insides.

"Let's load up," Abby Ruth said.

"Wait a minute," Maggie said. "We need to put this back in case Nash comes looking for it. Right now, he has no idea we're on to him."

Suddenly, the doorbell ding-donged and they all dropped into a crouch, with Maggie hugging the ledger to her chest.

"What do we do?" she whispered to Abby Ruth.

"Stay behind the island while I check it out."

"You're not answering the door, are you?"

"Do you think I'm stupid?" Abby Ruth peered around the corner of the kitchen island.

Two booming knocks came from the front door. "Talley, you in there?" a man called.

"Teague's always been too smart for his own damn good." Abby Ruth scrambled back like a long-legged crab.

Oh, Lord. Teague? He'd promised to stop by Nash's house, but why today when Abby Ruth had talked Maggie into waltzing into Nash's house?

Maggie studied Abby Ruth. Maybe she'd set this up.

No, her eyes were closed and her lips were moving.

"Are you praying?" Maggie asked.

"Lord's prayer never did any harm to anyone."

Amen to that.

"He's on the move," Abby Ruth said.

"He's coming inside?" Sera asked, her eyes as round as a plumbing gasket.

"No, circling the perimeter," Abby Ruth answered.

Maggie glanced over her shoulder. They were completely visible from the back door window. "Which way did he go?"

"Around the right side of the house."

"Then we also go right." Maggie nudged Sera, who nudged Abby Ruth. They all duck-walked to the opposite side of the island. Please let Abby Ruth be right because if

Teague had turned left, he would spot them through the window over the sink.

Seconds later, that same banging came from the back door. "Talley, if you're in there, open up."

Maggie held her breath and watched Sera sink into a yoga ball on the floor. "Don't get too comfortable down there. We're about to be on the move again."

Abby Ruth edged around the island's corner again. "Go, go, go. He's gone, coming around the side of the house."

Maggie crawled, pushing the ledger with her knee, almost mowing over Sera in her haste to hide herself from the view over the kitchen sink. They all leaned their backs against the island, chests heaving. Granted, Maggie had more to heave.

It seemed like the length of time it took Hollis Dooley to get across town on his walker before they heard Teague's car engine turn over.

By that time, Maggie was one big puddle of sour sweat and booming heart.

Barely able to form a word and still shaking, she said, "Give me a few seconds to take pictures of the ledger pages and then we better get the heck out of here in case Teague decides to come back."

She pulled out her phone, mashed virtual

buttons until the camera function finally popped up. Then she started snapping pictures one by one. Once she'd recorded everything, Abby Ruth served as lookout while she replaced the book in the drawer and slid it shut with a definitive click. When they returned to the kitchen, Sera had a warehouse package of toilet paper and an armful of soap.

"What in the world are you doing?" Maggie asked.

"You said yourself money is tight." She hugged the Ivory against her chest. "This could last us for a year."

Maggie gasped. "But...but that's stealing."

Abby Ruth patted Maggie's arm. "Sugar, as many hygiene products as that man has stored up, he's not gonna miss a few boxes."

Chapter Twenty

The gals were already piling out of the truck in front of Summer Haven carrying armloads of Nash's soap when Maggie caught sight of Angelina Broussard on the front veranda. Damn that woman. She was peeking in the windows of the house! "What in blazes are you up to?"

Angelina whirled around and waved a crumpled piece of paper in the air as she headed toward them. "Make a visit to the warehouse store, ladies?"

"Well, with three women in the house, you can never have enough bathroom supplies." Maggie strode up the steps as if she owned Summer Haven herself. "Is there something we can help you with today or were you just window shopping?" A little grin broke on her lips at Abby Ruth's snicker behind her.

Then Angelina thrust out her fist, revealing a crumpled tour flyer, one Sera had painstakingly lettered and sketched. Damn her, those were works of art.

"I stopped by to inform you that hosting tours in a house that hasn't yet been certified by the Bartell County Historic Preservation Committee isn't allowed." Angelina's tone was so snippy that it made Maggie want to form a committee to ban that committee.

"Where is Lillian?" Angelina tapped the toe of a high-heeled sandal that would have killed Maggie's arches.

"Excuse me?" Who was this woman to tell Maggie what she could do with Lil's home? She swallowed the sour guilt sitting on the back of her tongue that Lil hadn't approved the plan herself.

Angelina folded her arms. "I want to talk with her directly about this."

"She's away visiting relatives right now."

"I assume she'll return home in time for the committee visit because it simply can't be delayed."

"Not even if one of your precious committee members is missing?" Abby Ruth stood shoulder to shoulder with Maggie on the top step.

Angelina's mouth tightened. "I'm afraid I don't understand."

"And I'm afraid," Abby Ruth drawled through her big-as-Texas grin, "that Mr.

Talley is also on an extended vacation. Surely you wouldn't think of evaluating Summer Haven without all your members present."

"But...but..." Angelina gestured vaguely over her shoulder. "Even I can see you have a toilet sitting in the middle of the parlor. That's simply not—"

Abby Ruth sauntered over the window and peered inside. "I don't see a commode anywhere. What about you, Maggie?"

Joining Abby Ruth, she pressed her nose against the glass. "All I see is a velvet divan, a lovely piecrust side table and other parlorly furnishings."

Sera dumped her soap in a rocking chair and headed their way. They made a privacy fence in front of the parlor window, and when Angelina tried to skirt by them to head for the other window, Abby Ruth caught her elbow. "Sugar, I don't know what y'all call this here in Georgia, but where I'm from, if a body comes on our property uninvited, we call it trespassing." Her grin went as sharp as the edges of Nash Talley's desk. "And when that happens, we shoot first and ask questions later."

Angelina stepped back, stumbling as her heel caught in a gap in the porch boards. "This place is falling apart. It's surely not fit for the attention it gets." She straightened and looked

Maggie dead in the eye. "I don't know exactly what you three are up to, but—" she tossed the balled-up flyer to the ground, "—I will tear down every one of these you've posted around town."

As she stomped down the steps, Abby Ruth called out, "Y'all don't come back now, ya hear?"

Lillian sat at a metal table surrounded by nothing but shades of brown and gray, wishing she could have visitors every day. She smoothed her pants. These unflattering khakis sure looked different without Maggie Rawls' colorful tops. A few strategically placed rhinestones wouldn't even hurt.

Never thought I'd see the day that I was wishing for a shirt with appliqués and rhinestones on it à la Maggie style, but then I never realized just how much color my life had. Brown is not *the new black.*

She glanced over at the now familiar faces of the other women who had visitors this morning. The process was belittling. Being called out of a cluster of hopefuls to be handpicked to come to the visit room gave the winners survivor's guilt. She felt bad for those left standing alone every day. It had to be like being the last kid picked for dodge ball, only she'd never known that feeling. If these girls could have traded one week of their muted lives to be with her at a Summer Haven lawn event, she'd bet their lives would have been so different.

Maggie and Serendipity were first through the door.

Lillian's heart did a flip. She'd put Sera on the visitors' list this time even though she wasn't sure if Sera would still be around. It was good to know she was sticking it out and giving Maggie a hand. That lessened Lil's guilt a little. She motioned Sera and Maggie to the chairs in front of her.

"It's so good to see you, girls," Lillian said. "Sera, thank you for staying and helping Maggie with Summer Haven."

"We make a good team," Sera said. "Plus, now we have even more help."

Maggie nudged Sera with her knee.

"Whatever do you mean, dear?" She glanced from Sera to Maggie. Guilt was written all over Maggie's face as plain as if she'd used permanent marker. "Oh, Maggie, please tell me you didn't let Teague talk you into getting a live-in handyman. You know what I think of that idea."

"No. I didn't, but quite frankly, I don't think you're in a position to tell me what kind of help I can get. If I didn't have help, I'd be—"

"SOL," Lillian said.

"What?" Maggie slouched down in her chair.

"Shit out of luck," Sera said.

Lillian nodded. "Exactly. And you're right, Maggie. I shouldn't expect you to run Summer Haven the way I would. I'm sorry, so just fill me in."

"Are you saying I'm not doing a good job?"

"Maggie—"

"Because if you are, I could hop on a plane to Colorado. Pam's been hinting at me moving out there."

"You wouldn't!"

"Not if you add Abby Ruth Cady to the visitor list," Maggie said.

"Who in the world is Abby Ruth Cady?" Lillian said.

Sera spoke up. "She's staying with us."

Lillian lined her sights on Maggie. "What are y'all doing? Summer Haven is not a hotel."

Sera scooched forward in her chair. "You see, she's a friend of the sheriff's from his hometown. She's a wild woman. Lord, I'd never want to piss her off. She wears blue jeans and boots that cost more than my vehicle. Anyway, she saw the Torpedo and did you know that thing is worth like a million dollars? Did you know it's some special limited-edition car? You could have your debts done and paid for and probably be home if we could find someone rich enough to buy the darn thing."

"No. No. No. NO! Even if I paid the entire sum today, they wouldn't let me out of here. Daddy will not lose that car because of my screw-up, and there isn't a car in the world worth that kind of money."

Sera glanced at Maggie. "He's dead. He'll never know."

Lillian blinked in disbelief. "It was my one promise to Daddy. I will not break it." She hadn't meant to raise her voice. She glanced around. Several of the inmates were looking her way. *Hold yourself together.*

Big Martha stared in her direction. Had she heard?

Lillian lowered her voice. "Great...now she knows my business."

"Who?" Maggie started to turn, but Lillian grabbed her hand.

"Don't look. Her name is Martha and she's a real badass."

"You just said *ass* and you know what *SOL* means? What is this place doing to you?" Maggie withdrew her hand and rubbed her temples. "Geez, Lil, you've only been in here a short time and you've lost all your color, gained a potty mouth and some interesting acronyms. I'm afraid you'll be a Hell's Angel by the time you get out of here."

"I'll be me. I'm just trying to stay below the radar, and if a few potty-mouth remarks are needed, I can do that." Lillian breathed, trying to release the panic in her chest. Daddy's car wasn't up for grabs, no matter how bad things got. "Now, let's get back to our pleasant visit."

"Pleasant?" Maggie bit out. "We come in here and you want to chitchat about the weather, about the house. Honey, I miss you like there's no tomorrow, and I hate that you're in this place, but we've got some pressing things to discuss."

"More pressing than Summer Haven?" Lillian tsked. "I doubt it."

"Well then, let's start with your ring sitting in a pawnshop somewhere in Atlanta."

Maggie certainly wasn't feeble about throwing jabs. "Desperate times call for desperate measures."

"But your wedding ring meant everything to you."

"Well, Harlan's sack of scratcher tickets wasn't netting me much and I couldn't sell *everything* in the house. Don't worry about the ring. Just take care of the house, okay?"

"We also need to talk about Nash Talley," Maggie said, "and this whole thing about you being charged with taking way more money than what it cost you to bury Harlan."

"It would've saved all of us a lot of trouble if I'd just stuffed Harlan's sorry ass in one of those godforsaken lottery bags or buried him out in the back flowerbed. I bet that two-liter brand would've held him just fine. And he'd have made excellent fertilizer, he was so full of sh—"

"Four mil," Maggie mumbled. "And, yes, it would have, but all that aside. Nash dropped out of sight."

"So?"

"So, Sera and I went to see Warner Talley, but he's about lost all the marbles he had."

"Not all of them," Sera said. "He sure knew a beautiful woman when he saw one."

"True." Maggie's smile was secretive and a little sad.

Lillian watched the interaction between Maggie and Sera and her heart shrank. It made her feel small as a grain of sand to be left out of the inside joke. "Where is all this going? Is there even a point?"

"There is. Nash is up to something. I know it. And I plan to get to the bottom of it."

"Have you been out to check Momma and Daddy's graves?"

"Of course I have."

"Flowers are there? Everything in place?"

Maggie nodded.

Lillian let out a breath. "Well, then Nash is

around somewhere. He promised to take care of that for me. He's always been good to his word."

"I don't think he's as good as you think, Lil. I'm going to get to the bottom of it," Maggie said.

Lillian shook her head. "What are you going to do? Break into his house?" A light chuckle escaped her, but it frittered out at the unwavering look on her best friend's face.

"It's not breaking and entering if we've got a key," Maggie said.

Lillian lunged forward and asked in a hushed tone, "How did you get a key to Nash's house?"

"His dad gave it to Maggie," Sera said. "He's sweet on her."

"Well, it's not right. Leave Nash be. He helped me through a very difficult time and I do not want you treating him like the bad guy."

"But, Lil, I'm almost certain he took more than you think." Maggie glanced at Sera for support.

"It does look that way," Sera said.

"What do you mean?"

"Lil," Maggie said, "haven't you wondered—really wondered—why the government accused you of taking so much money?"

"Well, I just figured with penalties and

interest—"

Maggie's head shake was jerky. "No, ma'am. I'd bet you dollars to doughnuts that man kept depositing Harlan's checks after your funeral debt was covered. Sounds about right doesn't it—five years and ninety grand?"

"But...but how?"

"Did you ever receive any of Harlan's checks?"

"No, because I..."

"Because you set it up for that money to go directly to Nash, right?"

Lillian's head felt loose on her neck, but she tried to nod.

"I have a feeling Nash never told the Social Security folks Harlan was dead."

Lillian pushed her hair behind her ears and grabbed one of Sera's hands and one of Maggie's. "I appreciate all you're doing, but let it go. Please just concentrate on taking care of Summer Haven. It's the most important thing. As much as I'd like to spend time with you, I'd hate for you two to get into trouble and end up my roommates."

Maggie's voice rose. "But if he did something wrong, he should be paying for it too."

"It doesn't matter. No matter what you think Nash has done, it won't change me being in here. Let's just bide our time. If he's done something, he'll get his. That's for the big guy upstairs to handle. Not us."

"It's bigger than just you, Lil," Maggie said.

Maggie looked tired, and Lillian knew that was her fault. *I'm so sorry, Maggie.*

Sera said, "And what Maggie is politely not saying is that he might have scammed other people too."

"Excuse me?"

"Extra Social Security checks started showing up in folks' mailboxes about the time Nash skedaddled out of town."

Oh. Oh, no. "You mean to tell me—"

"Yes," Maggie said. "Nash Talley is a scheming, no-good, lying, liver-bellied cheat."

"You could be wrong." But the hard ball in Lillian's midsection told her *she* was the wrong one.

"We'll know soon enough." Maggie lowered her voice. "I'm going to use that key Warner gave me. It's the right thing to do."

"I doubt Teague would agree with you." Lillian held her gaze. "Breaking and entering will land you in here or worse. As prisons go, this may be the crème de la crème, but trust me, it still isn't home. Do us a both a favor and let Teague handle this if you insist on checking it out."

"If Nash has the money you're doing time for, then he needs to pay up, because we can use that money to help with Summer Haven."

Sera put a hand on Maggie's arm and they exchanged a glance. "It's true, Lillian. Things are falling apart like meteor showers when the Geminids peak."

Maggie folded her arms and Lillian knew better than to argue when her lip went all quivery like that.

"Our time is up," Sera said. "You ready, Maggie?"

"Yeah." Maggie and Sera both stood. "I love you, Lillian. We'll be back soon."

She watched them leave, worrying just what trouble they could get themselves into. Yes, Nash might have been up to no good. Might be the reason Lillian was wearing these hideous khaki clothes, but Maggie was putting herself at risk. She knew less than nothing about nefarious criminal-type activity.

Lillian looked up to catch Martha staring at her from across the room.

Oh, now wasn't this just perfect? Lillian smiled at her. If there was one person who either knew everything there was to know about B&E or knew someone who did, it was Martha.

Maybe a little etiquette bartering could work right about now.

As soon as Maggie and Sera exited the building, Sera grabbed Maggie's arm. "Why didn't you tell her we'd already been in Nash's house?"

"Because she'd worry, and I think she's got enough to worry about just being here. Besides, if we can't get around Angelina to give those darn tours, I think there's going to be way more for her to worry about."

"You really are a good friend, Maggie."

Maggie took Sera's hand and headed toward the truck. Suddenly, Maggie let go of Sera and broke out into an all-out sprint when she saw Abby Ruth slumped in the driver's seat of her truck.

Please don't let her be dead. I can't take one more bad thing happening. She yanked the passenger door open. "Abby Ruth!"

Abby Ruth sucked in a snore louder than a buzz saw.

Maggie reached across the seat and slapped Abby Ruth's arm. "You scared me. I thought you were dead."

"Don't slap me. Are you nuts?" Abby Ruth rubbed her arm and then sat up in the seat. "Y'all were in there an awful long time."

"Sorry." Sera climbed into the backseat. "Lillian had a lot to say."

"Great. So she's all in on the Nash thing I take it," Abby Ruth said.

"I wouldn't say that." Maggie clicked the seat belt and positioned the strap between her ample bosom.

"How could she not agree?" Abby Ruth fired up the truck and pulled out of the parking spot. "Well, how about the Tucker? Did she know what that thing is worth?"

"Nope." Sera kicked off her shoes, stretched out on the seat and put her feet up on the window. "Not sure she even believed us."

"She thinks we should turn investigating Nash over to Teague and just concentrate on taking care of Summer Haven."

"That's ridiculous. You need to get me on the visitor list."

"Why would you think she'll listen to you when she won't listen to me, her best friend?"

"Why wouldn't she?" Abby Ruth gave her a look that made her wonder the same thing.

Oh, to have this woman's confidence.

"Maggie, do you love your friend?"

"Of course, I do."

"Sometimes you have to go behind people's backs for their own good."

Maggie stared out the window. She didn't say a word until they passed the prison guard. "Maybe we should just turn everything we know over to Teague. What are we but three over-fifty women? We don't have experience with investigating a possible criminal. We're totally out of our league."

"Speak for yourself," Abby Ruth said. "I'm ready, willing and able."

Wait just a minute now. "I thought you wanted to run to Teague."

"I've decided I'm not ready to give up on the fun yet. What's poking around a little more going to hurt? It's not like this Nash guy is a murderer or something. We just think he's taking money that isn't his. How dangerous can it be?"

Maggie did feel more energetic and alive than she had for years. Maybe they could look a little more before letting it go. "So what do you suggest we do?"

"Make a plan."

"But what are the steps to the plan?" Maggie did like a step-by-step guide to building things.

"I had you pegged as one of those read-the-instructions types. I'm right, aren't I?" Abby Ruth pursed her lips. "Don't bother answering. I know I'm right. Let's brainstorm together." She glanced in the rearview mirror. "You in, Sera? And get your dirty hoofs off my window. Jesus, girl."

Sera swung her feet around and sat up. "Haven't you done this a million times as an investigative reporter?"

Abby Ruth tapped her fingers on the

steering wheel in an uneven rhythm, which sent a nervous tendril through Maggie. "Not exactly."

"What does that mean?"

"It means what I really did was interview guys in jockstraps my entire career. I broke stories about who was likely to win MVP, not big crimes."

Sera made a sound like she was clearing a fur ball from her throat. "So you're a liar? That's so *not* good for your karma."

"Well, karma's a bitch, and sugar, I have my moments, but I'm no liar. I'm an opportunist," Abby Ruth said. "What I do know about this little venture is that if we're going to poke around, we can't underestimate Teague. That boy is as smart as the day is long."

Great. She was discounting Lillian's wishes *and* deceiving the sheriff. Maggie's stomach swirled like it was filled with bubbling lava. "I'm not sure I even know where to begin."

"Maggie, why don't we start by looking through those ledger pictures?"

Why didn't I think of that? Nerves always made her go blank. Same as in college. She took her phone out of the pouch on her hip and started mashing buttons and icons on the screen.

Abby Ruth snatched the phone from her and tapped her finger twice and handed it back to her.

"Thanks," Maggie said, wishing she could figure out the stupid thing. She thumbed through the pictures. "Some of these are blurry." She enlarged a clearer one. "Okay, here we go."

Sera peered over Maggie's shoulder. "Low-hanging fruit first. What's obvious?"

Maggie and Abby Ruth exchanged a glance. Sera came up with the most lucid random comments. "Perfect. Okay, so there are entries on the same days of the month each month."

"How many months?" Abby Ruth asked.

Maggie flipped through the pictures. "A lot, not all of them are clear enough to tell for sure. My hand must've been a little shaky. And I didn't take pictures of every page."

"Once a fluke, twice a coincidence, three times a trend," Sera said.

"So, we have a pattern of dates," Abby Ruth repeated, then swerved into the highway's fast lane and gunned the engine. "What else?"

"The entries are all three letters followed by numbers and letters." Maggie counted aloud. "Thirteen positions. Three letters, two numbers, three letters, two numbers, three letters."

"He does like his orderly world, doesn't he?" Abby Ruth said.

"This is like math word problems." Sera's

voice held an excitement that was usually concealed by her Zen-like calm.

Maggie let out a sigh. "I always hated word problems." Just looking at the numbers made her seasick.

Abby Ruth tapped the screen. "It had to take him forever to keep all these records. Look how neat they are, like he stenciled each letter and number. With his meticulous need for order, there's got to be a pattern."

"Maybe that's why he was missing those Meals on Wheels deliveries. He was backed up on paperwork," Maggie said, half-joking.

"What?" Abby Ruth spun around, taking her attention off the road.

Maggie grabbed at the wheel. "What? What?"

"You said he was missing deliveries. That's it." Abby Ruth snapped her fingers. "The perfect way to chat people up without them being suspicious. We're going to put Sera on Meals on Wheels duty."

"Why her and not me?" Maggie asked.

Abby Ruth reached over and put her hand on Maggie's arm. "Because you promised Lillian you'd watch out for Summer Haven, and I don't want you to break your promise."

Chapter Twenty-One

If Lillian was going to keep her girls out of trouble, she needed to get them some help. And if Nash was in the middle of it, it didn't matter how nice he'd been to her over the years, he deserved to get his too.

Big Martha would be in the rec room. That woman never missed an episode of *TMZ*, and if there was a sure time she could corner her without a big audience, it would be as she left.

Butterflies did somersaults in Lillian's stomach as she stood at the back of the room waiting for the right moment. *Suck it up. I have to do this. After all, Maggie is saddled with Summer Haven and now she's been forced to take in more help just to keep my secret from the town. It's the least I can do.*

The closing credits rolled and Lillian made a beeline for Big Martha.

"May I have a moment?" Lillian whispered, then stood to the side.

Martha gave a nod of dismissal to the women sitting on either side of her, then patted the sofa cushion.

Lillian sat down. "I think we can help each other."

Big Martha sputtered and gave her a look of doubt. "Honey, I'm the one calling the shots around here. I don't know what you think you can do for me."

"You wanted my allegiance. I don't give anything away for free."

"I'm listening," Big Martha said.

"I kept your lack of participation in the etiquette class on the DL. That class is important to the warden and she wouldn't be pleased. If you need extra help, I'll do it on the side so no one else knows. To these other woman, you might pass yourself off as coming from money, from culture, but I can tell a fake a mile away. Honey, you are not the real deal."

Big Martha straightened, but she didn't argue.

"It's okay. Your secret could be safe with me." Lillian smiled sweetly.

"What do you want?"

"My girls are up to their elbows in something on the outside," Lillian said.

"Those grannies that were in here visiting you?" Big Martha laughed. "What's wrong? They stealing from the bingo fund or something?"

"No, and they may be old, but do not underestimate my girls." Lillian leveled a stare until Big Martha's smarty pants smirk fell from her face. "I need you to give them some advice on breaking and entering."

Big Martha swung around with a smile so wide it practically hit her ears. "Really?"

"Really. I do not want them to get caught, and they need some expert 4-1-1 on this. They think they have a key, but I know that still can be considered B&E, and should the key not work, they need a backup plan. Are you in?"

Big Martha lifted her chin. "I'm in, but you and I are going to talk further."

"I'm sure we will. I'll expect you to join me on the next visitors' day." Lillian got up and forced herself to walk, not run, out of the room. She'd just bargained with the baddest ass in prison camp. *Please don't let this backfire on me.*

Sitting across from the Twilight Breaks admissions coordinator, Nash pulled an ink pen from his pocket and signed the contract. Another line item completed. It wouldn't be long before the whole list was checked off.

The nine-thousand-dollar money order was tucked in his coat pocket. He reached for the crisp envelope and laid it on the table. The down payment.

The woman pulled the envelope to her side of the desk and looked inside. "This will do it. I think we're all done here, Mr. Warner."

"Excellent." He slid the pen back in his pocket and stood. "I'd like to make one last visit to the suite before I leave."

"Certainly. It's still unlocked." She stacked the papers and passed him a portfolio with the Twilight Breaks logo in gold-foil across the front. "Mr. Warner, we're so pleased you've decided to entrust us with your father's care. We're anxious to meet the senior Mr. Warner."

"Please. Just call me Theodore, but when Dad arrives you can call him Warner. Daddy's friends always called him Warner." If there were any lucid moments in Dad's future, the least Nash could do was be sure the people around him called him by the right name. He'd had to make up a new first name for Dad. It wasn't like he could tell them his father's name was Warner Warner.

"Since you've decided to furnish the unit with items from our inventory, we'll have his room ready tomorrow. You're welcome to move him in any time after that."

"Excellent." Only he wasn't going to be moving Daddy in with anything aside from the clothes on his back, and Lord knew those would probably have to be tossed out. A good clean start. Minimal furniture. Good art, and he'd stock that dresser with just the necessities. He wasn't about to fill this place up with a bunch of stuff his father wouldn't remember.

Nash let himself out of the office and rubbed antiseptic gel into his hands as he walked down the well-lit hallway. Except for the polished rails on each side of the hallway, it could have been any floor in any high-dollar oceanfront condominium.

The doorknob was as shiny as if it had just been installed, but he took out his handkerchief and covered it before entering just the same. It wasn't a large space, but it had lots of natural daylight.

He walked to the wide span of windows lining the wall. No balcony. No sliding doors. A bit of a waste, but under the circumstances he guessed they couldn't have senile seniors hanging off balconies either.

The view from the room at Twilight Breaks was nearly as lovely as the one from his own balcony here in Hilton Head. It was funny how timing had changed things. He'd have probably tried to keep Daddy right there at Dogwood Ridge as long as possible, and they'd have let him since he practically funded the darn place. Those people owed him. But the truth was, Dad wasn't going to get better, and Tina was the only one willing to say it out loud.

He'd been reintroduced to his own father more times than he cared to remember over the past six months. Tina had provided a reality check, and now with Lillian's friends poking around in his business, he knew moving Daddy was the right thing to do.

Nash made a mental note to get Tina to take down the paintings he'd put in his father's room. They were worth way too much to just leave behind at Dogwood Ridge, not that anyone there would ever realize it. There were sure enough poker-playing dogs and dime-store oils hanging on the walls in that place. At least Twilight Breaks was tastefully decorated. The staff all wore whites and the place smelled fresh and clean.

Moving Daddy. Now that was one thing he hadn't quite figured out how to do without raising a stir, but he'd just take it one perfectly planned step at a time. But then again, did it really matter if it caused a stir if he and his dad were no longer in Summer Shoals?

He closed the door behind him and headed home.

Back in his condo, sitting on his white couch, in his white pants, he conjured up another white lie to tell Tina. He'd gone back through every step, every communication, to be sure he was mitigating every risk.

His stomach burned. *I'll probably die of an ulcer after all this and not even be able to enjoy it.*

He only needed two things from Summer Shoals—his dad and the ledger. Everything else in his house could be tossed in the trash and he'd never miss it. Even his high-dollar suits weren't Theodore Warner's style. He was so close to leaving Nash Talley behind, and he knew without a shadow of a doubt that he'd never miss that guy.

Loose ends were the only things that could trip him up now. He'd already transferred responsibilities to the people who worked for him, and although they didn't know the funeral home would have a new owner soon, it wouldn't matter because their jobs wouldn't change. Things would move along like they always had. Not like anyone in Summer Shoals really gave a damn about him. There would be talk, but not for long.

He'd feel better if the ledger were under lock and key with him here though. That was the only loose end worrying him now. It was well hidden, but why tempt fate? If those snoopy old broads were asking about him, they could stir up trouble, and he didn't need the attention right now.

Once he had this last bit of business put to bed, he'd return to Summer Shoals for the final time. Nash pulled his phone from his pocket and dialed nine digits. Before he could hit number ten, he hung up. Dad would be so hurt if he knew what Nash had already set in motion.

He would never know. His mind was already gone. And it wasn't coming back. It was time to let the past go for good. Only the future mattered.

Nash took a breath and dialed the full number.

"Hello, Mercy Corporate Services, providing compassion to millions in times of grief."

"Good afternoon. This is Nash Talley. Please tell Mr. Richardson I'm ready to sell. I'll have the contracts to him in Chicago within the week."

When Teague slid into the booth at Earlene's Drinkery, Abby Ruth already had a draft beer sitting on the table for him.

He gave her hand a smacking kiss. "Have I told you lately how much I love you?"

"A woman can never hear that too much."

"So you settled in at Summer Haven?" He took a sip of his beer, skimming away the perfect quarter-inch of foam on it. "I know it's not exactly your kind of place."

"Oh, it'll do for now. The bed isn't bad, although with that Sera cooking, I might starve to death."

Teague motioned for a waitress, who rushed over with a menu, but he didn't even have to look at it. "We'll do the potato skins and the wings, atomic with ranch dressing."

The waitress grinned. "You got it."

He turned back to Abby Ruth. "What's Sera cooking that's so bad?"

"Fajitas made out of tofu." Her mouth turned down and she swigged her beer like she was trying to rid her mouth of a bad taste. "Can you imagine? I mean, shrimp is skirting the limit, but something that was never alive to begin with? No, thank you."

"Maggie's special tea could make up for that."

"Doubtful."

"So other than Sera's cooking, what do you think of them?" Jenny had told him her mom was never one for making friends with other women. Abby Ruth had played the good-ole-boys game for too long.

"Seem like nice enough ladies. And they don't suspect a thing about me. I'll have this where-in-the-world-is-Lillian-Fairview thing wrapped up in no time."

Lord, he hoped not. Abby Ruth needed to find a permanent place to land, both to keep herself out of trouble and to save Jenny's sanity. And his sanity would be much improved if he could persuade Jenny to come down for that visit before Abby Ruth hightailed it out of Georgia. "You had any time to just relax and wander the area? I bet you could talk shop with the folks at the newspaper. Maybe even do some freelancing for them."

"Sugar—" she lifted an eyebrow and shook her head, "—it's not like they cover the Texans or Cowboys here."

"There's always high school football in the fall."

At that, her mouth dropped open and her beer clunked to the table. "The hell you say."

A beep-beep-beep noise screeched in Teague's head. Yeah, backing up was the direction to take. "I just meant...that...you could...teach them a thing or two about real sports journalism."

The waitress slid two platters to the table and Teague let out a silent breath. He'd always sucked at undercover work.

He piled wings and skins on two small plates. His mind raced. What could keep Abby Ruth busy once she finished this little Summer Haven spy job? Anything to keep her from moving on. If she turned south and meandered off into Mexico, Jenny would have a hissy fit. Even worse, he would have no leverage to get Jenny to Summer Shoals.

Teague and Abby Ruth munched appetizers and sipped their beers while catching glances of *Sports Nation* and talking scores.

Finally, Abby Ruth wiped her sauce-covered fingers on her napkin and sat back in the booth. "You haven't even asked me what I've dug up out there at Summer Haven, and I've been in town over a week. What's with that? I thought you were so concerned about that Lillian woman and her mansion of a house."

Shit. Making her suspicious that he'd set her up was the last thing he could afford. "I didn't want to be too conspicuous."

"Well, first off, that old place is falling apart."

"Tell me something I don't know. What about Lillian? Is she really off visiting a friend?"

"As far as I can tell, Maggie's telling the truth. That woman doesn't have a lying bone in her body. But she did mention someone else in town is missing. Name's Nolen Talbert or some such thing."

"Nash Talley," Teague said. "Don't get all excited. I checked around. Apparently, Nash is just out of town for some funeral director business. Not uncommon according to the gal over at the old folks' home where Nash's daddy is living these days."

Abby's eyebrow shot up. "How much training does a funeral guy need? Just hang 'em and drain 'em."

That made being eaten by a shark a little more appealing as a way to go. Teague shook his head and finished off his beer. "You may not feel that way when it's you."

"Don't you worry." She toasted him with her mug. "When I go outta this world, I'll be kickin' up my heels and having a great time."

The thought of this world without Abby Ruth Cady punched a big old hole dead center of Teague's chest.

"So about this Talley guy..." she said. "What's he like?"

"Why all the interest in a man you don't know?" And just what did she know that he didn't? First, Maggie was all concerned about Nash and then changed her mind. But it was obvious Maggie was still on the guy's trail. Question was why?

"I heard he's got some OCD thing."

So the guy's neat, but then again, I think dust is a designer statement. What the hell do I know? "I never paid it all that much attention. What's it matter?"

"Nothing. Just trying to get to know the

folks in town like you recommended. Maybe I could do a story on him."

What did she care about a story when she wasn't even interested in talking with the *Dispatch?* "Nosiness and gossip are like Olympic sports in Summer Shoals," he told her. "Just because people are talking doesn't mean there's anything to it. I need you to concentrate on what's happening out at Summer Haven, you understand?"

Abby Ruth plastered a toothy grin on her face. "I understand, Tadpole." She laid her hand dramatically across her chest, raising the hair on the back of his neck. "Sugar, you know I'd never stir up trouble."

The alarm going off in his head now wasn't just the backup alarm. Abby Ruth Cady had a spoon big enough to stir a Guinness World Records-sized pot of trouble. And he'd just stuck her right into the middle of his kitchen.

Chapter Twenty-Two

Maggie eyed the wine bottle Sera placed on the table with caution. *She's crazy if she thinks I'm going there again. Only my special tea from now on. I know how much of that I can hold.*

"You better tell us the details of your day before you dive into that," Maggie warned Sera. "We need to keep our wits about us."

"I just want to celebrate a little. Delivering meals was so much fun," Sera said. "Everyone welcomed me right into their homes. No questions asked, and they were so appreciative for the meals. The Meals on Wheels people weren't very forthcoming with information but according to the neighbors I met today, Nash used to deliver meals once a week on the second, third and fourth Wednesdays, but he didn't deliver at all during the month of July."

Abby Ruth looked over her shoulder as she rolled out butcher paper against the wall. "So he's missed three Wednesdays?"

"Yep." Sera walked over and put her hands on the other end of the paper to hold it in place while Maggie duct taped it to the wall.

Maggie tugged another length of purple duct tape from her hip. *Schwick.* "That'll hold it."

Sera stepped back from the paper and turned to Maggie. "I don't know how he juggles it with a job though. It took me all day long. Those old people must not get many visitors because they were more than happy to tell me story after story."

"They aren't any older than us," Maggie said. She pulled a bag of scratcher tickets from where she'd stowed it behind the buffet. She needed something to do with her hands during this discussion, and there were only a few scratchers left.

"Well, some of them are. That food they serve could sure be a little more exciting too. Maybe I can help them create a more balanced and tasty variety."

Lordy, don't let her get a hold of their menu. That would never fare well.

Abby Ruth held a marker in her hand. "Time to get all our facts straight."

"Is that a Sharpie?" Maggie asked.

"Last I checked."

"You can't use that. You'll ruin the

wallpaper." Maggie ducked into the kitchen and returned with a plastic toolbox full of mismatched crayons.

"This is why I'd rather live in a horse trailer." Abby Ruth dipped her hand inside the tool box and scooped out a handful. "Okay, let's outline what we know."

Lord, the bits and pieces had been swirling around in Maggie's head for days. It would be a relief to get everything out in the open.

Abby Ruth drew a timeline and they each started filling in whatever random details they could remember. After about ten minutes of scribbling and memory bursts, the wall of white paper now looked like it had been tagged by a team of adolescents with a penchant for wall art.

Sera sipped her wine and said, "Nash helped Lillian steal $90,000 in Social Security."

Maggie pushed her glass away without a taste and winced. It just sounded so bad when stated aloud. "No, he *helped* Lillian borrow $12,000 from the government, which she will pay back in restitution."

"Okay, but she got busted for the whole 90k." Abby Ruth scribbled the figures on the paper.

It looked even worse written on the wall in big block print.

"Nash disappeared around July 5," Maggie added. "And we have pictures from his secret ledger if we could only figure out what those coded entries mean."

"Yeah," Abby Ruth said, "that ledger is the key."

Maggie's stomach dropped as if it had been shoved into an elevator shaft. Oh God, the key to Nash's house. The lottery ticket she was holding fluttered to the ground and she dropped her head back, clunking it against the dining room chair.

"What's wrong?" Sera asked.

Maggie shook her head. And here she'd thought she was doing so well, becoming so independent, so strong on her own. What a load of hogwash.

"Just spit it out." Abby Ruth tapped her boot against the floor. "Don't make us wait."

"I'm an idiot," Maggie finally croaked.

"No, you're not!" Oh, where had Sera been all Maggie's life when she'd needed someone on her side? And now she didn't deserve her.

"I left the key sitting in Nash's kitchen."

"You didn't." Abby Ruth knocked the heel of her hand against her forehead.

Sera slid down in her chair. "Oh, no."

"Oh, yes."

Abby Ruth sucked in a few breaths and finally looked up. "Okay, it's not ideal, but we'll figure out a way around it. First, let's finish talking about what we do have and then we'll handle the key issue. Sera, what about the Meals on Wheels folks? What did you get from them?"

"They're all just so sweet," Sera said, "and lonely. Which is not sweet."

"I'm sure they are, but you were supposed to gather information. Did you get anything?"

"Several of them mentioned they'd received extra Social Security checks this month."

Abby Ruth tapped her chin and then speared Maggie with a sharp look. "Let's flip through those ledger pictures again."

Maggie scrambled for her phone and fumbled to pull up the little photos. "It's still the same jumble of numbers and letters." She pinched and spread her fingers to enlarge the image. "Here's an example. This entry has a description of DEM04MOW91HAD."

Abby Ruth stared at the screen and then sounded out the jumbled characters. "Demmowhad? That means absolutely nothing."

"Here's another one dated in April," Maggie said. "FWH83TFH91LSF."

Sera tapped the phone screen. "They all have that 91 in them."

"Good catch," Abby Ruth said.

Sera drifted away in the dreamy-eyed state

of hers, swayed to the right and left and then jerked upright in her chair. "Maggie, what's Hollis Dooley's middle name?"

"I have no idea."

"Arnold? Augustine? Albert?"

Maggie just shook her head.

Sera grabbed the phone and paced around the dining room table mumbling to herself. "It could be...no...but what about...maybe if..."

Abby Ruth started to speak, but Maggie waved her off. If they interrupted Sera, it might ruin everything. Maybe she was on to something.

Finally, Sera stopped and gripped a chair back. "What about Harlan? What was his middle name?"

"Wayne." Maggie crossed her fingers. *Please let that be the right answer.*

Sera blew out a relieved sigh, and snapped her fingers. "I think I've got it."

"Well, bust out with it, dammit." Abby Ruth's volume went up a decibel.

Sera grabbed the crayon from Abby Ruth's hand, strode to the butcher paper on the wall and wrote *FWH —> HWF.*

"Oh my God! Harlan Wayne Fairview." Maggie jumped up and took the crayon from Sera. "And *LSF* is really *LSF.* Lillian Summer Fairview."

"And the numbers and other letters?" Abby

Ruth asked.

"What if it's not 91 but 19?" Sera asked.

Maggie clutched Sera's hands and danced her around in a tight circle. "You're a genius. The 91 is 19 and the 83 is 38. I'd bet you anything Harlan was born in 1938."

Sera snatched up Maggie's phone and scrolled back. "Those middle letters are...that rotten sonofa..."

"Bitch?" Abby Ruth offered.

"Exactly." Sera looked up. "The TFH is Talley Funeral Home and the MOW is Meals on Wheels."

Understanding crashed through Maggie. *Sonofabitch* was too good for the likes of Nash Talley. "He's stealing from people who can barely afford to feed themselves and from people who just want to bury their loved ones. We need to take this—" she stabbed a finger toward the phone, "—to Teague immediately."

"Whoa, whoa, whoa there, sugar britches. Wait just a minute now." Abby Ruth pulled the phone out of Maggie's reach. "By the looks of those entries, Talley has a shit-load of money stashed somewhere. What do you think happens to all that cash if the law gets involved?"

"Maybe Lillian would get out of prison!" Maggie's insides boogied at the thought.

But Abby Ruth was shaking her head.

"Highly doubtful. But if *we* find Talley, we find his money. And in case you haven't noticed it, Summer Haven is a money pit. Doesn't it make sense to have him pay to take care of this place Lillian loves so much?"

Why didn't I think of that? "But no one knows where Nash is," Maggie said. "And even after being inside his house, we didn't have a clue."

Abby Ruth jotted the findings on the paper, then plopped down in her chair. "Then we'll just have to try again, and while we're at it, we'll pick up that ledger as insurance." She crossed her leg and bobbed that fancy boot in the air.

"I just told you I screwed up and left the key," Maggie said. "I may not know much about crime, but even I know what we're thinking about is illegal."

"But if that ledger contains illegal stuff, what's the harm in stealing it? Who gets hurt? No one except the bad guy." Abby Ruth sat back and did that eyebrow thing. "Did you see just how many entries that book had? We can shake down that schmuck, grab a little cash for Lillian's house and give back to those he ripped off."

This wasn't just about Lil anymore.

Abby Ruth leaned forward with her elbows on her knees. "All we have to do is find Talley.

We can do that. It's three against one, and my money is on us."

Maggie's heart warmed with pride. They were about to get justice for every unsuspecting senior citizen Nash Talley had ever taken advantage of.

Lillian strolled into the dining hall, finally feeling more confident about her place in the prison food chain. Big Martha had agreed to help her. Navigating this new world wasn't so hard.

"Lil!" Dixie frantically motioned Lil to her table.

"I'll just get my lunch and—"

"No, get over here. Now!"

Lil was taken aback. Dixie had never spoken to her that way. Reluctantly, because today was hamburger day and they were actually quite decent, Lil left the lunch line.

Dixie pulled her down to the bench. "You need to get back to the pod."

"But the hamburger—"

"I heard some talk that Big Martha's girls were seen around our place earlier."

"So?"

"You need to go check your bed and your footlocker."

"Whatever for?"

"I don't trust that Martha any farther than I can toss her," Dixie said, taking a big bite of her burger and swallowing. "If they were hanging around our place, then they were up to no good."

Lil's stomach shrank. Not enough room in there for lunch now. "Fine. I'll go check it out."

She hustled out of the dining hall and back to the dormitory. Looking to her left and right, she checked for witnesses before she stepped into her and Dixie's sleeping area. First, she rifled though her footlocker, but all it contained were her extra clothes and a picture of Maggie and her back in their William & Mary days. But when she patted down her bed, she felt a suspicious lump at the far corner of her pillow case.

Lillian jammed her arm inside and pulled out a cheap black phone. Oh, Lord have mercy. If the guards caught her with this, she'd probably not only lose her teaching job but lose favor with the warden as well. Not something she could afford.

That damned Martha. This had her touch all over it. She'd just acted like she was willing to help Lillian, but it was obvious the woman still had it out for her.

Lillian shoved the phone into the front of her bra, but it poked out, making her look like one of those multi-breasted Picasso paintings.

Where, where to hide this thing?

Shoot, there was only one other place. She shoved it down the back of her underwear. Humiliating to have to hide something there and not too comfortable either. Sweat pooled at the base of her spine and began trickling down.

Hope the dad-burned thing doesn't electrocute me.

She had to find Big Martha and not only return her phone, but to give her a piece of her mind at the same time.

So as not to attract attention, Lillian strolled out of the dormitory and slowly made her way across the courtyard to the cottages. And with every step, that damned cell phone ooched lower. She tried to hitch up her pants, but that only made the thing stick to one butt cheek. Finally, she made it to the cottage and knocked on Martha's door.

"Enter," a voice called from inside.

Lillian walked in to find Martha cramming a book under her own pillow. What in the world? She'd caught sight of one word: *Post.* Was Martha actually reading Emily Post?

"Is that—"

"What do you need now, Grammy Lil, advice on knocking over a convenience store?"

Lil's back muscles tensed. "Certainly not." She shoved her hand down the back of her pants and fished out the phone. "I thought we'd come to some understanding, and yet I found this in my pillowcase today. If you think you're going to stay top dog around here by getting me in trouble, then you can just think again. I may be old, but I'm not feeble." She'd already been taken in by Nash Talley and she was done playing the patsy.

"But—"

Lil held up a hand traffic cop style. "Martha, I don't want excuses. I told you if you would help me, help my girls, that I would be loyal to you. Stop while you're ahead." Lillian tossed the phone at Martha, who snatched it out of the air with one swipe.

"You're welcome," Lillian said as she slammed the door behind her.

Before they could move forward with their plan to find Nash, Lillian called asking Maggie to come to the prison camp for visiting hours. Now Maggie watched Sera relaxing in the backseat of Abby Ruth's crew cab dually, having one of those doggone Zen moments and humming what sounded like *On The Road Again*.

Maggie fluffed her shirt, praying for some relief from the summer heat. Didn't these other women ever sweat?

"And we need to be sure Lillian understands that finding Nash and his money may not get her out of Walter Stiles, but will at least help us save her precious Summer Haven," Abby Ruth said, then rattled off three other things she thought they needed to tell Lillian.

Maggie reached over and turned off the sports radio Abby Ruth had on. "Look," she said a little too loudly. "I don't know that you'll even get in to see Lil. Just because I asked her to put you on the list doesn't mean she'll do it. And as far as what we need to say to her, she's my best friend. I'll do the talking."

Abby Ruth gave her a what-the-heck look, then turned on a smile and an accent like the heavy syrup in canned peaches for the gate guard at Walter Stiles Prison Camp. "Yes, sugar. We're here to see Lillian Summer Fairview." She took the parking pass and tossed it in the dash, then maneuvered her massive truck through the packed parking lot.

"What is it? Some kind of prison holiday or something?" Sera asked.

"This is crazy," Maggie said. "How about over there?"

Abby Ruth floored the truck and headed to the farthest corner of the lot. "I'm not going to go up and down every blessed aisle. We can walk."

The three of them piled out of the truck and began the hike up to the main building.

About a third of the way to the building, Maggie realized she wasn't huffing or puffing. In all the recent chaos, her body seemed a little more...right. When she walked, that *swish-swish* of her inner thighs had disappeared. Her mood lifted, pushing away some of the worry that had been weighing her down about talking with Lillian today.

Abby Ruth stopped abruptly and flung both arms out, stopping Sera and Maggie in their tracks.

Maggie felt her left boob wrap around the woman's bony arm. Okay, so not everything was skinnier.

"What?" Sera asked.

Abby Ruth shushed them both, then pulled them back between the scraggly red tips lining the sidewalk. "Look!"

Maggie batted the twigs from her face, then peered out to take a look. A man in a dark uniform and cowboy hat was leaving the building they were headed toward. "Is that Teague? Oh, my God. That's Teague." She faced Sera. "He knows."

Abby Ruth shook her head. "We don't know *what* he knows. He's the sheriff. His visit could be totally unrelated to Lillian."

Maggie started sucking air. "We're over an

hour from Summer Shoals. I highly doubt it. He knows she's here and he's going to..."

"Stop it. Just simmer down." Abby Ruth grabbed Maggie's hand. "Seriously. Slow down. Breathe. All I need is you having a heart attack here in the bushes."

Sera rubbed Maggie's shoulders. "It's okay. Even if he knows, it doesn't mean he knows everything. We've got this, Maggie."

They hunched in the bushes and watched as Teague made his way through the parking lot and got in his car. When he finally turned out of the main gate, they broke free from the cover.

"That was close," Abby Ruth said. "We sure didn't want him to see us here."

"Come on," Maggie said. "Let's get this over with."

Inside, the prison guard who'd checked Maggie and Sera in before was on duty again. "Names?"

"Maggie Rawls." She handed over her license.

"Clear."

Abby Ruth stood with her legs braced and thrust her ID at the guard. "Abby Ruth Cady."

"Clear."

Maggie goggled at both women, but Abby Ruth just lifted a shoulder and strolled around the table.

The guard glanced up at Sera. "Reverend Marcus, go right in."

"Bless you, my child."

"What the hell was that?" Abby Ruth demanded. "Reverend Marcus?"

"Long story," Maggie told her. Then she spotted Lil sitting at a table with another inmate. The woman was younger, probably in her forties. Dark hair pulled back in a wide headband, high cheekbones, no smile. She was pretty in a harsh sort of way. But why the heck was she sitting at Lil's table?

Lil stood and although her posture was as straight as ever, she seemed to have shrunk since they locked her up in this place a little over a month ago. She hugged Sera and then Maggie. Her arms wrapped around Lil's shoulders, Maggie couldn't help but feel the sharp bones.

"Lil, are they treating you okay?"

Lil smiled, but it seemed forced. "It's not the Ritz, but I'm making do." She turned to Abby Ruth. "Lillian Summer Fairview."

"I've heard a lot about you." Abby Ruth gestured at Maggie and Sera. "You've got some real loyal friends here."

Lillian swallowed. "Don't know what I'd do without them. Thanks to all three of you for coming today."

They settled at the table and Maggie asked,

"What did Teague want?"

"Teague Castro?" Lil's eyebrows winged up.

Maggie nodded. "Is he the reason you called us to come visit? And by the way, I didn't even know you *could* call."

"I can't do it often." She glanced over at the dark-haired woman. "The regular phone costs money, but I had a little help."

"Oh, Lil." Maggie started to stand and dig in her pocket. "I can—"

"No, save any money for Summer Haven and don't expect me to call often."

Maggie plopped back down and eyed the inmate who'd yet to do more than look them all up and down as if they were from another planet. "Want to introduce us to your friend, Lil?"

"Oh! This is B—" Lillian paused midintro, "—Martha. Now, what's this about Teague?"

"He was here," Sera said. "We just saw him come out of the building and then drive off."

"Well, he wasn't here to visit me."

"We don't need the sheriff poking his nose in your business," Sera said. "We need to get him out of the way."

"I like the way you think, blondie," Lil's buddy said. "I could teach you a thing or two about how to do that."

"That's all we need," Abby Ruth grumbled. "Y'all don't worry about Teague. I'll figure out a way to handle him if it comes down to it."

"Fine," Lil said. "About going to Nash-ville—"

Maggie cut her off. "We haven't been there." *Again. Yet.* Lil didn't need to know they'd already been inside once and that they already had their next visit planned down to the minute. Maggie hated lying to her, but Lil had enough to worry about in this place. "But if we do, I have the...um...tools for the job."

"That's a start, but the tools are one thing," Lil said. "Knowing how to use them is another. My new friend, Martha, knows a thing or two about how to help you get to Nash-ville and what to do once you get there. So I want you to listen up."

New friend? Maggie didn't like the sound of that but she loved hearing the take-charge tone in Lillian's voice. This was the Lillian she knew. Not that droopy do-the-time-no-questions-asked chick she saw last time. But Lord a mercy, Lil had rounded up a specialist to help them. She'd sure changed her tune since the last visit.

Abby Ruth arched an eyebrow at Maggie. *Suck it up, sugar.* Abby Ruth might already have a plan lined out, but they would listen to Lillian and her friend, no matter how much Abby Ruth hated being told what to do.

Maggie made a slicing motion under the

cover of the table, and Abby Ruth pulled back. She might not like it, but at least she wouldn't cause a scene.

"So," Martha said, "you think you're all packed for your vacation to Nash-ville, right?"

Maggie nodded.

"Couple things you want to be sure and put in your bag."

Maggie dug for a piece of scrap paper, but Martha snatched it out of her hand. "None of that." The guard glanced over, but the paper had disappeared into Martha's fist. "We don't do packing lists. You get me?"

"I think so," Maggie said.

Martha proceeded to spout about a hundred and fifty tips for a successful breaking and entering, all in code. *Like I'm supposed to remember all this?* By the time the woman wound down, Maggie's head was one big whirling ache.

Lillian leaned toward her. "I'm worried. Maybe you shouldn't—"

"Lil, you trusted me with Summer Haven, trust me with this."

"If you're sure."

No, I'm not sure, but that's not going to stop me anymore. "We're heading to Nash-ville tomorrow night."

Lillian drew back and covered her mouth. "So soon?"

"The sooner we go, the better."

"What time?"

"After dark. The driving's easier then."

The visiting room guard strode over. "Ladies, I have to ask you to wrap this up. Visiting hours are over."

They all stood and Lil hugged Maggie hard. "I'll call you to check in while you're on the road. Be sure to pick up at 9:30 p.m. or I'll get worried."

Maggie nodded. "I'll answer, no matter what."

Chapter Twenty-Three

With muted conversations as background noise, Teague sat at his usual table at the diner staring at his usual breakfast—two eggs over easy, bacon, hash browns and a biscuit. Only that feeling in his gut wasn't the usual. No, it was more like indigestion because if he let Abby Ruth go hog wild crazy on his watch, Jenny Cady wasn't going to be happy. The last thing he wanted was to disappoint Jenny. Again. But he was the one who'd put Abby Ruth in the Summer Haven mix and now she wasn't telling him everything.

Maggie walked into the diner and took a seat at the counter across from where Teague sat. She picked up a menu, but in the mirror lining the wall he caught her eyeing him over the top of the plastic folder.

"Teague!" A broad smile on her face, Maggie spun around on the red vinyl-topped stool. "Good morning."

Why did he get the feeling she wasn't really surprised to see him?

Teague pushed his plate to the center of the table. "How're things out at Summer Haven?"

"Good. Real good."

Teague smiled and paused just to make her a little nervous. "No more branches or flying toilets?"

She rapped her knuckles in the counter. "Knock on wood, we haven't had any more surprises. Just trying to keep everything shipshape so when Lillian gets back she's pleasantly surprised."

"I'm sure you'll have plenty of time to get it all done before she gets back." Teague watched for her reaction to see if she was picking up his subtle hints. "I bet she'll be so happy to be back home it won't even matter."

Maggie's lips tightened.

She knows I know. That'll teach them to try to keep things from me. Teague smiled broadly. "Let me know if there's something I can do for you."

"Well, now that you mention it, there is one little thing." Maggie slid off the stool and sat down at his table. "Aren't you hungry?"

"Had a little heartburn lately," he said. "Now what can I help you with?"

"Oh, it's nothing really. If you're not feeling well, I can take care of it myself."

Yeah, kinda like you took care of the tree limbs?

"Maggie, help is my middle name."

"Well...it's time to get all that money out of the fountain again. I never realized how heavy coins were until I filled a bucket the other day. Darn thing is still sitting there in the fountain. I could barely lift it, much less tote it to the truck."

For God's sake, maybe they would decide to raise a barn by themselves next. "Don't you go lifting those heavy buckets."

"Well, I need it cleared out today. I know it's short notice, but I need to turn that money in to fund a couple of the projects, else—"

He raised a hand. "I'll come over after my shift."

"Perfect! We'll make supper for you."

"You cooking?" Teague tried to not sound unappreciative. "I've heard about some of the things Sera has been cooking over there. I don't think I could stomach tofu."

"Oh, honey, I'd never put you through that. I'll make you my special chicken pot pie. It was George's favorite." Maggie jumped up from the table and headed for the door.

"Maggie?"

She turned back. "Yes?"

"Aren't you having breakfast?"

"Oh...um...you know, I think I'll just grab

something on the run and get on over to the market and buy those pot pie fixings." She hurried out.

What? Did she think there was gonna be a run on chickens at eight in the morning?

It was just a few minutes after five when Teague pulled up in front of the Summer Haven fountain in his sheriff's car. Maggie hunched over the fountain and dipped a scoop of coins into a bucket. This had seemed like a foolproof plan this morning, but now her fingers tingled and it was probably more from nearly hyperventilating over what she was about to do than from dipping coins out of the stupid fountain.

The pitcher of her *special* tea was set up on the tailgate of Abby Ruth's truck. Teague loved that concoction so she knew he wouldn't refuse it, even though she'd kicked the bourbon up a notch to be sure it would mask the taste of the extra little something. The mixture Sera had put together felt like an *arrest me* neon sign flashing across her forehead. *Lord, please forgive me. I swear it's all for good.*

Maggie wiped her brow, pretending she couldn't scoop another cupful, although she was feeling quite invigorated from the activity.

It was nice to fake it rather than feel it. Maybe all that tofu and natural food Sera was cooking for them, coupled with the exercise class at the fitness center, was finally paying off.

"Teague, I poured us a couple of glasses of special tea. Would you mind fetching me my mug, getting yourself a glass and joining me for a quick break?"

She didn't have to ask twice. He trotted right over there like a service dog and delivered hers, sipping his own along the way.

Her stomach clenched. Would he taste the difference? Spit it out? Not take another sip? Lord, this plan had as many holes as Baby Swiss.

"You make the best tea around, Maggie." Teague handed her the mug and she took a long swig, encouraging him to do the same.

Monkey see. Monkey do. Monkey Maggie is drugging you. Sorry.

She gulped down a few big swallows, and then watched him mirror her actions. It was like she'd become the sheriff whisperer or something. With the ice knocking around in their empty glasses, she turned and began scooping pennies and hoping whatever little concoction Sera had whipped up would kick in quick.

Teague grabbed a bucket in each hand and hoisted them over the side of the truck bed with ease. He was making quick work of it, and within a half hour, the fountain was darn near empty of the coins normally hiding most of the sexy mosaic-tiled scenes.

Worry gnawed at Maggie's insides. Maybe the tea wasn't going to work. At the thought, the partially filled bucket she held dropped to the ground and spilled coins all over the place.

"Let me get those, and you rest a minute," he said.

Maggie perched on the side of the fountain and watched him toss water-slimed coins now coated with dirt back into the bucket. "That chicken pot pie is going to taste good after all this work."

"Yeah. I've been looking forward to it all day." Teague stood and heaved the bucket of coins into the truck.

"Abby Ruth will be here for supper."

"Goo...good," he said slowly, staggering against the tailgate. He pulled a handkerchief from his back pocket and wiped his brow.

"You okay?"

He blinked and nodded, but the movement was slow, unsure.

Perfect.

"You don't look so good." She rushed to his side. "Here, sit down in the truck. Maybe you're overheated." She helped him to the passenger seat and then ran around to the driver side and blasted the AC. At least if he passed out she could move him if he was already in the truck. Thank goodness, Abby Ruth had thought of that. "You sit tight for a minute. We're almost done anyway."

He nodded, but he didn't look too steady.

Maggie felt a little lightheaded herself as she walked back to the fountain and tidied up the rest of the things. How could they do this to Teague?

By the time she returned to the truck, her heart was thumping in her ears like the *rum-pum-pum* of a bass drum in the Fourth of July parade.

She sucked in a deep breath and stepped to the open passenger side door.

Teague had one leg hanging out. His eyes were shut and his head lolled over to his left shoulder. At least his chest was moving up and down. If she didn't know better, she'd have thought he was enjoying a deep sleep. No telling what kind of psychedelic dreams Sera's secret syrup was inspiring inside his head.

"Teague?"

He didn't rustle.

She snapped her fingers and called his name again, but he didn't respond. She lifted his leg inside the truck and slammed the door.

She ran around to the driver's seat, climbed behind the wheel and cranked the engine.

Teague lifted his head just a smidgen.

"You okay?"

He nodded.

Men. They never would admit when things weren't right. She drove straight to the house. Sera and Abby Ruth ran out the front door and helped her get Teague inside. They took him to Lillian's downstairs bedroom and tipped him against the bed. Sera jumped from the floor to the mattress and spotted his clumsy sprawl back onto the frilly chenille spread. His shoes might soil the fabric, but that was just too darn bad.

Maggie had bigger things than keeping the whites bright to worry about right now.

"Are you sure he's going to be all right?" Maggie fanned Teague's face and looked to Sera for reassurance. "I feel bad about this."

"He's fine. Trust me, he's probably having a *Fantasia* dream right about now," Sera said with a giggle. "Besides you're the one who's convinced he knows about Lillian. That didn't leave us much choice."

Maggie sat back on her heels. "I know. He made a couple comments at the diner. He knows. I'm telling you. He knows."

"Don't be a worrywart, Maggie." Abby Ruth, wearing a black button-down shirt, held

Teague's wrist and looked at her watch. "His pulse is fine. We've got work to do." She waved them out of the room and to the front door. "Load up, gals. It's time."

Maggie was surprised to see Abby Ruth in something besides a white shirt. Darned if she didn't look like a female Johnny Cash in her dark jeans and boots too.

All Maggie had been able to find was a black sweatshirt faded to grayish color and she was already regretting the choice because she was sweating like she was going through menopause again.

Maggie fanned herself as Sera whisked by in a flowing sleeveless maxi dress. *What I'd give to be wearing that right now.*

Abby Ruth pointed at Sera. "You're gonna want to cover up those arms."

Sera pulled a delicate crocheted shrug from the huge hobo bag on her shoulder. "Better?"

Great. No wonder I feel like a frump next to Mrs. Johnny Cash and a New Age version of Stevie Nicks. But this was no Fleetwood Mac or country song moment. *As soon as we're done with Nash Talley, I'm buying a decent breaking–and-entering outfit come hell, hail or high water.*

Maggie sucked in her stomach and followed along.

Abby Ruth checked something behind her

truck's backseat and Maggie's suspicion-o-meter rang like a fire bell. "What's back there?"

"Insurance."

Yeah, right. You're not hiding a good hands agent behind the backseat. Maggie elbowed her aside and peeked behind the seat. Abby Ruth's *insurance* was long and black and looked like something a SWAT guy would have strapped to his back. "What is that thing?" Maggie screeched. "Whatever it is, you can't take it."

"It's just my little ole AR-15."

"No, no, a thousand times no."

"Fine—" Abby Ruth pulled the gun from the truck, "—but I'm not going anywhere without my backup."

All the blood drained from Maggie's head. Sure as anything that was what she'd seen Abby Ruth hiding under her mattress soon after she arrived at Summer Haven. "Where's the other one?"

Abby Ruth stuck out her right leg. "That's why I have my boots custom-made."

"Even I know that a weapon takes this from breaking and entering to armed robbery."

Abby Ruth reached down, hitched up her jeans to pull a pistol from her boot. She stuffed it in the back of her jeans. "I'm not going anywhere unprotected."

Maggie stood her ground. "Maybe we should just stop this whole thing right now then."

Abby Ruth's shoulders dropped marginally. "Fine, I'll leave the rifle here and the Glock in the truck."

Maggie already knew this woman well enough to know that was about as much as she'd get from her.

Abby Ruth trotted back inside with the SWAT gun. Maggie climbed in the passenger seat, wondering if it was normal for women their age to go crazy like this, but before she could answer her own question, Abby Ruth was back in the truck and they were headed for Nash's place.

Since they had Teague comfortably ensconced in Lillian's bedroom, Abby Ruth didn't bother to park two streets over this time. She just pulled her rig right up in front of Nash's house, even running it up on the curb so one tire sat on his grass. She grinned like a little kid climbing on the roof wearing a Superman cape. One day, Maggie was going to be that ballsy.

They went around to the side door, and Maggie pulled out her new tools, a knife and her phone to watch that locksmith YouTube video one more time.

Abby Ruth sighed and kept lookout. "I

thought you knew what you were doing."

Maggie stuck her tongue out at Abby Ruth's back. "I do. I didn't go out and buy a professional set of tools without some research, but I just want to be sure." She shoved her phone in Sera's direction. "Hold this while I get the lock."

She peered into the lock, poked it a couple of times with one of her new tools. Not worth her time to pick it. She flipped open the knife and ran it between the door and jamb, and with a quick flip of her wrist, the door opened.

Abby Ruth looked utterly amazed, and that made Maggie's day. She gestured inside. "After you, ladies."

"Good work, Mags." Abby Ruth stepped inside, then turned to Maggie. "Since you know where the ledger is, why don't you get that while Sera and I poke around for anything we might've missed?"

Maggie nodded and raced back to get the ledger. She hunkered down on hands and knees under Nash's desk. Fumbling around for the magic spot on the kick plate, she froze at the sound of a car pulling up in front of the house.

A litany of those words her momma had always said a lady never used scrolled through Maggie's brain. Some even popped out of her mouth.

"Everybody hit the deck," Abby Ruth called from somewhere else in the house.

She couldn't get any closer to the deck. She was a sitting duck under Nash's desk, and there was very little other furniture in the room. Dang the man for being a minimalist. She crawled as fast as she could and scrambled to her feet with her heart sitting on the back of her tongue. *Where, where, where?*

There.

She ran to the corner of the room and wedged herself behind a funky black leather chaise and crouched low. God help Sera and Abby Ruth.

The footsteps were slow and cautious and echoed off the white tile Nash had floored his entire house in.

"I called 9-1-1 as soon as I saw the truck with the Texas plates outside," Nash called out. "The sheriff is on his way."

If he thought he was going to flush them out with that lie, he was off his rocker. He wasn't stupid enough to put himself in Teague's sights.

Maggie held herself like a freeze-tag victim and prayed her butt wasn't hanging out in plain sight. So help her God, if she got out of this, she was never again going to touch another cupcake.

The footsteps drew closer.

When they turned into the room where she was hiding, Maggie held her breath.

Nash walked to the center of the room.

She could see him standing there. *If I can see him, he probably can see me. Please don't look over here.*

He cocked his head, listening.

Apparently satisfied, he headed for his desk, kicked his foot underneath, then reached under and withdrew the ledger. He tucked it under his arm and hurried out.

Maggie almost collapsed but held herself upright because they weren't out of the woods yet. He could still find Sera or Abby Ruth.

The minutes stretched out until Maggie was sure she would scream from the tension.

Finally, the door closed and an engine turned over outside. By that time, Maggie's knees were like custard filling, and the best she could do was crawl across the room and out the door. The headlights swept across the window and she didn't move until the sound of the car had disappeared, then she raced into the hallway.

Abby Ruth stepped out of the bathroom. "Thank God he didn't have to take a piss because I'm taller than his damn shower curtain."

"Where's Sera?"

"Sera!" they both called.

They searched the house, even their own hiding places, but Sera was in none of them.

"The carport," Abby Ruth said. They rushed out, but apparently Nash wasn't the handyman type because there was nothing out there, not even a grease stain on the concrete.

Sera was gone.

Chapter Twenty-Four

"Serendipity? Where are you?" Maggie prayed, "Please be here."

"Maybe she's just gone Zen-moment on us in a deep state of meditation. Or he scared the bejeebies out of her and she's hiding. Just call her," Abby Ruth pointed out.

"She doesn't have a cell phone." Misery sloshed in Maggie's stomach. Why hadn't she insisted Sera get a phone before they started all this craziness? Not having a cell was like going swimming in the ocean without a buddy.

Abby Ruth scrunched up her face. "Who doesn't have a cell phone in this day and age?"

"Remember, this is Sera we're talking about."

"Dammit."

A little light bulb flashed inside Maggie's head. "Wait a minute! She had mine."

"Why didn't you say so in the first place?"

Abby Ruth pulled out her phone and stared at Maggie expectantly. "Give me your number."

Shoot. She didn't ever call herself. She closed her eyes and recited a number.

Abby Ruth stabbed at her phone and it blared out that *da-da-da* tone. "Not a working number."

"Try a six instead of an eight."

They both heard the call connect and the phone rang.

"I don't hear it in the house," Maggie said.

Abby Ruth held the phone to her ear. "Sera, if you get this message, call us back immediately at 281-555-9797."

"She was just here. What could've possibly happened to her?" As soon as the words passed Maggie's lips, she regretted asking the question.

"Sugar, I think there's only one answer to that question." Abby Ruth's shoulders slumped. "Nash Talley has her."

Lillian paced back and forth up and down the dormitory hallway, waiting on her turn at the telephone. Although she'd gotten in line two hours ago, three inmates were still in front of her and with only fifteen minutes allowed per phone call, most people used every precious second.

She wasn't going to make it on time for her check-in phone call to Maggie at nine-thirty at this rate. What if they'd run in to trouble at Nash's? Why had she helped them prepare to break in? Maybe she shouldn't have given in to them. Nash sure had put himself on the line for her when she needed his help. What if he was innocent?

Lillian would've chewed her nails if she had any left after her former job cleaning toilets. When she finally got out of this place, her manicurist was going to pitch a fit.

She looked up to see Big Martha ambling down the hall like she had nowhere to go and had no plans to get there quickly. But as she passed Lillian, she pitched her voice low and said, "Come with me."

"But I've been waiting on the phone for—"

"I said c'mon, Miss H&M." She strolled on by and headed toward the bathrooms.

Lillian glanced around to make sure no one was paying attention and slipped out of line to follow. When she opened the restroom door, Big Martha yanked her inside and wedged something under the door to keep it secure from anyone else entering.

Oh, Lordy. Maybe she'd been wrong and Big Martha's help with the B&E plans wasn't a proclamation of undying friendship. What if she'd lured her in here to—

"Here." She shoved something into Lil's hand.

Her heart clenched. "Oh." Lillian looked down to find a cell phone. It was the one she'd recently found in her bed. Lordy, Martha hadn't been trying to set her up. She'd been trying to help. Shame burned the thin skin on Lillian's cheeks. She reached out to hug the other woman, but Martha did a quick shuffle step out of reach. "I'm sorr—"

"Just call 'em."

"How did you know—"

"Because you damn near paced a hole in that floor out there. You make a crappy criminal, you know that?"

Lil's lips twitched. Coming from Martha, that could be either a compliment or an insult. Lillian punched in Maggie's number on the contraband phone and held her breath. The call went through, but only gave a half ring before it went live and she heard nothing. Her stomach dropped.

Then shuffling came from the line, like Maggie was trying to work the phone from her pocket.

"Mags?"

More rustling and a strange moan. Then the line went dead.

"What is it?" Big Martha asked.

"I don't know, but it didn't sound good."

She immediately tried to call back, but got one of those *The caller you are trying to reach* messages.

The tuna casserole the dining hall had served for dinner swam in Lillian's stomach and she clicked the off button on the cheap phone. Held it out to Martha. "They're not answering."

"You already lost your place in line. There's no way you're gonna get another call out on the community line before phone privileges are done for the night, so keep that one."

Lillian's throat closed so tight she couldn't force out a thank-you, but Big Martha seemed to understand. She just nodded and walked out.

Lillian had never felt so helpless—and grateful—before in her life.

Leaving his Summer Shoals house for the final time, Nash drove directly to Dogwood Ridge. The staff wouldn't be overjoyed at him showing up—unplanned—to remove his dad at this late hour of the night. But tough cookies, because although Nash had found his ledger untouched, something had been *off* about his house.

Worry bubbled up, forcing him to burp. *Disgusting.*

He inhaled and exhaled a few calming breaths. Maybe he would just bypass the staff altogether, tell them he was taking Dad out for ice cream or something. The fewer questions, the better because something told him he needed to put this town in his rearview mirror as quickly as possible.

It was time. Time to move forward with the plan. Dad would never be Dad again, and Nash wasn't getting any younger.

He parked his sedan perfectly between the lines two spaces down from the door. He climbed out, feeling somewhat relieved to have finally made the decision. He had a blanket and travel pillow in the trunk that would make Dad's ride out to the island more comfortable. With a quick press of the key fob, the taillights flashed and the trunk popped.

As he lifted the trunk, that bubbling feeling stormed back as though he'd chugged a case of Perrier.

The parking security light illuminated a heap lying in the middle of his bottles of all-purpose cleaner, four-ply toilet paper and wet wipes. It was the strawberry blonde hippy-girl he'd seen at Lillian's on the Fourth of July.

She lifted her head, but her hair was a mess and her skin was the green color of a body delivered from the coroner's office into the care of Talley Funeral Home.

In a reflex response, he grabbed the trunk to slam it closed again. But she must have been fresh enough to sense his motivation because she rose like a cobra, then tumbled from the trunk to the ground in a swirl of black fabric.

She leaped to her bare feet, gulping in air.

"Why the hell were you in my trunk?"

She held up a finger and then, as elegant as a princess might curtsy, she leaned over and heaved on his best dock shoes.

The stench rose and filled his nose. He tried not to look at the fluorescent green-colored goop splattered on his clothes, but the sight and smell got the best of him and he dry-heaved. Bile crawled up his throat and burned his nose. He gagged again.

"I'm so sorry." She swept at the chunks on her dress and wrung out her hem. "I get carsick if I don't...have...enough a...air." She hunched over and vomited again.

This time he had the presence of mind to jump back. "Stop it. You're spewing toxic waste."

She wiped her mouth with a clean patch of her dress and leaned on his car for support. "I haven't had a toxic thing in my body in over thirty years, unless you count Mike & Ike or my college boyfriend."

She staggered a few steps from the car.

"Oh, no you don't." Nash grabbed her arm, but his hand slid from her elbow to wrist thanks to the puke coating her skin. "Where do you think you're going?" Panic and bile rushed up his throat. This wasn't the way this is supposed to happen.

"My friend, I'm leaving. I got the ride I needed. I'm going to find a place to get my chakras back in good order and meditate for a while."

If he let her walk away, he might never make it out of this town. *What am I supposed to do? Let her go and take Dad as planned? Or leave Dad here and run like hell?*

This nut job had left him no choice. He yanked on her arm, swinging around the rear of the car. Before she could regain her balance or her chakras, he toppled her back into his trunk and slammed it shut.

Nash stood there in the lot, his chest heaving. His head pivoted like an owl. No one was around. *Thank God.* Only, with every puke-tainted breath he took in, his desperation ratcheted up another notch. He could not, under any circumstances, drive the entire way back to the island like *this*. He'd never get the smell out of his car if he did. Hell, he'd have to stop every five miles to vomit himself. He glanced toward Dogwood Ridge's front door but saw no movement inside either.

Thank God for small favors.

He trotted around to the driver's side to shield himself from the view of the door and the road. Shoot, he should've retrieved that blanket. Couldn't be helped now, though.

Nash worked his smooth cotton polo over his head, all the while holding his breath and trying to keep the woman's bodily fluids away from his skin. He flung it to the pavement and went to work on his belt. Thirty seconds later, he was standing there in nothing but his boxer shorts. Even his coveted shoes had to go. He picked his clothes up with his fingertips and quickly dropped them into an outside trashcan.

In that split second, he knew how a person could lose all control and kill someone.

Chapter Twenty-Five

Standing there in Nash's carport, Maggie had never felt more helpless.

"It's probably time to bring Teague in on this whole thing," Abby Ruth admitted.

"Did you conveniently forget that we drugged him? We don't even know what I put in that tea. Sera said it was better if we didn't."

Abby Ruth flipped a hand in the air. "Cold water can do wonders."

"I don't think we have time. We've got to track down Sera."

"How do you propose we do that when Sera won't answer your phone and we don't have the slightest idea where Nash might be headed?"

Suddenly, Abby Ruth's phone lit up in her hand. "It's a text from your number."

"What does it say?"

Abby Ruth's eyebrows lowered into a vee between her eyes. "*In truck.*"

"Thank God." Maggie took off across the

lawn and yanked open the truck door. She climbed in and peered over the seat to see if Sera had taken refuge in the back floorboard. Nothing.

She hopped out and climbed on the tire. The bed of the truck was also empty except for the buckets of pennies that Teague had loaded up earlier.

Abby Ruth's phone beeped again.

"Wait a minute. I've got another text message," Abby Ruth called. "*In trunk.*"

"Text her back."

"Already did and no response."

Maggie trudged back toward the carport, and the muggy breeze swirling around her did nothing to cool her armpit sweat. But it did set off a high-pitched tinkling over Abby Ruth's head. Maggie glanced up and spied a wind chime hanging from the house's eaves.

"What's that?" She pointed to the dangling snarl of assorted shells. The longer middle string had a seashell anchoring it, and it darn near brushed the top of Abby Ruth's head.

Abby Ruth looked up. "Ugly. Sugar, we don't have time to stand around jawing about Talley's lawn ornaments. We need to head back to Summer Haven pronto."

"You're right," Maggie said. "It doesn't match anything else around the man's house. Don't you think that's odd?"

"I'm pretty damn sure Nash Talley is about the oddest bird I've ever come across," Abby Ruth stated. "And I've met some doozies in my day."

Maggie stood on tiptoes to get a closer look. "Can you pull it down for me?"

"I think you'd be better off with another load of soap, but suit yourself." Abby Ruth reached up and yanked the whole mess of shells and string and wood down. She shoved it into Maggie's hands. "Let's take it to go."

They climbed into the truck and hightailed it toward Summer Haven. Abby Ruth's phone lit up again and a little box appeared in the center of the screen. She shoved it across the seat to Maggie.

"Sera says *car suck*." Maggie looked closer. "Wait a minute. *Car sick*."

"Tell her we need to know where the hell she is."

Maggie texted back and waited. "She says she doesn't know. I told her we're going to find her."

"Damn straight, we are." The tires squealed as Abby Ruth took a sharp turn.

"These are lettered olive shells. They're common on this coast." Maggie fingered the wind chime and sorted through the mess of seashells to inspect the round wood piece that held the wind chime together. It was stamped with a C shape with two vertical lines slashed through it, making it resemble a cent symbol. "Haskell Cumperton made this."

"Guess nobody's ever told him he should keep his day job."

"Might not be your cup of tea, but—"

"Hardly Nash Talley's either, if you ask me."

"Exactly my point," Maggie said. "This didn't match the style of his house, if you can call empty a style. Why would Nash own this type of tchotchke?"

"Could have been a gift," Abby Ruth said.

A gift. Warner Talley liked stringing macaroni, maybe he liked shells too. Whatever else Nash was, he sounded like a good son so he would proudly display a gift from his dad. It hit Maggie like midnight lightning from a summer thunderstorm. "I think Nash is bound for Hilton Head."

Abby Ruth glanced over, disbelief clear on her face. "How in the world would you know that?"

"Haskell Cumperton's gallery is there. My late husband George and I visited that gallery when we were vacationing years ago. Haskell's quite a celebrity around there. Something tells me Nash and Warner have spent time at Hilton Head in the past. Hit the highway. We've got to catch up with them."

"You mean people actually pay good money

for that crap?" By this time, they were pulling into Summer Haven's driveway. Abby Ruth screeched to a stop in front of the house and was already bailing out of the truck. "It won't take me a sec to check on Teague and then we'll hit the road."

When they walked into Lillian's bedroom the collective gasp could have sucked all the air right of the space. They both rushed to Teague's side.

"Get me some water," Abby Ruth shrieked.

Instead of his earlier comfy place on Lil's bed, he was now sprawled on the hardwood floor beside it.

Abby Ruth knelt and pressed her fingers to his throat. "Thank God, he's alive." She ran her hands over his head and winced.

Maggie raced out to the kitchen and returned with a big plastic jug of water. "Here. Is he okay?"

"He's got a goose egg back here."

As if Sera's drugs weren't enough to knock him out cold. Lord, when this man woke up, he would go three shades of crazy on them.

Abby Ruth splattered water on Teague's face, but he barely reacted.

"Think we should lift him back onto the bed?" Maggie asked.

"I'm afraid we'll hurt him worse if we try to wrestle him back up there." Abby Ruth smoothed her hand over his shirtfront, straightened his badge and patted his chest. "Teague, sugar, I promise to buy you a new felt cowboy hat after this is all over. The sky's the limit."

His response was a snore.

Maggie's insides were one big ball of snarled rubber bands. *Nash dropping in on us. Sera disappearing. And now Teague lying unconscious. I'm going to hell for all this.*

"I thought you said you could revive him."

"I don't know what Sera whipped up, but it's waterproof." She sucked in a breath and leveled a stare at Maggie. "We're on our own, Mags."

Maggie knelt down beside Teague. "You're sure he'll be okay if we leave him?"

"Yeah, this was the kid who broke both arms in a dirt bike race and then climbed a pine tree in my backyard to zip-line into his. Granted, he ended up back in the ER, but only with a sprained ankle."

Maggie looked at the sheriff with new respect.

"C'mon," Abby Ruth said, "we'll be back before he sleeps this off. He'll never know a thing about it."

Maggie bit her lip, but there was really no

other option but to leave him. Sera's life could depend on it.

Lillian tucked her head under the blanket and grappled for the cheap burner phone Big Martha had given her. Four times in the past hour she'd called Maggie's phone, but it had rolled to voice mail every time, forcing her to leave this number and beg Maggie to call back.

Maybe this phone wasn't working. She flipped it open to check the battery level and signal, and the screen displayed 10:32 p.m. and the picture of women drifting in a boat.

Up the creek without a paddle. That's about how I'm feeling right now. God, please let everything be okay. I don't care about Summer Haven if it means any harm to Maggie.

Lillian popped her head out from under the covers. Dixie was still asleep on the top bunk, mumbling something about "Leroy" and "right there." Snores, snuffles and coughs pierced the dormitory's darkness and somehow reassured Lillian.

Ten more minutes. That was all she was giving them. She couldn't let them get hurt while trying to help her.

Lillian tucked the phone under pillow, praying for that vibration. She closed her eyes and counted imaginary sheep that looked exactly like the ones on Maggie's shirt. Once six hundred made the leap, she would dial Teague Castro's number.

What if Nash showed up at his house?

What if Maggie was hurt?

What if...?

Five hundred and ninety-eight, five hundred and ninety-nine. She didn't bother with the six hundred. She eased from under the covers, but didn't even slip into her shower shoes. They'd just make noise. With her pillow under one arm and the cell phone in her hand, she tiptoed over the cold dormitory floor toward the bathrooms.

She went to the far end of the lavatory and ducked into the last shower stall. None of them had doors, so she went still and quiet, listening for any sound indicating she'd woken someone.

After what felt like five decades of silence, she opened the phone and checked it one last time.

Still no call and it was 10:51 p.m.

Lillian crouched down, tucking herself into the shower's corner and making herself as small as possible. Based on what Big Martha said worked for her, Lillian propped the pillow before her to hopefully mute the sound of her voice and dialed Teague's number.

Please don't let her have set me up. And please don't let her have set Maggie and the others up. She might do such a thing just to stay top dog at Walter Stiles.

The phone rang. And rang.

And rang some more.

With every unanswered ring, the tight feeling in Lillian's midsection clenched harder.

She counted seventeen rings.

Where was Teague and why didn't he have voice mail?

Just as she was getting ready to hang up and redial, a garbled voice came on the line. "Tongue Custard."

Oh Lord, maybe she'd misdialed. "Teague? Is this Teague Castro?"

A moan and a grunt from the other end echoed against the shower walls and Lillian huddled into a ball.

After several heavy breaths, he said, "This is Teague."

What did I interrupt? This is about the time of night Harlan had always wanted to—

"I said this is Teague."

"You sound...busy."

"Who the hell is this?"

Well, there was no cause to be rude. "Lillian Summer Fairview."

"Miss Lillian? What are you doing—"

"I need your help. Now."

"How are you calling me?"

"That isn't important." If he did know she was in this place, he didn't need to know she was probably breaking another law by having a phone in prison. The less he knew, the better. Only as much as he needed to find Maggie and bring her home safely. "I need you to go to Nash Talley's house immediately."

"What?"

"Listen up. I'm serious," Lillian said then rattled out all the details she could.

"Wait a second," Teague said. A shuffle and a thump came from the phone. "Ouch. Dammit."

"What in the world are you doing?"

"Whoa." She heard him blow and sputter. "I think I'm being attacked by a giant ruffle."

"Potato chip or skirt?" The question popped out before she could contain it. "Never mind. I do not need to know."

"Actually, ma'am," Teague said. "I'm pretty sure I'm lying under your bed at Summer Haven."

Lord have mercy on them all. What had Maggie done now?

Chapter Twenty-Six

Hell and damnation. Teague's head hurt like a mother. From Lillian's hardwood floor, he eased himself to a seated position and rested his back against her bed. When he tried to get his feet under him, they slid out again and he plopped to his butt. If any of his deputies saw him like this, he'd never live it down.

What had Maggie done to him? The last he felt like this had been his sophomore year in college, the one and only time he'd smoked...*sonofabitch!*

She'd slipped something into his tea. Abby Ruth had to be in on the scheme too.

Lord help him at the department's next drug test. If he pissed out something illegal, these three grannies were going to pay.

How could Aunt Bibi blindside me like this? Because she's Abby Ruth Cady, that's how. Damned if she hadn't switched teams on him. And he wasn't the least bit surprised. In fact, he'd bet she was as happy as a rat with a gold tooth.

Finally, he pulled himself up and sat panting on the side of Miss Lillian's bed. His shirt was soaked through with sweat, and his mouth felt like a skunk had up and died in there. Jesus, he needed a shower and a toothbrush. Yesterday.

But hygiene would have to get in line behind a trip to Nash Talley's house. That slimy shit was going down after everything Lillian had just divulged to him on the phone. Not only for what Talley had done to her, but other elderly folks in this county. Teague shook his head and the movement set his stomach rocking.

He lumbered toward the front door. As soon as he opened it, the humid summer air hit like him like a slap with a wet fish.

With one hand on the door jamb, he fumbled for his cell phone and dialed Abby Ruth's number. It rang four times before it went to voice mail. "Aunt Bibi, if you don't stop whatever the hell you're doing, I'm gonna be forced to throw you in jail." For what, he wasn't 100% sure, but if it slowed her crazy ass down, he'd figure out some charge to slap on her. "Call me immediately."

Something tangled around his right foot, and he stumbled. He tried to kick it away, but a length of string followed in his wake all the way down the driveway to his car.

He collapsed into his cruiser and tugged at the wad around his ankle. It was a string of seashells. "Where the heck did these come from?" He untangled himself and tossed the whole mess into the floorboard.

He reached to crank the ignition, but his phone burned against his palm. As much as he dreaded it, he had to make another call. No way around it. He punched the button he always programmed into his phone first, even though he never used it.

He swallowed back the dizzying nausea and cleared his throat.

"Teague?" Jenny's tone was clipped. "What's wrong?"

His insides warmed even though she didn't sound happy. If Jenny knew it was him calling, she had him programmed into her phone too. He tried to make his voice light and asked, "By chance, have you talked with your mom today?"

"You lost her," Jenny accused.

"*I* didn't lose her."

"You were supposed to keep her under control."

Yeah, like that's a cakewalk.

"This isn't good," Jenny said. He could just picture her, pacing back and forth with her cell phone clutched so tight her knuckles were white. "No telling what she's up to. After the newspaper gave her the golden parachute, she was at a loss with nothing to keep her busy. When she's not busy, she can so easily get herself into trouble."

Oh, he was pretty sure Aunt Bibi was up to her pretty little .22 shell casing necklace in trouble. "Don't worry so much. She's already made friends here. In fact, she's staying with some nice older ladies at the estate of the town's founding family."

"*My* mom?"

"She said something the other day about developing a new hobby."

"Besides guns?"

"Mighta been collecting coins."

Jenny snorted. "Good try. You're going to track her down, right?"

"Of course." *Damn.* Why had he called Jenny in the first place? No way Abby Ruth would have told her daughter what she was up to if it was no good. But when it came to Jenny Cady, he'd never been able to think straight. That woman had messed up his head and heart years ago and had always been able to see right through him, especially when he was keeping the truth from her. "Jenny, when have I ever let you down?"

The quiet on both ends of the phone

stretched out until it vibrated from the tension. He'd let Jenny—and two other people—down ten years ago. Neither he nor Jenny would ever forget that.

Finally, she sighed and said, "Call me when you find her."

Relief and regret warred inside his already woozy head. "Will do."

They hung up, and he peered through his windshield at the dark Georgia night. He blinked half a dozen times, but his vision was still fuzzy around the edges.

Screw it.

He cranked the engine and tore out of the driveway, heading toward Nash's. With the car straddling the center line, he made it to the house in less than five minutes.

When he pulled up, no cars were around, but a fresh set of dually tracks ripped through the yard. The whole place had an abandoned feeling around it, not surprising since those three women moved faster than most women a third their age, but still he got out to check the house.

The back door hung open, so he went inside and scanned every room. Nothing seemed out of place, but his stomach was still a pit of uneasiness.

He punched in Abby Ruth's number again.

Voice mail. He didn't bother to leave

another threat.

He strode out through the carport and something crunched under his boot. He stooped down to investigate. A seashell was now in fragments on the concrete.

More shells. He scooped up what was left and took it back to the car. It was a match to the string of shells that had tripped him up back at Summer Haven.

By the looks of them, they were those long skinny shells you could find up and down the southeast coast. Good Lord, if these things were any clue to where Aunt Bibi and her friends had taken off to, he was in a heap of hurt.

Two hours after the debacle at Dogwood Ridge, Nash pulled into his condo's garage. He killed the ignition and rested his head against the steering wheel, but rather than soothing him, the leather was hot and slick from his hands. Ugh. He pulled away only to hear a muffled banging from his trunk.

Her.

He should leave her in there. Would serve her right, but that wasn't part of the plan. Heck, nothing had been part of the plan since he opened his trunk to find her inside. But just his luck, she'd find the inside release and escape.

He grabbed his ledger from the passenger seat and scooted out. Damn, he needed both hands to control that wild woman. He tucked the ledger into the back waistband of his boxers.

Positioned where she couldn't get past him, Nash popped the trunk. This time, the woman looked worse than a dead body, lolling there amid his cleaning supplies. Those would have to be dumped now. "Get out."

She lifted her head and rolled forward. But this time, Nash moved faster. He sidestepped as she heaved down his bumper. He reached around her to grab the soiled blanket, poked her with one clean edge. "Move. Now."

"Can't you see I'm sick?"

She was going to be a heck of a lot more than sick if she didn't move. He grabbed a four-pack of toilet paper and whapped her on the shoulder. "Do you want me to toss you back in the trunk and drive around some more?"

"God, no." She slithered out, landing in a mound at his feet.

"Up with you." He nudged her again.

She wobbled to her feet and weaved toward the garage's outer wall to hang her head over the rail. "Need air," she gasped.

He grabbed another package of toilet paper,

jammed them both into the small of her back to force her away from the wall and toward the building. She stumbled and he thwapped her on the shoulder. "None of that. March."

"You're cranky," she complained. "And in case you don't know, your chakras are a mess. You might—"

"Well, you reek, and I don't need any advice from the likes of you." Thank God there was only a keycard entry into the building from the garage, so he didn't have to explain to a security guard why he was forcing her inside. And why he was wearing nothing more than his now not-so-pressed underwear.

She craned her neck to look around, but it didn't matter what she saw. There'd be no way for her to know where they were after that long drive. "Then why are you dragging me along? I don't want to come with you. You got nothing I want."

"I don't believe that for a minute." He hustled her into the elevator and they rode to the top floor. "What's your name?

"Serendipity."

Stupid name, and there isn't one thing serendipitous about you being in my trunk.

The elevator doors slid open and he prodded Serendipity toward his condo. "Get inside."

She breezed through the door. "Wow, this

place is—"

"Stop!"

She jerked. "Geez. I was going to say gorgeous. What's up your butt, dude?"

"Do not take a step. Not a single one."

She stood in his foyer, with one foot pointed and the opposite arm frozen midflourish. "Whatever you say."

Yes, she would do whatever he said.

She could not, under any circumstances, walk on his carpet. But what should *he* do? If he left her here to clean himself up, she would bolt. *Think, Nash. Think.* This was not part of the plan. Or the contingency plan. *Breathe.*

He locked the front door and pulled out the key.

"If you move from this spot, I'll be forced to...to..."

"To what?"

"Do something you won't like." Nash whisked past her and trotted down the hall. In less than sixty seconds, he returned with the plastic liner from his guest shower flowing behind him like a sail.

He fluffed it into the air and dropped it to the ground in front of her. "Sit."

She started to squat on the tile.

"No. On this."

"Well, you should have said so." She clomped forward two steps and dropped to a cross-legged pose with her feet atop her thighs.

"I don't want you touching anything I own." He grabbed the two corners and dragged her onto the carpet.

"Whoa." She tipped over to her side and grappled for the edges of the plastic. "Little warning would've been nice."

Nash's nerves popped. "Shut. Up."

He dragged her through the living room on the marshmallow-soft carpet, past the white couch and his statues, then down the hall to the master suite.

He looked up to find the damned woman with her arms out like she was flying on a magic carpet. "Stop that."

"What?" She dropped her arms and he pulled her from the carpet to the bathroom's marble floor. Her tailbone made a thud when she hit the tile. "Ooomph."

"Get cleaned up." He slammed the door and rammed a transparent acrylic chair under the knob.

So there.

Maggie and Abby Ruth were on the road hell-bent for Hilton Head and closing in fast. Maggie wouldn't even glance at the speedometer, but the telephone poles and trees outside her window were a blur.

"I sure hope you're right about this," Abby Ruth said. "Because if not, we've just wasted almost two hours going in the wrong direction."

"Me too," Maggie said. Doubt was sneaking in, but she was out of other ideas.

Abby Ruth's phone signaled a text.

"It's from Sera." Maggie thumbed down to the message. *Out of car.*

Maggie texted back. *Where are you?*

Okra & Man w Nash.

Huh? "She says she's at Okra and Man streets with Nash."

Maggie texted her back. *Does he know you're there?*

Yes. Busted. Hurry.

Abby Ruth glanced over at Maggie. "See if you can get a house number."

"821."

"And ask her if she can keep him occupied while we're on our way."

Maggie didn't bother with the last request. "She'll think of something. Sera has a way with people."

"She better or her ass could be in deep shit before we get there." Abby Ruth stabbed at the buttons on the fancy built-in GPS in the dashboard. "Okra and Man," Abby Ruth muttered. The GPS squawked, "Recalculating.

Recalculating. Recalculating."

Wouldn't have surprised Maggie to hear the automated voice start spitting out cuss words at Abby Ruth. "Maybe Sera didn't mean Okra and Man."

"Well, seeing as neither of those streets seem to exist in Hilton Head, I'm betting you're right."

Abby Ruth's phone rang for what seemed like the millionth time since they'd left Teague conked out on Lil's floor. "It's him again, isn't it?" Maggie asked.

"Yup."

"He's going to kill us when he finds us, isn't he?"

"Yup."

"Then we can't let him find us."

"You're growing on me every day, Mags." Abby Ruth grinned even while she stabbed at the navigation system. "Who names a street for a fried vegetable?"

Maggie's stomach growled at the thought of a big old plate of fried okra. *Wait a minute.* She snapped her fingers. "Not Okra and Man! She meant Oak and Main."

"Makes a helluva a lot more sense."

This time the GPS cooperated and directed them to a complex of high-rise condos near the water. Maggie checked the address. "It's not 821, though. Not on Main or Oak."

"I've got a bad feeling that we need to find her soon." Abby Ruth drummed her fingers on the steering wheel. "A man with that much Ivory Soap and toilet bowl cleaner? You just don't know what his kind will do."

Sera hadn't been in Maggie's life for long, but they were already lifelong friends. They had to find her. Maggie rolled down her window and craned her neck out. "I don't think 821 is the street address. It's the apartment number."

"Damn, you would've made a great journalist." Abby Ruth wedged the dually between a BMW and a Cadillac SUV. Maggie was careful not to open her door too wide, and hot dog, she was able to squeeze out with only a little wiggling.

Chapter Twenty-Seven

After hopping in the shower himself, Nash quickly dressed in a pressed pair of shorts and crisp polo shirt. Sometimes it really paid to have his *little problem*. That crazy Serendipity chick was still in the master bathroom with the water running and singing what sounded like "Stand Back" by Stevie Nicks.

And people think I'm strange?

He rolled a large Tumi suitcase into his spotless living room. White leather couch, immaculate carpet and wide windows. The life-size nude statues standing on pedestals had been commissioned and he'd handpicked every art piece for a specific reason. He would miss this condo. These things. It was the only place he'd ever felt like himself.

The Theodore Warner self he was so proud of.

Too bad Theodore Warner was about to disappear.

Nash hurried into the kitchen and pulled a cereal box from the cabinet. He ripped open the wax liner and pulled out a manila envelope. Even though he'd known the envelope was safe in there all this time, relief still streamed through him. He scooped up a box of stuffing and a packaged hamburger meal, shuddered at the thought of ever eating what used to be inside them. Once he had the envelopes out, he returned to the living room and tucked them into the suitcase.

Step one of the plan complete. Nash breathed, a deliberate inhalation and exhalation to clear his mind for step two. Every step in order and no skipped steps. The woman in his bathroom had already inserted a step that he didn't know where to place. His breath hitched. *No. She will not throw me off stride.*

He tugged on the edge of the abstract painting on the wall. From the safe behind it, he removed a stack of envelopes, a small box and a leather-bound journal. The envelopes went in one pile on the coffee table where he'd already placed the ledger. The small box sat lined up with the journal.

He tipped out the bills from the top envelope and counted. *One hundred. Two hundred.* He was up to seven hundred when from behind him someone said, "All done."

The money flew from Nash's grip and rained down like green ash. He whirled around to find Serendipity standing there in his plush robe.

She was an escape artist.

"How did you get out of the bathroom?"

She ducked her head a little. "Sorry about your chair."

"You broke it? That was a Kesstermann acrylic!"

"Maybe next time you should go for natural materials."

Forget it. A chair didn't matter at this point. Nash knelt to gather the cash he'd dropped. He glanced up to catch the woman trailing her fingers over a statue's man parts. "No touching!"

She snatched her hand back. "Sorry."

The bills crumpled in Nash's tight grip and his heartbeat tripped. "Sit on the couch and don't move," he ordered.

Unbelievably, she sat.

Nash smoothed the cash, tucked it back in the envelope and marked off a tally in the journal. He'd spend that money first so he didn't have to live with wrinkled bills in his wallet.

No time to count what was in the rest of the envelopes. He flipped to the back page of his journal, carefully tabbed with a red flag.

CONTINGENCY PLAN was printed in perfect block print across the top of the page. The steps were specific and clear.

Step one: *Secure money.*

He slid ten envelopes into a larger one. One thousand in each small envelope. Ten thousand in each set. In the end, he had one small envelope left over. Damn that Twilight Breaks asking for a nine-thousand-dollar deposit. Money down the drain since there was no way he could move his dad now.

What could he do with the extra thousand dollars?

He arranged all the envelopes but that one in the suitcase.

Step two didn't say anything about leftover money.

And it didn't say anything about dealing with a trunk hitchhiker.

It said: *Retrieve second suitcase from hall closet.*

"How did that woman get in my trunk?" he muttered as he walked down the hall to retrieve the matching bag he'd packed months ago. "Damn it all. She's not on my list. Can't she just disappear?"

When he cleared the corner rolling the suitcase behind him, she was standing again, staring at him with a poleaxed expression.

He'd said that disappear thing aloud, hadn't he?

I hate it when that happens.

She tugged the robe tight around her body but the bottom gaped a little. Her legs were long and tan and her left ankle sported a tattoo. Kind of sexy. *Stop it, Nash. No time for this. Stick to the contingency plan. But she isn't on the contingency plan!*

The chaos that had just invaded his perfect place was eating at him like maggots on a hunk of raw beef. He stared down at the still open bag filled with envelopes.

"Are they all filled with money?" she asked.

"Letters."

"Must be special letters if you're packing them up. Are you going on vacation?"

Maybe she could come with me. No. No. She's a loose end.

He had what he needed to take care of that too. On another journal page, he'd outlined an *In case of loose ends.* Too bad he'd have to use that plan. He'd hoped he'd never need it.

Just as he was about to check off *Get gun from safe*, a sudden movement caught his attention. The woman was rising from the couch, lifting her arms as if they were angel wings and letting his robe fall to the ground like a cloud. She flexed her foot, grabbed her big toe and lifted one leg into the air.

Who knew a woman her age could look that good without clothes on?

Oh hell yeah, she can come with me.

Abby Ruth strode toward the front door of the fancy condominium at the corner of Oak and Main like she owned the place. Maggie trotted along trying to appear like at least a princess to Abby Ruth's queen. They stopped by the security desk.

"We're here to see the hot hunk in 821," Abby Ruth told the guard.

"Warner?" He reached for the phone.

Maggie almost squealed with excitement. Talley might be using a fake name, but creativity wasn't his thing if the best he could do was use his daddy's name. It was him. Sera was here.

The guard cast a suspicious look their way. "This is awfully late. I'll just give him a call and see—"

Abby Ruth placed her hand over his, leaned over the desk and before Maggie's eyes she became a sultry sex kitten. "Sugar, it's the man's birthday, and we're—" she gestured between Maggie and herself, "—his surprise present. Now you wouldn't want to ruin that, would you?"

The guard swallowed and eyed them both.

Who in tarnation would believe she was in some kind of threesome with Abby Ruth and Nash Talley?

"It's highly unusual, but since it's his birthday..."

Abby Ruth gave him a smile that could've boiled ice cubes and then sauntered away to the elevator. Maggie shot after her.

Maggie felt the guard gawking at them as they walked away.

When the doors closed, Maggie said, "What was that?"

"I was actually a double major in college—journalism and drama."

"God help us all."

The elevator whooshed them up eight floors, and they stepped out into a hallway tiled in slate and lined with muted gray wallpaper. This was no criminal hidey-hole, it was a retreat. Nash Talley deserved to pay—and pay big—if this was how he'd spent the money he'd stolen. They found number 821, no problems.

Maggie stuck her ear to the door. "I don't hear anything. What if they're not here?"

"What if he's in there carving Sera up while you're jacking around with the door?"

"Fine." Maggie pulled out her supplies and knelt to study the door.

"Why don't you do it with that knife again?"

"Because he's engaged the deadbolt." Maggie inserted her tension wrench and worked her pick inside. Slowly. Slowly.

Abby Ruth paced in jerky little circles. After all of forty-five seconds, she pulled the gun from the small of her back and aimed it at the lock.

Maggie jerked upright and felt the pins give. "Dammit, Abby Ruth. You made me lock it again."

"Lemme just blow it off."

"No! If we walk in there with guns blazing, we've lost the element of surprise."

"I could surprise him with my little friend here." But Abby Ruth reluctantly reholstered the gun and patted it.

Maggie wound up her plug spinner and slid it inside the lock. She regulated her breathing like Sera had taught her and became one with the lock. Gave the plug spinner a quick snap and...

Click.

"We're in." Maggie slowly turned the knob. "Cover me." She'd always wanted to say that.

When they swung open the door, Abby Ruth stayed high while Maggie ducked low.

Chapter Twenty-Eight

Maggie and Abby Ruth turned the corner into Nash's living room, almost blinded by the white *everything*. If the decor hadn't done the job, seeing Sera buck nekkid in what she'd described to Maggie just the other day as a Standing Hand to Big Toe was enough to cause anyone to stop and stare.

Nash was frozen, gawking at Sera.

Jackpot.

"It's over, Talley," Abby Ruth said with more gusto than Dirty Harry.

He spun around. His hair was ruffled in little ducktails and his eyes were wide and glassy. "What do you people want? First, this wacko—" he flicked a hand toward Sera, "—is in my trunk—"

Abby Ruth motioned him away from Sera with her gun and then kept it trained on him.

"How did you get in here?" He practically tripped over his feet trying to move. "And now you're standing in my house waving a gun at me. Why?"

Maggie advanced on Nash, one deliberate footstep at a time. "Justice. Not only did you set Lillian up—" she lifted her finger and pointed it straight at him, "—you stole from old people, people who need every dime just to make ends meet."

"You don't know what you're talking about."

"I know you're a dirty rotten scoundrel. How could you do this to your father?" Maggie asked. "He would be so disappointed in what you've been up to. Thank God, he won't ever know. That sweet man loves you, misses you, and this is the way you repay him?"

Nash swept a hand through his hair. "You don't understand."

"We understand perfectly," she told him. "We saw the ledger, Nash."

"Wh-what ledger?" Only his stammering didn't hide the panic rising in his voice. He edged toward the coffee table.

Maggie tracked his movement. "The one sitting right there on the table. The one you're about to hand over to us," she demanded. *Wow, I like this giving orders. No wonder Abby Ruth is addicted to it.*

"Don't forget the money," Abby Ruth added.

Nash's expression sharpened. "What

money?"

Sera finally lowered her leg. "He packed the money in that suitcase over there. There's another ledger in there too."

"Shut up," he screeched. "Don't you ever shut up?" He dove forward and grabbed the suitcase.

Maggie dove, too, but he had the suitcase and Sera in his arms before she got there. He pulled naked Sera against his chest, creating a shield in front of himself. "I'll hurt her." His eyes went wild. "I swear I will."

"With what, your hand sanitizer?" Abby Ruth didn't look impressed. She took two steps toward him. "May as well just give it up, Nash. I'm in no mood to put up with this kind of crap."

He turned Sera and backed out of the living room as if they were engaged in some perverted waltz. Peering over Sera's shoulder, he shouted as they waddled away, "You won't use that thing. You old ladies are softies and easy marks. Lillian was the easiest of all."

Pressure built in Maggie's head. *Wanna see just what kind of softie I am?*

"Think I won't?" Abby Ruth laughed and took aim at one of the sinuous statues in Nash's foyer.

"You wouldn't," he sneered.

She squeezed the trigger. And just that

quick, the male statue was a eunuch. "Then think again."

"What the hell are you doing?" Nash hopped around in a circle, dragging Sera with him.

But his distress and momentary distraction was all it took.

Sera broke away, kicked up into a Downward Facing Dog Planning to Pee and clocked him right in the jaw.

He staggered back and bounced off the wall.

"What do you think you're—"

Maggie darted forward, caught Nash in the side and tackled him facedown on the floor. But in her hurry, she must've brushed the now penis-less statue because it teetered off its perch and toppled, clunking Nash on the head.

Before he could shake it off, Maggie whipped out her duct tape. She slapped a piece of duct tape over the wound on his head before it could start bleeding, then grabbed his wrists and one ankle—quite forcefully, if she said so herself—and trussed him up like a bawling calf.

Maggie patted her handy duct tape dispenser like it was a gun in holster. "He won't be going anywhere."

Abby Ruth set her fancy boots into a wide stance and took aim. "I got a bead on the back of his head."

Sure enough, right there in front of Maggie's eyes, a red dot marked a spot in the middle of Nash Talley's tousled hair.

He groaned and tried to turn his head.

Abby Ruth spoke low and steady. "Flip him over, girls. I'll line up a shot on him like I did that big-ass Casper boy in the living room." She hitched her chin toward the now smashed statue.

"You won't kill me." Nash's words sounded like they'd been put through a meat grinder, but they still had a cocky edge to them.

"Didn't say I would. Said I'd blow your boy parts to nethers." Abby Ruth's laugh made Maggie a little nervous, but it wasn't enough to dull the anger she was feeling for Nash right now.

Maggie rocked on her heels and shoved him to his back. "I wouldn't tempt her, pretty boy."

When Abby Ruth moved the laser dot from his head to the fly of his shorts, his smug attitude wilted.

"Fine," he practically squealed. "Tell me what you want."

"Answers," Maggie barked out.

His gaze darted from Maggie to Abby Ruth and back to Maggie. "Then call off your gun-crazy psycho Annie Oakley, would you?"

Reluctantly, Abby Ruth lowered her gun.

"How?" Maggie asked.

"How what?"

She nudged him in the ribs with her toe. Okay, maybe it was a kick. "How did you hornswoggle all those nice old folks? We know you were running some kind scam through Meals on Wheels."

"If I tell you everything, will you let me go?"

Abby Ruth flipped the laser back on and waved it toward him. "Don't push your luck, Tidy Boy."

Maggie grabbed Abby Ruth's arm and pushed the gun back down. "We'll see."

He slumped a little, but it only took a moment—and another of Maggie's toe nudges—for him to start talking. "I drove the Meals on Wheels van on the days Social Security checks showed up in the mailboxes."

"Didn't people ever miss the money?"

"No. Those people were dead. I just skipped a step in the paperwork at the funeral home. The checks kept coming and I only took the ones from the deceased spouses. No one was looking for them anyway. I wasn't hurting anyone, not really."

"So you call Lillian being in federal prison camp not hurting anyone? Same thing could have easily happened to everyone else you were stealing from."

"That wasn't part of the plan," he mumbled,

his gaze cast toward the floor.

Abby Ruth looked doubtful. "That doesn't seem like it would net him that much money." She tapped her chin with one finger. "Because how many people get actual checks these days? Everything's gone direct deposit."

"True." Maggie turned to Nash. "So, what about that?"

Nash huffed a sigh. "Isn't it obvious? All I had to do once someone died was to request a change of banks."

"So the money was diverted to your account."

"Accounts," he said. "It wouldn't do to have just one."

Evil, evil man.

"You're going to let me go, right? I'll be out of here in five minutes and you'll never hear from me again. I promise."

"I don't think so. Settle down there."

"What? Do you want the money? If it's about the money I'll split it with you. Fifty-fifty. Just let me go. A man like me would never make it in prison."

Abby Ruth laughed. "You got that right, pretty boy."

"Stop antagonizing him. Come here, girls. Let us talk about it," Maggie said.

Sera and Abby Ruth followed her back into the living room and out of Nash's earshot, but as soon as they were out of sight he started making a racket.

"What if he gets loose?" Sera asked.

Abby Ruth waved a dismissive hand. "He ain't goin' nowhere. You're pretty good with that duct tape, Maggie."

"Thanks." Maggie shook a finger at Sera. "What were you thinking, doing naked yoga when we came in?"

"A thank-you would be nice here." Sera propped her hands on her still-naked hips. "You two took forever to get here and then you were noisy. I could hear you at the door, and he would have heard you too. I had to do something to save your butt, and that was the best I could come up with on short notice."

Her best was pretty good. "Could you put some clothes on now?"

Sera grabbed the robe from the couch and slipped into it. From the pocket, she pulled out Maggie's phone. "By the way, someone's been trying to call you all night, but I didn't know how to pick up the messages."

Maggie grabbed it and checked the screen. Oh, no. Lillian. Lord, it was after one in the morning. She couldn't call this number and risk getting Lillian in trouble.

"I'm going to find something else to wear." Sera headed down the hall to what Maggie assumed were the bedrooms.

She took a breath and asked Abby Ruth, "What are we going to do with him?"

"Looks pretty damn clear to me."

"You talk a big game, but you're saying you'd pull the trigger and kill a man in cold blood?"

"Well..."

"Never mind. There are some things about you I don't need to know." Maggie rubbed the center of her forehead. "It sure doesn't seem right to just let him up and walk out of here, even if we take the money, or just call the cops on him. That's going too easy on him."

"He needs to be punished," Abby Ruth said. "Taught a lesson he'll never forget."

Nash thumped around in the other room and she heard him gag. He was one tender-bellied OCD man. Looked like poor Angelina Broussard was going to have to find herself another historic preservation committee member.

"We may not be able to get Lil out of jail, but we can at least help save Summer Haven if we take back every penny Lil's doing time for."

Sera came back wearing a man's shirt. "What are we going to do?"

Maggie snapped. *Oh, I have just the thing.* "I have an idea about how to give Nash Talley what he's got coming to him. Follow me."

They trooped back into the foyer and circled

Nash.

"Y'all grab his leg and flip him back over," Maggie instructed.

Abby Ruth and Sera wrestled him back to his stomach and grabbed his untied ankle. "Ready."

"Pull him back that way." Maggie pointed down the hall. "Sera, you know where the bathroom is?"

"Yep."

"Then let's go."

They tugged and slid him slowly across the carpet while Maggie strolled alongside. She winked at Sera and said casually, "Sera, have you ever heard about the kind of things that hide in carpet?"

"Like what?"

"I read somewhere that carpet is one of the top five places in a home that harbors germs."

Nash struggled in their hold and tried to spit. "I know what you're doing."

"And another thing." Maggie grinned down at him. "A person sheds about one point five million skin flakes an hour. Most of those fall to the floor and sink into the carpet."

Nash's head thunked against the wall as they made the turn into the hallway. "Just kill me now."

Sera patted him on the leg and he shivered. "Our friend here doesn't like germs much. Has a bit of weak stomach. By the way, did you know I get carsick if I don't have enough air?"

"Oh, Sera." Maggie mock-sympathized. "Did you get sick?"

"Sugar, are you okay?" Abby Ruth added.

Nash coughed and sputtered, finally going limp. "What about me? Doesn't anyone care if I'm okay?"

"No," they all said in chorus.

They dragged him into the guest bathroom and Maggie said, "This'll do, girls. Sera, why don't you keep our friend company while Abby Ruth and I run an errand?"

"Happy to." Sera eased down beside Nash in a cross-legged pose.

Maggie walked over to the two suitcases in the living room and opened the first one. She dumped out his clothes and started to wheel it toward the door.

Abby Ruth grabbed the other one. "Do you need this one too? What's the plan?"

"Yes, empty that one too."

Abby Ruth unzipped the bag and then took one of the envelopes out. "Well, lookie here. Even a blind hog finds an acorn now and again, but it looks like Nash packed us a whole dang picnic." She reached down and picked up a stack of similar envelopes. "We are *not* dumping this out. Look at this."

Abby Ruth fanned out a stack of bills that made Maggie feel like one of those jackpot slot machines.

"Holy Moses! That's thousands of dollars! I thought Sera said the money and ledger were in the other suitcase."

Sera popped her head out in the hallway. "Everything okay... Jesus, that's a lot of cash. That's not even the one I saw him put cash in."

"Wait. Stop. I'll cut you in," Nash cried out. "Don't leave me. Serendipity. You have to help me."

Sera turned back toward Nash. "Now you just need to settle down. Your aura is all convoluted."

Maggie laughed. "If Sera's aura talk doesn't freak him out before we get back, Nash is going to be in for a heckuva night."

She nodded toward the bag. If that thing was filled with cash like Sera claimed, surely she could skim a little off the top for Lil's ring. "Count out the ninety thousand that Lillian is doing time for and three thousand more."

"Why don't we just take it all?" Abby Ruth said. "Not like he can report it stolen."

"It's not Lil's money and it's certainly not mine."

Abby Ruth rolled her eyes. "Well, then how about an even one hundred thousand? They're already in ten thousand dollar bundles."

"Fine." Maybe there would be a future for her in that carriage house after all. "Leave the rest on the counter along with that darned ledger. Then come with me to the truck."

When Maggie and Abby Ruth returned to the condo, they each had a suitcase filled with damp rank-smelling pennies. They wheeled the bags into the bathroom to a sweating and disheveled Nash Talley.

He looked relieved to see his suitcases. "Thank you. When I split this out, I promise I'll be fair."

"Fair?" Abby Ruth shook her head. "Y'all should've let me take care of him the way I wanted to."

He sucked in a breath as they wheeled past him.

They unzipped the bags and dumped the coins into the tub with a loud metallic thunder.

"That's a pretty sound isn't it?" Maggie asked.

Abby Ruth sniffed. "Sounds nice, but that scent... How would you describe it?"

"It's stinky in here," Sera said.

"Kind of like a sewer if you ask me," Abby Ruth said.

"I don't know." Maggie sniffed the air.

"Smells green to me."

"No," Nash moaned. "Nothing else green." His stomach gurgled like a bubbling drain.

"I think we're all set," Maggie said with a slap to the back of her pants.

Nash lifted his head slightly and said in a dull tone, "Get it over with already."

"It's time. You're nearly done, Nash Talley, but don't you ever do anything to Lillian Summer Fairview or anyone in Summer Shoals again. You hear me?"

The three of them slid him closer to the tub and Nash's head whapped against the side.

"Oops," Abby Ruth said.

They surrounded him and grabbed his arms and flailing leg.

"On three," Maggie said. "One, two, three." They hoisted him up and over the side of the tub, dropping him into the penny-filled fiberglass.

Maggie stood there with her arms folded, watching him shiver and wretch.

"You know," Sera told him, "if you did the locust pose it would help with your neck strength."

Abby Ruth snickered. "Sure you don't want to just shoot his ass?"

"No, I think our work here is nearly done." Maggie reached into her pocket and pulled out four pennies. She handed one to Abby Ruth and one to Sera and held one in each of her own hands. "Heads we win, tails you lose," she said to Nash.

Abby Ruth flipped hers into the air and let it thud onto Nash's back. "Heads."

Sera did the same. "Heads."

"One for me," Maggie said, flipping the coin with an expert flick of her thumb. She bent over and peered at hers. "Heads."

"And Nash Talley, this last one is for Lillian." Maggie's phone rang before she could toss the last one. She answered, "Lillian!"

"Maggie Rawls, you've scared the fire out of me. I told you to answer the phone when I called and—"

"Lil, we're in the middle of something here. Later you can nag me all you want, but first I need to finish this." Maggie held out the phone, flipped the penny in the air and watched it land on his spine. "Four for four. Heads, we win."

"What's going on there?" Lillian asked. "Maggie, if I put you in trouble, I couldn't live with myself. All those things I said about Summer Haven being the most important thing in my life, well, that was just silly. I've realized friends are way more important than money or a house or—"

"Lil, hon, I've known that all along, but we're kinda busy right now and—"

"Oh Lord, you found Nash!"

"Don't worry, everything's under control. Watch the news tomorrow and we'll visit on Friday. Love you, Lil."

Maggie leaned over and whispered into Nash's ear. "Sorry. It just ain't your day." Then she and the others hightailed it out of the bathroom, leaving Nash in the pile of filthy coins.

"Hang on one sec," Maggie said as she paused at the counter. She scribbled a note and left it on top of the ledger next to the stacks of money.

Abby Ruth went back into the living room and picked up the statue's unmentionables, flipped them in the air and caught them.

Maggie gave her a wink. "It was a nice shot. Souvenir?"

"You betcha."

Chapter Twenty-Nine

Teague had sat up nearly all night waiting for those women to show back up in Summer Shoals. Even called in a BOLO to the counties near the coast, but by four in the morning he'd given up and gone home. Whatever had landed him in Miss Lillian's bedroom had sunk him into the hardest sleep he'd ever had, and it'd been nearly eleven o'clock when he woke up.

Still a little fuzzy-headed, he walked into the diner just before noon. Today was chicken-fried steak on the lunch plate special, and he still had the damn munchies from last night.

He scanned the place for a booth, and there they were—the three boils on his butt—sitting in a booth smiling and laughing. Smiling and laughing spelled no good with that crew.

He moseyed over. "How's lunch today, ladies?"

The laughter died a quick death and they pokered up at his words. Now that he was closer, he could see the bags under their eyes and the fatigue weighting their shoulders. Where all had they been between last night and noon today and just what had they done?

"Mind if I join you?" Not waiting for an answer, he nudged Abby Ruth in the shoulder and she slid over to make room.

Maggie fiddled with the wedding ring she wore on her right-hand pinkie. The big center diamond glinted in the sun streaming through the front window. "Teague, about that tea—"

"What tea?" He channeled his best clueless act, and it seemed to be working.

Six eyes around the table widened and he held in his laughter. It would worry them more if they didn't know for sure what he knew for sure.

"Where were you last night about ten o'clock?" Abby Ruth said.

"At home in bed, I imagine, since that's where I woke up this morning. Why?"

"Oh, no reason. I noticed you looked a little tired lately, that's all."

Umm-hmm.

"Turn up the noon news, will you, Dottie?" someone from across the room called out.

Dottie picked up the remote from behind the counter and pumped up the volume. A male reporter with a serious face stood in front of The Condominiums at Camelot on Hilton Head Island and rattled off the breaking story.

Everyone in the booth straightened a little, including Teague.

"Just minutes ago, a man was found facedown in his bathtub, his arms and leg restrained with duct tape. Although he claimed to be unharmed, emergency personnel took him to the hospital where he was treated for a severe allergic reaction allegedly caused by the approximately five-hundred dollars in loose change also in the tub. The man has been identified as one Nash Talley from Summer Shoals, Georgia."

Everyone in the diner gasped and a murmur rippled through the room.

"He's now being investigated for connection to Social Security fraud. A meticulously annotated financial ledger and a journal outlining Talley's plan to flee the country under an assumed identity, along with thousands of dollars in cash and fine art have been confiscated as the investigation continues. We'll be bringing you the latest updates right here on News Channel Three. Sandra, back to you."

The buzz grew louder as the newscaster moved on to another story. But Teague's table

366 Kelsey Browning and Nancy Naigle

was silent.

"Looks like you ladies were on to something." And sure as he was sitting here, they'd done something about it too. But what proof did he have? He couldn't tell anyone they'd drugged him, and his only other evidence was a broken seashell. Didn't exactly make a case. And as for Lillian Summer Fairview *vacationing* at a federal prison camp, he wasn't going to spread that around town. That was Lillian's business.

"Who would've ever guessed?" Maggie gripped her tea glass as if it might try to run away. "Wonder who will run Talley's Funeral Home now?"

Sera and Abby Ruth fumbled for their drinks.

Teague was enjoying watching them squirm. "I guess you just never know what people are capable of, do you?" He slowly moved his gaze from one granny to the next and settled on Abby Ruth, who smiled the sweetest smile he'd ever seen on that woman.

"If you ladies would excuse me for a minute," Teague said, "I need to step outside and make a quick call." He scooted out of the booth and headed for the door, but he heard the frantic whispers behind him.

"Lordy goodness, do you think he knows?"

"He didn't act suspicious and I think that

tea might have even helped his sacral chakra."

"Whatever you do," Abby Ruth said, "do not let that boy fool you. You underestimate him and *bam,* you could find yourself in a pile of crap faster than you can say *boo*. Caution and stealth. That's the name of the game when it comes to Teague Castro."

Since his back was to them, he didn't bother to hide his broad grin. If they thought they could pull anything over on him, they were battier than a belfry. But damned if it wouldn't be fun to see them try.

Once outside, he pulled out his phone and hit the key to call Jenny.

"Teague, tell me you found her."

"I found her."

"Where, for God's sake?"

"At the local diner."

"Do you mean to tell me she wasn't off somewhere getting into trouble last night?"

"All I can tell you is that she's safe and sound in Summer Shoals today, but you should probably come see for yourself."

She sighed and that one sound carried the weight of the world on it. "It's not a good time with my job and Grayson and Daniel."

"Daniel?" So help him God, if that pansy-assed ex-husband of hers was giving her problems, he would get on a plane to Boston and show him how Texans handled pains-in-the-ass.

"Yeah, he's just, you know…"

No, he didn't know. "I bet Grayson would love to see his grandma," he said. "And I could take him fishing while y'all are here."

"You'd do that?" God, the way she asked, with a layer of disbelief on her words, about punched a hole in his heart.

"Sure, I would. And hey, the holidays will be coming up before you know it so—"

"Where would we stay? I'm pretty sure there's not enough room for us and Mom's guns in the horse trailer."

"Don't you worry, we'll figure out something." Yeah, something like Jenny staying in his bed the whole visit. Teague shook his head, but the picture hung on.

"Okay, but I don't know when. I need to look at my schedule, so don't say anything to Mom yet."

It was as if someone had just filled that hole in his heart with a blast of helium. "If I don't hear back from you in two weeks with some kind of plan, just know I will call and I will get you down here if I have to come up there and pack your bags myself."

Jenny laughed. "I wouldn't expect anything less."

As Teague hung up, his whole body felt looser, more relaxed than it had in a long time, even with the aid of a six-pack and a fishing pole.

When he walked back into the diner, Maggie called, "Dottie, could we have our cake now?"

Dottie hustled over to the table with a cake, three plates and forks. "Maggie, hon, you're looking mighty fit these days. Sure you want to blow whatever diet you're on with this here treat?"

Maggie eyed the cake like a man sinking in quicksand might look at a rope he was about to latch onto with both hands. "I think my diet can handle it."

Dottie sliced into the cake, showing five layers—chocolate, white, pink, yellow and green. She asked Teague, "Did you want some too?"

He considered the cake sitting in the middle of the table. Five layers. That was a special occasion cake, like for a wedding or a milestone birthday. That wasn't an everyday lunch dessert.

"Why not?" He looked at Sera, Abby Ruth and Maggie in turn and then smiled at Dottie. "Because apparently, these ladies have something to celebrate."

The midday news blared from the television

screen in the rec room at Walter Stiles Prison Camp, where Lillian sat hemming a pair of khaki pants for Dixie and trying desperately to remember to breathe as they waited for the afternoon news to come on. She'd already pricked her fingers more this morning than she had in her whole blessed lifetime.

Big Martha walked in with her posse flanking her sides like giant wings. They commandeered the front table and all the chairs around it, and Big Martha shot Lillian a conspiratorial look.

Suddenly, the news anchor cut in. "We've got a late-breaking story from Hilton Head, South Carolina. Kevin Travis is there to tell us more."

A young dark-haired man stood before a tall building. "Thanks, Sandra. This is Kevin Travis here at the Condominiums at Camelot on Hilton Head Island. Just moments ago, police were forced to break down the door on an eighth floor condo after receiving an anonymous lead about a possible Social Security fraud scheme."

Lillian leaned forward and dropped the pants to her lap, where they slid to the floor. All her talk about Summer Haven these past few weeks and Maggie had taken up Lil's cause like a soldier rather than giving her a knock upside the head like she deserved. Not everyone had friends like that and it appeared she was making some new ones who were pretty darn fantastic too.

The screen switched from the handsome reporter to a shot of two city police officers storming a door into a home decorated in all white and littered with what looked like marble fragments.

An audible gasp escaped Lillian and she coughed to camouflage it.

The reporter continued, "Sandra, details are still coming together, but an anonymous call to the Hilton Head Island police in the early morning hours led officers to believe the owner of this condo swindled thousands of dollars from senior citizens in Georgia."

Footage cut to a scene of Nash Talley being escorted to an ambulance in handcuffs. Instead of his normal snappy suit and tie, he wore a grimy pink golf shirt, boat shoes and shorts that had possibly once been white. His hair stood up every which way and he appeared to be mumbling to himself in a state of confusion.

Lord have mercy. My girls certainly took him down a notch or two. I bet he never saw that coming, but then I never saw him as the type to pull off a senior-citizen-cheating scheme either.

The reporter's voice became more

animated. "Strangely enough, the man had been restrained with duct tape and left in a bathtub full of coins. Possibly an appropriate punishment as sources are saying this man allegedly used Meals on Wheels and his family's funeral home to gain access to unsuspecting elderly and a pipeline of federal money."

When they spoke on the phone last night, Maggie had been so confident, so...happy. That was her Maggie. Never mess with a woman with duct tape.

Lillian glanced at Big Martha to find her smiling, a genuine smile of enjoyment, rather than her normal toothy smirk.

"Lillian, what in the world is wrong with people these days? Taking money from the elderly." She shook her head in mock sadness, but her eyes were bright as she strolled toward Lillian. "But whoever took him down a peg did a mighty fine job of it."

Pride bloomed in Lillian's chest. Those were *her* girls. "Not everyone could pull off such a slick strategy. Must've been some smart folks with the right firepower behind them."

"No doubt about that. Sure wish I knew some goodhearted Robin Hoods like them." Martha leaned close to Lil and pitched her voice low. "Boy, could I tell them some stories. Stories that might even earn 'em a little extra jingle."

Lillian eased out of her chair, motioned for Martha to follow her from the room. "I'd surely give a penny for your thoughts."

THE END...

of this adventure

Acknowledgements

We are so grateful to the fabulous team of people who helped make this first Granny Series book possible and hope to share the entire series journey with them.

A big 21-gun salute to Adam Firestone, who outfitted Abby Ruth with her gun collection and taught us about antique Spanish firearms.

Thanks to super-editor Deb Nemeth, who saw the humor in our grannies and allowed us to hang on to as many southernisms as possible. You make us and the grannies look good!

To Kimberly Cannon, thanks so much for cleaning up the little grammar things. Maggie, especially, likes everything in its place.

To Michelle Preast, who brought our vision of the grannies to life. So much so that we made paper dolls out of them that helped us through the re-writes and traveled with us on those crazy trips to Atlanta. We still have them today! And yes, there's a whole other story about that.

About the Authors

Kelsey Browning writes sass kickin' love stories and Southern crime capers. Originally from a small Texas town, Kelsey has also lived in the Middle East and Los Angeles, proving she's either adventurous or downright nuts. These days, she hangs out in northeast Georgia with Tech Guy, Smarty Boy, Bad Dog and Pharaoh, a Canine Companions for Independence puppy. She's currently at work on the next book in her Texas Nights contemporary romance series and The Granny Series. For info on her upcoming single title releases, drop by www.KelseyBrowning.com.

Nancy Naigle writes love stories from the crossroad of small town and suspense. Born and raised in Virginia Beach, Nancy now calls a small farm in southern Virginia home. She's currently at work on the next book in her Adams Grove series and The Granny Series. Stay in touch with Nancy on facebook, twitter or subscribe to her newsletter on her website ~ www.NancyNaigle.com.

Also by Kelsey Browning::

TEXAS ★ NIGHTS Series
Book 1:: Personal Assets
Book 2:: Running the Red Light (2014)
Book 3:: Problems in Paradise (2014)
Book 4:: Designs to Die For (2014)

Also by Nancy Naigle::

The Adams Grove Series
Book 1:: Sweet Tea and Secrets
Book 2:: Wedding Cake and Big Mistakes
Book 3:: Out of Focus
Book 4:: Pecan Pie and Deadly Lies
Book 5:: Mint Juleps and Justice (2014)

Young Adult Mystery
inkBLOT – co-written with Phyllis Johnson